Elsie Burch Donald worked as an editor in London before becoming a novelist. Her first novel was published in 2001. She was born in the USA, attended Sweet Briar College in Virginia and completed her studies at Edinburgh University. She currently divides her time between London and southwest France.

A ROPE OF SAND

A chance encounter in a French town brings dark memories flooding back to fifty-five-year-old Kate. As a student in the 1950s, she'd been one of five girls from Sweet Briar College, Virginia, to take a life-changing grand tour of Europe. Flung headlong into the dangerous freedom of the old world, Kate and her friends giddily soak up all that's on offer. When, one by one, three intriguing but very different young men latch on to the party, what seems to be a privileged and sophisticated clique is formed. But nobody is quite as they appear, and as façades crumble, the grand tour will prove eye-opening in ways the girls couldn't possibly have imagined.

ELSIE BURCH DONALD

◆

A ROPE
OF SAND

Complete and Unabridged

ULVERSCROFT
Leicester

First published in Great Britain in 2004 by
Doubleday, a division of Transworld Publishers
London

First Large Print Edition
published 2005
by arrangement with Transworld Publishers
a division of The Random House Group Limited
London

The moral right of the author has been asserted

British Library CIP Data

Donald, Elsie Burch
  A rope of sand.—Large print ed.—
  Ulverscroft large print series: romance
  1. Voyages and travels—Fiction
  2. Large type books
  I. Title
  813.5'4 [F]

  ISBN 1–84395–553–9

Published by   F
F. A. Thorpe (Publishing)
Anstey, Leicestershire

Set by Words & Graphics Ltd.
Anstey, Leicestershire
Printed and bound in Great Britain by
T. J. International Ltd., Padstow, Cornwall

This book is printed on acid-free paper

To Sarah

'Nothing is certain then or even remotely stable, but an illusion that learning and our senses keep in place. Yet when it works, such happy moments open up, precious intervals, little paradises, you could say; none of them permanent.'

Thinking It Over, K. Preston

1

When you die, they say your whole life passes before you, like a speeded-up motion picture, I suppose — just as mine is doing right this minute; and I can only pray it isn't going to kill me. I mean metaphorically, of course. But I have had a shock, a primal surprise, and mentally it's as if a table holding a laboriously completed jigsaw puzzle has been violently upended and the carefully assembled pieces are scattered chaotically across the floor.

Yesterday, for the first time in over thirty years, I saw Olivia. So improbable, so hideously unexpected. No time at all for preparation — ostensibly no need for any. No need to gird myself or start digging up the past. And yet . . . and yet, like that dunked biscuit that set Marcel Proust back decades in his thoughts and feelings, the past has come crowding in of its own accord, pushing out the present — the present which, after all, *is* me; what I am now, at this particular moment in time, the doggedly assembled personal jigsaw puzzle that is my reality. Or was.

But I am gabbling, which most assuredly is not my nature; yet the effort to pull sensible order out of such confusion has indeed opened up a vein of something like garrulity. Does this mean the notorious talking cure has something to it? That talking a thing through from the beginning, reassembling all the pieces logically, then stepping back to take a good hard look, can restore perspective? For it's perspective that neurotics lack. Mind you, I am not a neurotic; but subjected to severe emotional upheaval, we all display the symptoms: obsession, suspicion, irrational fears, loss of identity, even physical illness. Only with non-neurotics it is temporary and, mercifully, as I understand, non-recurring.

But I do feel the strongest urge to talk, to go through this extraordinary and frankly, for I must warn you, terrible story from beginning to end. I want to make something useful out of it — a cathartic silk purse, if you will — I want to put myself back together again, restore my outlook and my general view of myself. I want to mount a re-assembly.

It was here in Bordeaux that I saw Olivia. Was it fortuitous or fated? A silly question; we understand so very little in the universe. Ostensibly I'm here because my husband is attending an economics conference, working out problems to do with a proposed European currency. And yesterday, having time to waste, I wandered about the city. Strolling past the magnificent opera house and through streets lined with elegant, Parisian-like stone buildings, I eventually wandered into the Place St Michel, which is, in fact, not very far from our hotel. Although architecturally like most of *vieux* Bordeaux, St Michel's character is different. The soot-covered fifteenth-century church rises at one end of a long esplanade. Its unattached bell tower, like a cascade of blackened candle wax, still dominates the city skyline. But otherwise its importance must be much reduced: today the church is in the Arab quarter. Watch your handbag, I was warned in the hotel.

Church and esplanade are encircled by decaying eighteenth-century houses: tall, narrow, doubtless occupying medieval sites, the windows with faded louvre shutters gazing out forlornly on the esplanade, the wrought-iron balconies sporting an occasional sickly-looking geranium. But the esplanade itself was chock-a-block with umbrella-shaded stalls selling spices, old clothes, defunct kitchen utensils, chipped pottery and cast-off bric-à-brac — the detritus of other and invisible lives. It's the sort of market where one secretly hopes to unearth genuine treasure.

Many of the vendors and clientele were dark, small-boned men in jellabas and pillbox caps, whose diminutive elegance undermines our rougher Western style, and whose presence added the exotic flavour of a Byzantine or Egyptian souk. It was charming, this improbable mix of East and West, surrounded by a sprinkling of street cafés, some French, some Arabic — the latter not selling alcohol, of course: a pronounced irony in Bordeaux.

I sat down and ordered a Turkish coffee. I had a copy of the *Herald Tribune* to read in the September sun, but I never opened it. For suddenly, not ten yards in front of me, was Olivia. I tell you, my heart stopped. She stood there, examining casually a piece of bric-à-brac at one of the stalls. Tall, slender, no make-up — well, she never needed any — her long neck, perfect Grecian profile and straight blond hair pulled back simply on the nape of her neck were engraved upon my brain like an exquisitely carved cameo.

What on earth to do? I had to do *something*. This sort of moment can't be allowed to enter one's life then fade out again without any response, as if it had never happened. That would be cowardly, that wouldn't be living. Or might it still have been the wisest course? At fifty-five, why subject

4

life to deep questioning? At fifty-five, usually, the die is cast, the aspic set, and we are most of us just plodding on, doing the best we can.

I paid up quickly, not knowing how to proceed, but at any rate preparing for eventualities.

Like everyone, Olivia seemed in no particular hurry. She was chatting, bargaining perhaps, with the young *brocanteur*, always such an agreeable pastime in southern France. Then, as I moved towards her, she suddenly looked up. It must have been intuitive, I thought, she must have felt the pressure of my gaze, sensed my concentrated presence. Something like that, because she looked right at me, but then sort of through me, as though I wasn't remotely in focus, as though whatever prompted her gaze had proved to be a false alarm, and she returned to her bargaining.

Good God, it was all so strange! I stood there literally open-mouthed, for I had been about to speak. And that was when, as the English used to say, the penny dropped. It couldn't possibly be Olivia. Thirty years on and virtually unchanged — not even Olivia could have achieved that. Nor could I envisage Olivia wearing jeans, as this leggy young woman was doing. Though in this I might simply have been out of date.

But under the spell of it having been Olivia, I watched, enthralled, as the young woman paid for and pocketed her treasure — an ugly faience sugar bowl, it looked like. My eyes still followed as she sauntered towards the one smart café, its green awning fronting what was also an 'antiques cave' entrance. She looked back once, saw me charting her progress and frowned slightly. I didn't care. Why should I?

Why? Because sitting in the sun at one of the painted metal tables, peering briefly at a bill the waiter had laid down, was indeed Olivia; and this time there was no mistake. Olivia, who had once, with consummate success, totally wrecked my life and changed its course and me for ever — yes, that *can* happen, such catalysts, even inadvertent ones, *do* exist — Olivia, whose life I vengefully must have helped to wreck as well; and suddenly here we were, two former ship-wrecks, apparently re-caulked and under full sail again, crossing, fortuitously or not, each other's paths.

My nerve was rapidly dwindling in this see-saw of discovery and error. Fear weakened me like a fever; but clutching my bag in front of me with both hands, I marched resolutely forward. No soldier going into battle could have been more brave, I thought.

6

The girl, a dead ringer for her mother thirty-five years ago, saw me first. She looked uneasy, as though some lunatic was bearing down on her, and moved closer to her mother's chair.

'Olivia!' I called out in a voice that most certainly was not my own.

Searching for change in her purse, she looked up. For a moment there was blankness, mild bewilderment. She put her hand to her brow to shield her eyes for a closer look.

'Kate . . . ' It was somewhere between a question and an exclamation. 'Why, Kate!' She stood up.

'Hello, Olivia,' I said coolly, coming alongside the table.

And falling into a conventional greeting, we kissed.

'I saw your daughter in the market a minute ago, and I thought it was you. The resemblance is simply amazing.'

'I'm immensely flattered.' Olivia smiled her Mona Lisa smile, and introduced me to Caroline.

'How on earth did you know my married name?' I asked.

She said she'd read of my marriage in our alumna magazine.

I was smiling warmly now. We both were.

'And you?' I asked.

'Lanier,' she replied. 'Olivia Lanier.'

'You live here, then? In Bordeaux?' It was fairly obvious, but I had to say something, and preferably something banal. That would be safer.

'In the country, about an hour from here.' She had left money for the waiter and, still standing, she regarded me solemnly. Bordeaux was her city, so of course the social shoe was on her foot.

'I'm afraid Caroline has a dental appointment.' She glanced rapidly at her watch; there was another pause. I could almost hear the neural cogs clicking, and to give her time I quickly explained my presence in Bordeaux.

'Why don't you come and see us, Kate?' Another pause. 'I mean it. Why don't you come for lunch tomorrow? It's the *vendange*, grape-gathering time, but Sunday lunch is always Sunday lunch, and afterwards it might be nice to have a chat.'

'I should like that very much,' I said. I meant it too; my long-nourished animosity had mysteriously evaporated, or else it was on hold. Hers too, it seemed. Or were we letting bygones be bygones, just like that? If so, it struck me as a rare event. After a crash, friends, unlike families, almost never make it up. The chance to meet and do so is removed.

But a shared past inexorably connects and, when one is older, can become almost a family connection; the years do it automatically, without any help from us.

I said I would hire a car, the hotel could easily arrange that; but because of the conference, I would have to come alone.

Again she looked at me a little oddly, again the Mona Lisa smile, as she drew up a quick map with some instructions. Had she thought I would refuse? Well then, she was mistaken. We'd both made a decision and were sticking to it. At long last we were, it seemed, going to see the whole thing through; though never did I remotely suspect what that would mean.

I watched the pair of them disappear among the stalls, and then I sat down and, though it was only eleven o'clock, ordered a gin and tonic. I needed it. I felt deadbeat.

The first thing I thought about was how Olivia, at Caroline's age, had seemed so goddess-like, in a quiet and regal way, so full of elegance and sophistication — so full of mystery. Yet any grown-up would probably have seen what I saw in her daughter: beauty as fresh as rainwater on a peach; a lovely face, exquisite, yes, but also placid, empty — a *tabula rasa* that would require considerable imagination to render interesting.

Now, however, Olivia's face had genuine

definition. There was character as well as beauty in it, the poignant evidence of beauty's slow erosion, the visible lines of experience, even of pain and disappointment, perhaps. Or was I reading too much in again? At any rate, I now saw that when young I'd worshipped a sort of graven image. Well, people do that, don't they?

I noticed too that she had kept her excellent figure. It was not the sort that comes from dieting, health clubs and personal trainers, but one derived more naturally, out of doors: horse riding, tennis, walking, that sort of thing. She was quite brown. I could imagine the well-stocked stable, the tennis court and discreetly hidden swimming pool, the ancient château flanked by its seigneurial *pigeonnier*, the flats in Paris and Bordeaux. For whatever her husband's wealth, there was to boot all that Rockefeller money.

'My French isn't very good, it isn't *couramment*,' I'd said, thinking of Monsieur Lanier.

'Then we'll speak English,' she promised.

★ ★ ★

That was yesterday. And now I sit in an anonymous hotel suite, distraught, my mind

10

in shreds, gabbling maniacally away, aware only that I must get this story straight, make sense of it once and for all, and put things back into perspective. What I need, ideally, is the impartial confidence of a stranger. So much better than a friend, who would be judging, building up her secret interpretation based on previously formed views; or for that matter, *in extremis*, a psychiatrist, who would be looking for personal cracks and flaws requiring remedial attention. A stranger on a train, that's what I need!

I might even imagine that I am on a long train journey, instead of sitting here alone, writing this in an opulent, overly furnished hotel suite. I could imagine I am crossing the great expanse of Russia's steppes — that's something I've always wanted to do — travelling in a closed, well-heated compartment, the clumps of white birch trees adding to the reassuring monotony of the snow-flecked plain and pale white-silver sky — a dull and repetitive background against which my story may be welcomingly projected.

And you are seated opposite. Perhaps you are a foreigner, it's hard to tell, but by your clothes and demeanour you are evidently from a similar milieu, so there is much that can be mutually understood without elaboration, even between strangers.

11

I like the idea of our cosy isolated intimacy, uninterrupted except for the occasional clatter of a tea trolley passing along the corridor, bearing a steaming copper samovar and plate of little sticky cakes. I anticipate the expression of surprise, also of wonder and compassion, of incredulity and dismay, as your gaze moves from the window alongside to rest on me, back and forth, as my story unfolds. I relish our special intimacy, the intimacy of the confessional, as it were — while at the same time and with equal pleasure I foresee the resumption later on of our separate, non-intersecting lives.

But listen, I can hear the tea trolley right now, rattling noisily in our direction, the vendor calling out something repeatedly in Russian, in a loud voice, the adjacent compartment doors being opened by eager customers.

Well then, shall we begin our own communion over a glass of steaming lemon tea?

2

If you haven't already guessed, and many don't at first, I am American. So this story begins in America. It begins in 1954, when I was in my junior — that is to say third — year at Sweet Briar College in Virginia. Sweet Briar was in those days, together with Bennington, the most expensive women's college in America. It cost two thousand dollars a year. But there the similarity ended. Bennington was highbrow and progressive, while Sweet Briar's reputation depended on what part of the country you were from. If you were a Southerner, it was thought the finest education a young woman could get. If you were from the North, however, you went there if you hadn't got into an Ivy League college and your parents could afford to pay the fees. This gave it the reputation of a 'debutante school'.

I was from Kansas. My father owned a small farm-machinery business in Wichita, but, significantly, my mother was from the South. She was from the mysteriously dismembered branch of an old and distinguished Southern family, and Mother's

13

dearest wish was somehow to graft our near-moribund appendage back on to its venerable Southern trunk, which meant, essentially, retrieving an established position in Society. Sweet Briar being a repository of well-to-do Southern girls seemed to her therefore a step in the right direction. Yes, Mother had strong social ambitions and I was taught them early on in life. An only child, I was, you see, her sole investment in the future, and my admission to Sweet Briar the first promise of growth in her investment's capital value.

Of course, we could never have paid the two-thousand-dollar tuition, but I had won a full scholarship — the only full scholarship the college offered. It meant I had to wait on tables in the refectory, but all the scholarship girls did that; it wasn't in the least demeaning. The girls weren't snobbish; they were much too well-behaved and innocent for that. And, naturally, I had to keep my grades up, which wasn't hard: learning was mainly by rote and I was blessed with a near-photographic memory — an eidetic memory, I believe it's properly called. But in any case, female education was mainly decorative, a sort of polish designed to give a pretty surface extra sparkle. It was also, indirectly, about learning tribal values and displaying them with feminine charm, and being agreeable and competent in social life. We weren't taught to think, to scrutinize or question things, chiefly because already our paths were fixed. Marriage and rearing a family comprised our destiny. There were no two ways about it; everyone accepted that and aspired to it. Nothing else was on the menu. Going to work, even having a career, especially after marriage, carried a stigma of social inferiority or, at best, financial embarrassment. It all seems very silly now, but, as I expect you know, that's the way things were — and how they had been for well-bred girls since history began. The really remarkable thing isn't that, therefore, but that it changed so fast. And mine, I see now, was the in-between generation.

Mother's first dividend on her investment appeared when in my sophomore year I came to room with Polly Brydonne. Polly — Gollypolly, we called her — was from Nashville, Tennessee. Her family had produced a Confederate general and they were fourth-generation owners of an ante-bellum house. From Mother's point of view, therefore, Polly was quite a catch, and subconsciously I must have felt so too. But it also happened that we got on extremely well together. Dear lovable Polly! You can never imagine what will happen in life. And what did happen — that awful accident, if you could call it an accident . . . But wait, I'm running ahead, when I must keep to chronology, tell everything in order, exactly as it happened, since it's precisely order that I'm trying to achieve — and through it, perspective. But I must explain some of the background first, because it's central to understanding so much that subsequently occurred.

Mother's hopes for a Southern re-graft rocketed when a romance started between Polly's brother Billy and myself. Billy Brydonne was at the University of Virginia law school and his infrequent visits to his sister had suddenly switched to frequent visits to his sister's roommate. I felt flattered and excited, and yes, there was a secret triumph in it too, while Mother I am sure was overjoyed, and Polly took it, as she did so much else, with bemused good nature.

Billy was an exceptionally nice young man: able, honest, upright, and handsome in a chiselled-chin, blue-eyed American way. And who knows, if I hadn't gone abroad that summer I might have married him. Though it's true Mary-Moore Montague went abroad at the same time, and she *did* marry him.

But first, more of Polly, Gollypolly, who is of such importance in this story. Polly was very petite, no more than five foot three. She had short curly brown hair, a gamine face and a minute doll-like mouth. Her big hazel-coloured eyes never seemed to blink, and she rarely laughed or even smiled. Her mouth was too small to spread that far, we said. But behind Polly's doll-like fragility reposed a natural sceptic. She thought a lot of things were rum, and it caused her to say unexpected and outrageous things, deadpan, which was why we called her Gollypolly. 'Golly, Polly, you don't mean it!' the girls would cry in response to one of Polly's dry, cynical-sounding ripostes.

Mind you, outrageousness was, in the 1950s, pretty mild, and in Polly, I see now, it was partly an affected cynicism, overlaying the emergence of something else. But no doubt we often got impressions wrong. Our self-knowledge — and so our knowledge of others — was almost non-existent. We rarely ever thought of 'self'. I don't mean we weren't sometimes selfish — that's instinctive — but we were devoid of self-awareness. We never examined our motives or made a rational study of our desires. What tadpoles we were! That the sixties were just around the corner was inconceivable, and I still don't know how that deep abyss separating the two decades was breached. It required a gigantic

17

leap or else a long slow crawl. And even then not everybody made it.

Principally, the deep abyss, as you know, was sex. More than any other thing, sex governs life: origins, inclinations, passions, offspring. And yet — isn't it extraordinary? — the subject was never mentioned. It was never discussed, either objectively or theoretically, nor were sexual experiences secretly confided. By some sort of bush-telegraph code we knew that 'petting' was acceptable, but not 'going too far'. Boys did not respect fast girls, that was axiomatic. And so, dedicated to this temple of high respectability, we intended, rather like Roman vestals, to enter our calling, which was marriage, as virgins. And it's my belief most of us did. But you couldn't be sure, since no-one ever said. The subject, being taboo, lay hidden below ground, like a buried landmine awaiting willy-nilly the wrong-footed. The truth is, I suspect, that before the Pill people simply didn't know how best to treat this primitive but crucial and potentially explosive issue. So they hid it under the carpet or cursorily locked their daughters up, keeping them innocent and brainwashed, so as to lower temptation. And it largely worked. Even Sigmund Freud was taken in. He declared that young women, after sexually alert

18

childhoods, normally went through a period devoid of sexual interest. He thought it might be biologically inherent. But ask any young woman today!

Another Sweet Briar taboo, and in its way a more surprising one, was talk of money and background, which was deemed vulgar and ostentatious, also undemocratic. This levelling of the playing field meant that nastier instincts, therefore, having less need to grow, were often nipped in the bud, and the better, more tender ones, saved from these tough weeds, flourished more easily. It all went to create a homogenous, egalitarian tribe of well-brought-up young women: polite, considerate, largely free of malice, truthful; and thus equipped, ready to face our adult lives as ladies — a word that, rightly or wrongly, has virtually disappeared today, together with much of its philosophy and trappings.

3

It was right after Christmas in the middle of our third year that Olivia Hartfield arrived at Sweet Briar. A big limousine delivered her and a great mound of luggage to our dormitory front door. I was on my way to the library and, fascinated, I couldn't help dawdling on the sidewalk, looking over my shoulder and pretending to search for papers in my book bag.

A full-length beaver coat exaggerated Olivia's willowy figure, her pale silky hair hung loose about her shoulders, and she carried a little crocodile case for jewellery or cosmetics or something. To the fingertips she looked like a svelte *Vogue* model about to enter an expensive metropolitan hotel. Other girls, passing by in their polo coats, saddle oxfords and white bobby socks, stared too at this cosmopolitan vision, convinced she was a visiting celebrity and wondering how they might see more of her. Their interest wasn't entirely gratuitous: we were forever on the lookout for role models, and here was one straight off the pages of a glossy magazine.

When Olivia reached the front door, Vivien

Doakes, our dorm president, who had been forewarned, was there to welcome her.

'It's very pretty here,' Olivia apparently said, looking around with some surprise. 'We're on a former plantation, aren't we?'

'It's a farm now,' Vivien, as she told us later, had answered with a shrug. 'I don't know why, but plantations went out with slavery.'

'Ah, *c'est un mot démodé*,' breathed Olivia.

'What?'

'Oh, I meant it's an unfashionable word. You must excuse me, please; I've just come back from France. I was in school there,' she volunteered after a pause. 'At the Sorbonne.'

'We have our own fresh milk and beef and there are horses and things,' Vivien had ploughed on. 'Do you ride?'

'Why, yes, but I didn't expect to here. How very nice to know one can.'

' "One," ' Vivien repeated with emphasis that afternoon in the smoker. 'That's what she calls herself. Very singular!' Vivien said Olivia knew nothing whatever about Sweet Briar; evidently she'd simply been shipped there, but her face had lit up a bit as she took it in. 'I think she was expecting Sing Sing.'

The smoker was crowded. Olivia's arrival had created a stir and everyone was curious

21

and hoping for news, Polly and I included, since Olivia had been given the room opposite ours. It was free because Susy Pelham had been in a car crash over Christmas and wasn't coming back that term.

'What's she doing here?' Mary-Moore Montague asked in a show of mild confusion that was typical. 'I didn't think students were permitted to enrol this late.'

Vivien shrugged. 'Special dispensation, maybe. All I know is Dean Allen told me to look out for her and make sure she got a friendly welcome.'

Pookie Payne, playing bridge at a corner table, leaned sideways and, pushing the smoker door shut, lowered her voice to a whisper. 'Special dispensation is right. I know all about it.'

Nobody said a word. We just waited.

'Her father's very distinguished: he was our ambassador to Egypt till a year or so ago. And they're rich as Croesus: Mrs Hartfield is a Rockefeller, no less.' (Pookie, like the Hartfields, was from Philadelphia.)

This caused a predictable buzz. It was odd enough to arrive so late in the year, but it was odder still, in light of this news, that Olivia wasn't at Bennington or Vassar. The mystery was all the greater.

'Her French is exquisite,' Vivien informed

us. 'She was in school at the Sorbonne.'

That popped a few eyes previously bent over books or knitting, and Sally James, a great leveller, was moved to say, 'Maybe she flunked out.'

'Stick to your knitting, Sally, dear,' said Pookie. 'Mother's told me the whole story. I spoke to her not half an hour ago. She says Olivia was yanked out of school by her parents — overnight, just like that. She'd got into the clutches of some fortune-hunter — and had fallen for him. Her family got wind of it in the nick of time.'

I know I've said money and background were never talked about, but Olivia's case was exceptional. Her father having recently been posted to Washington might easily have explained her presence at Sweet Briar, due to Washington's proximity. But that didn't suit our speculations in the smoker that afternoon, and frankly no-one really knew the truth. The point was, Olivia's background being international, not provincial like ours, and Rockefeller money being on such a superhuman scale, would have made her different in any case. For those reasons alone she would have been a sort of foreigner, and the emerging mysteries only added to the impression. But the fact is, I believe we felt unconsciously that she was too good for us.

Like a diamond sparkling in a parure of semi-precious stones, she simply didn't fit.

★ ★ ★

That evening, shortly before dinner, Olivia knocked lightly on our open door and, coming in, shyly introduced herself, formally shaking hands, which seemed to us so elegant and European.

'I'm so sorry to bother you,' she said. 'I hope I'm not the person from Porlock, but I wonder if I could borrow a safety pin. I don't seem to have one, which is very silly of me.' That was all she said, she didn't add what for. Olivia never said more than was absolutely necessary.

We thought of her great mound of luggage: safety pins would be like needles in that piled-up stack.

'Oh, I'm sure we've got one,' I insisted, already dying to please. 'I'll dig it out and bring it right over.'

'That's very kind of you,' she said, as though it really was a considerable favour I was doing her. I felt as pleased as Punch.

Polly, sitting propped up on her bed, more solemn and round-eyed than usual, had said absolutely nothing. She was busy sizing Olivia up, trying critically to put her into a safe pigeonhole, I suspect, thinking about it now.

'Who's the person from Porlock?' she asked me suspiciously.

'It's to do with Coleridge. He got interrupted by someone from there when he was writing 'Kubla Khan', and he could never finish it.'

'He was looped on dope, is why,' said Polly knowingly, watching my enthusiastic searching with disdain. 'Are you going to bear it over to her on a pincushion?'

In fact we bore it over together, out of curiosity (and without the pincushion). That was how we got to see the room. I think we were expecting something stylish: a good rug, chintz curtains, framed pictures on the walls. But to our surprise, a nun-like austerity prevailed. There weren't even the Impressionist posters, frilly bed cushions and cluttered bulletin board with which girls generally softened dormitory life. There were some books, but the walls were bare. On top of the chest of drawers, however, was this extraordinary Egyptian bas-relief. You didn't have to know anything about Egyptian art to see that it was something fine, a work of museum quality. It was about a foot square, in honey-coloured limestone, with two standing figures in profile finely carved in low relief, and surrounded by a delicate hieroglyphic script incised in the stone.

Olivia was visibly pleased at our interest. 'It's from a tomb near the step-pyramid at Saqqara,' she said. 'It's Isis and Osiris.' She even told us the story: how Osiris was murdered by his envious brother Seth, and Osiris's wife Isis wandered over Egypt collecting pieces of his body, and, putting him back together, had restored his life. 'A tale of fidelity and passion — one of the earliest, I think,' she concluded, looking with marked compassion at the bas-relief, on which a few streaks of paint still remained.

Yet the rigid, mummified figures showed no signs of passion, or even life — quite the reverse. Clearly we were in the kingdom of the dead.

'Passion and fidelity, what an imagination!' we agreed afterwards. 'Corpses in swaddling clothes, more like.'

Yet despite our disparagement, the intensity of Olivia's story stayed with us. She'd gazed at that bas-relief as if it were a sacred icon or a pietà reposing in some church. And mulling this over we decided that, like Isis, Olivia too was deep in mourning. She was pining for her awful young man in Paris.

'Maybe he isn't so awful,' Polly offered. 'Maybe her parents are. Maybe they're being tyrannical.' Polly's own parents were notoriously tyrannical. Correct or not, this thesis had immediate appeal. A maltreated and unhappy Olivia contained the dimension of suffering needed to change her from remote ice-goddess into a figure of affection in our impressionable young minds. For gods and goddesses who can suffer like humans receive the deepest devotion. Christianity picked up on that one pretty quick, and maybe the Egyptians had too, which is why the Isis and Osiris myth has lasted for so long.

★ ★ ★

'She never gets any letters,' Polly said a few days later. Olivia's letterbox was next to Polly's and Polly could see through the glass.

'And she never goes out.'

Worried that she was lonely, we considered introducing Olivia to one of Billy's friends, or Jimmy Hills's, the UVA undergraduate who was Polly's young man. But something told us she'd be bored or, worse, the boys might look dull in comparison, losing some of their necessary glitter in our eyes.

As it turned out, Olivia met them anyhow only a few days later.

Billy and Jimmy had come down from UVA to take Polly and me out, sharing the long drive. I was with them in the dormitory parlour, waiting for Polly, and I had just signed out for the evening when Olivia came in the front door, her head down, reading something. As usual, she wore no make-up and her pale straight hair, held back on the nape of her neck, had a few strands loose about her face. Instead of looking unkempt it had an appealing Botticelli effect.

I called out, out of politeness, and she came over, stuffing the letter she was reading back into its envelope.

Of course the boys, having heard much of Olivia, were intrigued.

'Polly's brother!' she exclaimed in wonder when I introduced Billy. It was such a warm smile, so full of friendliness and fellow feeling, like sunshine bursting from behind the clouds — really dazzling, and the first time I had seen it. Olivia said she too had a brother. In fact, she'd just received a letter from him. She said he was an archaeologist in Egypt, or there studying to be one. 'We were brought up in Egypt,' she added. 'It's a wonderful country.'

'King Farouk didn't do it much good,' Jimmy announced, trying to impress or simply to hold his own. 'Their last pharaoh, let's hope.'

'He did seem self-indulgent,' she agreed.

'But there's a nationalist movement now, you know — a man named Naguib. But I know so little of politics; it's inexcusable, really.' Olivia wasn't a diplomat's daughter for nothing.

'She's something of a loner,' I told Billy and Jimmy later on at Tommie's, the local college dive. 'We still don't know what she's doing here.'

The four of us were sitting in a high-backed booth, eating hamburgers and drinking 3.2 per cent beer. Normally beer is stronger, but Tommie's, catering to students, was in cahoots with the college.

'She's more the Vassar type, all right,' said Billy, who found Yankee girls a disappointment. Impervious to Southern gallantry, they could never recognize a model gentleman when they saw one.

'Guess what, Polly — Olivia got a letter,' I teased. 'You haven't been on the ball. It was from her brother.'

'It's been known to happen.' Polly eyed her own brother accusingly. 'Or so I've heard tell.'

'He's living in Egypt,' I said.

'What, I wonder, is the Eiffel Tower doing on an Egyptian postage stamp?' Billy was smiling broadly, rightly proud of this forensic observation.

And we all leapt eagerly in.

'She's covering up for her young man in

Paris. They're secretly in touch.'

'And planning to elope. She's biding her time here, just waiting for the chance.'

'I doubt it.' Billy's good-humoured pragmatism reasserted itself. He would, I thought, make a fine lawyer — as eventually he did. 'If she's come home under duress, her parents will almost certainly have taken her passport; and she's under age.'

'Then she's doing time, sequestered in our oh-so-genteel convent.'

'Maybe she wasn't dragged home,' Jimmy, who had thought her very beautiful, opined. 'Maybe she fled a bad situation of her own accord, and she's here recuperating. Maybe Sweet Briar is her sanatorium — sort of like in *The Magic Mountain*.' Having recently struggled through Thomas Mann's great tome, he was pleased to find some use for what had seemed a tedious and futile labour. 'That letter could have been from anyone. She must have lots of friends in Paris.'

'Then why *say* it's from her brother? She *must* be covering up,' I said. 'But maybe they had a lovers' quarrel and now they're trying to patch it up. Maybe that's why she left Paris.'

'Or she found him with another woman.'

'And shot him. *Crime passionel*. There's a lot of that in France, and, unlike here, you can get away with it,' said Billy, again reaching, if facetiously, for a legal angle.

'So she's murdered him?' Polly cheerfully proposed.

'Or wounded him, and she has to lie low for a while. Maybe this is her hideout. Like you said, there's got to be *some* reason why she's here.'

'Maybe he *is* dead,' Polly went on, 'and she's collected all the bits and stashed them in that big trunk she put in storage. Just like Isis.'

'Gollypolly!' I said.

'My sister is very ghoulish tonight,' grinned Billy approvingly.

'And we are all of us extremely silly. Come on, Polly, let's dance.'

Dean Martin, singing 'That's Amore', had just come on the juke box and Polly and Jimmy, silently mouthing the words in an exaggerated mimicry, fox-trotted smoothly down the linoleum aisle between the two rows of booths, adding a flourished dip, where he swooped her backwards almost to the floor, whenever Martin crooned 'That's amore!'

'I do think she lied about that letter,' I said to Billy, as he lit my cigarette. 'You're right, of course, it must have come from France, so there must still be an illicit connection there.'

I reminded him of the bas-relief in Olivia's room and how she had told the story of Isis and Osiris with such ardour. 'Polly and I were convinced that she's in love.'

'Isis and Osiris isn't a love story, really; it's a fertility story,' said Billy, who had picked this up in comparative religion when he was at Princeton. He said Osiris was a corn god, and as king of the underworld granted eternal life to whoever he believed deserved it. But essentially it was a myth about regeneration.

I looked at him admiringly: Billy had some impressive back pockets of extraneous knowledge.

'Fertility was what life was about back then,' he went on. 'Every living thing was in the multiplication business. People as well as plants and animals. But eventually people wanted more than just to reproduce; they wanted to branch out, enlarge their opportunities. Leaving paradise behind wasn't to do with sex: sex was endemic there. It was to do with curiosity and self-improvement. That's where man came unstuck, because, having rejected one modus vivendi, he desperately needed another one. And finding it hasn't been easy, as Sartre so brilliantly points out.'

Sartre and existentialism were all the rage. Few of us had read him, but his ideas were received knowledge, carried like clouds of

32

summer pollen on the collegiate winds. We are born into this world without a purpose, so we have to find one for ourselves — or else. Moreover, being free, we are also alone, which makes us sad. Altogether a depressing philosophy.

Another couple had come in; the boy was a friend of Jimmy's, so when the record finished he and Polly went over to their booth and squeezed in.

'Why don't we go out to the car and wait for them?' suggested Billy with a sly smile, pocketing his cigarettes and leaving some money on the table.

So we did.

4

Despite Olivia living across the corridor, Polly and I saw little of her over the next two months. We had no reason to visit each other's rooms and Olivia never set foot in the smoker. At meals she was one of the last to enter the refectory, and unlike the other girls, who had more or less fixed places among their friends, she took whatever chair was empty. If I was waiting on that table, she always greeted me with a smile and never took anything without saying please and thank you; but I noticed she rarely joined in the conversation.

When we met in passing she was always kind, solicitous even, and remarkably modest, but behind an invisible barrier of reserve. This, I've subsequently learned, is a subtle accomplishment of fine manners, and, once you know how, can build as secure a barrier as any castle wall. But behind Olivia's wall there lay the further isolation of unhappiness; and yet she sought no comfort. Her aloofness wasn't due to pride or superiority, I think; rather, she was used to going it alone and never suspected that support might be on offer. It wasn't that she was too proud to take it. Polly and I were longing to be useful in some way, but our desire was nipped by her impeccable reserve, added to which so much elegance and dignity made us shy. So we watched from afar and Olivia bore her grief alone, shrouded heroically in a mantle of solitude and pricking with a sharp tenderness our idolatrous hearts.

'It's medieval!' Polly declared, watching from our window Olivia crossing the campus alone, as others walked together in twos and threes. 'Her parents have locked her up here exactly like in some tower, till she does as they say.' By nature a champion of the oppressed, Polly longed for a metaphorical chisel with which to break the bars and set the prisoner free. It wasn't possible, though.

Olivia spent most of her time in the library, where there was a reading room with comfortable chairs. She was a great reader. We had, however, the same art-history class, and that term we were studying the Italian Renaissance. Mr Joll would project magnificent palaces and churches, paintings and frescoes on to a screen and talk about them, highlighting salient points. But Olivia knew them all already and at first hand. She never said so, it just oozed out. For instance, when Mr Joll showed us some pictures by

Carpaccio in the Accademia gallery, depicting St Ursula, Olivia compared them with another series by him in some Venetian church (Scuola San Giorgio, I later learned). I couldn't tell if Mr Joll was pleased by that or not. I think it cut both ways. But it was pretty obvious Olivia was too advanced for such an introductory class. Why, then, was she in it? Was she killing time and didn't care? Perhaps. But it was also true, I think, that there was little on offer for her. She was deeply interested in archaeology and ancient history, but she stayed out of those classes, and if the Renaissance was anything to go by, it was just as well. As to languages, she could read Latin and was fluent in French and Italian; she even spoke Arabic — so languages were out. Nor could I see her cutting up frogs in the biology lab or wrangling with the abstractions of algebra or trigonometry. While English, she claimed, was simply a matter of reading: you didn't need to go to classes for that. An English major myself, I found this pretty surprising. I'd no idea that European universities simply gave you a list of books, you read them, then wrote an essay on the subject, occasionally going to a lecture and to see a tutor. We, on the other hand, were being spoon-fed in appropriate doses, the topic thoroughly mashed up first for easier digestion. Toddler food.

'There's a mythology seminar starting that might interest you,' Pookie Payne told Olivia one night at dinner. Waiting table, I slowed down to hear her response.

'The syllabus does look tempting,' she agreed. 'In fact I'm reading one of the books right now: *The Golden Bough*. It's fascinating.'

'Oh yeah,' said Pookie, 'we're starting to study that.'

'The idea of sympathetic magic, of seeing things as interconnected like that, is surprisingly abstract, isn't it? One wonders people conceived of it so early.'

'But it's so stupid!' Pookie answered. 'Believing you can put a curse on somebody if you get a lock of their hair or a fingernail clipping.'

'Desperate people have desperate hopes sometimes,' said Olivia wistfully.

'Besides, it works,' insisted Polly. 'Through suggestion. It happens all the time in Africa. People can die from having a curse put on them; they believe it works and so it often does.'

'Well, what do you expect from a bunch of ignorant savages?' Pookie rudely returned.

Polly didn't let go. 'You Yankees were burning people for witchcraft not so long ago in Massachusetts. That's ignorant and savage, all right.'

'And you Southerners still lynch Negroes,' Pookie riposted, seizing the moral high ground for herself.

At this, Mary-Moore Montague diplomatically changed the subject, saying she and Sally James had just signed up to go to Europe with Miss Grist that summer and was anybody else interested? They needed at least three others, because there was a minimum of five.

'What about you, Kate?' said Pookie, helping herself to mashed potatoes. 'I thought you were crazy to go.'

I was indeed. I'd tried hard to take my junior year abroad. I'd even got accepted at London University, but my scholarship, it transpired, couldn't be twisted legally to cover foreign tuition, so that was the end of it. But I still yearned to go. My entire education had been, if unintentionally, a preparation: history, literature, philosophy — all of it was European. In other words, Europe was where the cake we all consumed was baked. America, too young for much past, possessed an enormous future, but it was the past that had captured my imagination, because it was the past my education was about. An equally strong influence, of course, was Hollywood.

But the upshot was that all my perceptions of life were derived from books and movies, rather than from any direct experience or perceived reality — something I would never wholly surmount.

★ ★ ★

That night I wrote home, begging my parents' permission to go to Europe and promising to wait tables in Wichita's grill-room for the rest of the summer to help pay my expenses.

Happily, Mother pushed hard for it. Having always yearned to see Europe herself, she now resolved to get some pleasure at one remove. A European tour was important for any young lady, she insisted. It put a patina of French polish on her education.

It made me sad to think that so much Mother would have enjoyed in life was closed to her. 'Don't ever marry foolishly,' she used to tell me. 'Love needs money.' It was a very un-American notion, but Mother felt strongly the constrictions of her lot. She never once openly complained, however. Her generation accepted such things, while today such a nature would, I think, up sticks.

When the *Kansas City Star* agreed to take three articles called 'Wichita Girl Abroad',

Daddy was at last persuaded, and I immediately went to work on Polly, who, in turn, half-heartedly put the squeeze on her parents. Money wasn't the problem *chez* Brydonne, it was indifference. Polly's parents couldn't see the point of sending her to Europe. However, they were going to Mexico themselves, Billy would be working in a New York law firm that summer, and Polly must be put somewhere. Eventually therefore they agreed, convinced it was a waste of money, and putting her on such a tight financial rein that in the end she had less money than even myself.

That was when Olivia went to Washington. She'd hardly left college except to go into Lynchburg, our nearest town, once or twice. Now she boarded the train in Lynchburg and went to see her parents for the weekend. Though we didn't know that. We only found out when she returned and, knocking on our open door, came in and, for the first time, sat down. She was unusually animated.

'I hope this will be agreeable to you, and to the others,' she began. 'Perhaps I should have consulted you first, but I've just been to see my parents and they've given me permission to go to Europe with your group — if you will have me, that is.'

Declaring our delight, we were in fact

completely flabbergasted. Of course we were flattered and excited, highly complimented by the prospect of so glamorous a companion; but we were uneasy too, even a bit suspicious — or I was, because, frankly, the thing just didn't make any sense. Why on earth, when her parents had prised her forcibly out of Europe, would they turn around now and give their consent? Was it a pay-off for good behaviour, or was there perhaps a hidden bribe? Had she made certain promises — promises she mightn't be able to keep? Above all, why choose to go with *us*? Olivia knew Europe and we didn't. She wouldn't want to see the same things as us, and we almost certainly would bore her and be self-conscious in her company as a result. For the first time I experienced a frisson of ambivalence, because it looked suspiciously as though we were being set up to provide unsuspecting cover, even to become 'fall guys' in some mysterious, possibly even sinister scheme.

'Miss Grist can't possibly keep her in check,' I told Polly, 'if that's what her parents imagine. Besides, she'll have her passport — so who knows?'

Pointedly Polly picked up her notebook and began to study it. 'Maybe we've got the whole thing wrong. Maybe there isn't any mystery, and maybe there never was an awful young man or egregious French pickpocket. Who started that rumour anyhow? Does anyone know?'

I said I thought it was Pookie Payne.

'Pookie Payne doesn't know shit from Shinola. Well, she doesn't,' Polly responded to my look of surprise. 'That's a fact. She doesn't.'

Clearly, then, the flag was up to let the whole thing go. Olivia was coming with us and that was that. Everyone would have to make the best of it, Olivia included. And though I brimmed with doubts, I'd no alternative but to wait and see; while Polly, to my surprise, seemed genuinely pleased.

* * *

Another incident is worth recounting:

I was coming back from the library one night. I'd been researching a term paper on Henry James. It was very warm, the sky covered with stars and the campus lit by a nearly full moon, so that I was able to take a short cut across the lawn. There was a clump of trees and as I emerged beyond them I suddenly saw Olivia sitting on a bench. She was just sitting there quietly by herself looking up at the sky. I felt embarrassed intruding on such a private reverie, but I was too close to pretend I hadn't seen her, and for her not to be aware of it.

'Oh, hello,' I said. 'Isn't the moon lovely?'

'Lovely,' she repeated.

I had stopped a little in front of the bench.

'I was just thinking that the sun illuminating it must be shining over Africa right now. Or is that how it works? I'm so vague about the heavens.'

'You mean the African sun is beaming down on us right now, via the moon?' The idea was charmingly poetic and the evening instantly felt warmer, the world smaller, an integrated community of wondrous simplicity.

'In Egypt,' she went on, 'the sun is everything — that and the Nile. When the Nile floods and the sun shines they can eat. The sun always does shine but the Nile doesn't always flood. That's what gives the edge.'

'Egyptian religion had a lot to do with fertility, didn't it?' I ventured, cribbing Billy's information. 'I guess it's not surprising, since so much depended on it.'

'Come and sit for a minute, won't you? It's so nice out. Do you like mythology?' she asked.

'I don't know,' I said. 'I like its symbolism.

It's such an imaginative way of explaining things; it throws light on them even if it doesn't really explain, I mean like science does. And it's so *poetic*. Yes, I like mythology,' I went on, trying unconsciously to please. 'Though Greek and Roman are the only ones I know a thing about.'

'You're right, you know,' she said reflectively. 'Myth does seek to explain, at the same time as throwing out a veil of mystery, so that the wonder stays. The divine mysteries, didn't they use to call them? A need for wonder and mystery must be in our blood, part of human nature.'

'Part of our spiritual instinct,' I suggested, gazing self-consciously at the moon; 'our capacity for faith. But isn't mythology also a euphemism for out-of-date religious beliefs?' I'd recently lost my own faith (we were Methodists). It had fallen away before the rational premises of science, like chaff from an ear of wheat. As a result I felt freer, but a dimension was lost. 'The love of God sweetens the universe, I read somewhere,' I said. It had struck me as odd, because religion was surely about security — an attempt to gain some control over life — or to believe that one has, through faith. 'It's strange love got mixed in, and yet it's worked very well,' the new-born atheist pursued.

'Maybe Christian love is one of the great inventions.'

'Oh, the capacity to love . . . ' Olivia trailed off.

'Older civilizations often saw love as a kind of illness, didn't they?' I rabbited nervously on. 'They wouldn't have dreamt of including it in their marriages, let alone their religion. Whereas today it's what we want most of all, in life and in religion. I mean, for instance, everybody wants to fall in love and to marry for love. That's the great thing, isn't it?'

'If you're in love you're stuck with it, that's all,' said Olivia quietly.

This really surprised me. I couldn't tell if it was desperate or dismissive or blandly philosophical. Her tone held no emotion, something I later learned was true of many Europeans, making them so much more difficult to read than us.

Now it may sound ridiculous but this exchange was the nearest I had ever come at college to a philosophical discussion. Perhaps it was my fault, but as I've said, life was so agreeably blinkered. We really were immured in a sort of Eden with no reason to question things or pluck metaphorical apples — which at college means to engage in speculative thought. But my brain was excited and I wanted more.

45

Olivia and I walked back to the dormitory together and for the first time I felt a friendly, even relaxed connection. I'd learned nothing at all about her, but a gap had somehow been bridged, and I stole a sidelong glance to see whether she felt so too. Instead, an unmistakable sadness swathed her perfect features, but gazing up at that moon mirroring the African sun, they instantly recomposed into a goddess-like serenity. Africa must be in her blood, I thought.

5

Teaching European history, Miss Grist was well placed to monitor fledglings' trips abroad, and she was popular with the girls who had accompanied her previously. Miss Grist was in her fifties. She had bright blue eyes framed by fine gold-rimmed spectacles and her greying hair, set in a cold wave, a style fashionable in the 1930s, gripped her head like a moulded bronze helmet. She favoured flowered dresses and insisted on sensible shoes, her own were lace-up English oxfords worn with nylon stockings. She had a broad moon face and a decidedly flat behind, which we were to see a great deal of; for Miss Grist's popularity as guide and chaperone, we soon learned, came from her having no intention of shepherding her charges around the sites of Europe. She had interests of her own and she viewed her summer undertaking as had Little Bo Peep: left alone we would come home, etc., being well-bred girls and therefore remarkably sheep-like.

Before disembarking at Southampton, Miss Grist set this out in a short speech, her hands clasped firmly before her as she confronted our little semi-circle in the ship's saloon.

'In everything you see, girls, always remember the importance of history,' she said. 'History is the foundation on which the present reposes, and you are yourselves its product. Drink it in. Let it go to your head and to your heart. Then you will know better who you are.' She said we were on our honour to observe the college rules. Moreover, we should not talk to strange men, a point she couldn't stress enough where Italy was concerned; and we must take care to keep our money safe. She would hold on to our passports herself. At which Polly and I exchanged a rapid glance. 'Remember, if you behave like ladies you can expect to be treated as such.'

She said that we could find her in her room between five and six every evening, if needed. Otherwise we could go about as we pleased. 'Each of you has a guidebook, annotated by myself, and five days in which to digest a morsel of England and English life. Have at it, girls. We leave for Paris on the eighth.' And that said, Miss Grist marched off the boat in her sensible oxfords, her young lambs tripping along behind her in stiletto heels.

Oh, the ecstasy of Europe! I felt its intoxication as did none of the others, I think, rushing breathlessly off that first day to

48

Westminster Abbey, the next day taking in the National Gallery, then St Paul's, the Tower of London. I couldn't stop: this might be my only chance. And I thought repeatedly how much my mother would have loved it all.

Polly took London in her stride, as she might a summer storm or a flourishing vegetable patch; to her all things seemed equal under the sun. Olivia went off to the British Museum every day and did some sort of research. As to Mary-Moore and Sally, strolling nonchalantly on the ramparts history had so obligingly thrown up, Harrods was the cathedral to which their worship turned.

Each night we dined at our hotel, where we were on half-board. Roast lamb or meat pie, and dessert lost in an ugly yellow custard, made up the menu, preceded as a first course by the strangest corn-on-the-cob. It was the size of your little finger and seemingly grown under-ground, it was so pale, so anaemic looking. Now that was something to tell them about in Kansas!

London's austerity and general shabbiness was a big surprise. For us, the war had been over a long time, it was part of childhood, but in England rationing had only ceased the previous year. The handsome stuccoed houses badly needed paint and the famous monuments and buildings, blackened with soot from London's coal fires, appeared to be swathed in veils of heavy mourning. Outside our small Mayfair hotel was another surprise. The prostitutes abounded. We eyed these painted biblical harlots, who lolled in doorways or strolled impudently in the streets, with fascination and an innocent scorn. They were the antithesis of all that was ladylike, all we had been brought up to think was right and proper, and we were astonished they should so brazenly walk in the same streets as ourselves. Yes, we were certainly little prigs, so often an underpinning of youthful self-assurance, I'm afraid.

But it was Polly who introduced me so unforgettably to my morsel of English life. She had English cousins and she'd been ordered by her parents to look them up. When they invited her to their house in Oxfordshire for the day, she took me with her. That visit, undertaken so haphazardly, would influence the course of my whole life, but I could never have remotely guessed it then.

Polly had said nothing about her cousins except that her parents had sent them a few Care packages in the war. 'Bars of soap, aspirin, that sort of thing. So they owe us, and they're getting me,' she said.

Our taxi from the train station was

traversing alongside an interminable stone wall, so broken down it could not have kept anything in, or out. Beyond it, thick woods alternated with rolling farmland. I could see an old John Deere tractor, circa 1930s, trundling noisily along in the fields. 'That's Brydonne Park,' the driver announced. 'Lord Brydonne owns just about everything around here.'

'He ought to fix it up,' said Polly pertly. 'What does Lord Brydonne do?'

Gollypolly, I thought. It seemed an inappropriate question to ask a taxi driver. Nor had she told me that her cousins were titled. Uneasiness stirred, together with mounting excitement.

'*Do?*' There was a pause. 'Oh, his lordship judges at the agricultural shows, and he sits on local committees.' Another pause. 'He does a bit of shooting and fishing. His lordship is a proper gentleman,' he added finally, by way of a full explanation.

A litter of leaves and branches covered the road, as though a festive procession had passed by, an arboreal path having been laid down specially for it. 'We had a big storm last night, the electricity was out for two hours. It was almost like in the blitz,' the driver said. He sounded nostalgic.

The gates were grand indeed. A stone

escutcheon over the arched entry showed a pair of rearing dogs holding up a shield with what looked like some turnips on it. Leeks, I later learned; the Brydonnes had a Welsh connection. The gatehouse alongside stood empty, its door open. I held my breath as the taxi wound through the big park. Sentinel oaks like vast umbrellas sheltered a few horses, and the grass was spotted with grazing sheep, which, I was to discover, the English gentry used as lawnmowers.

Beside the drive, two young men were engaged in cutting up a tree that must have fallen in the storm. The taxi slowed to a halt. One young man, very tall, thin, a shock of pale yellow hair hanging over his brow, stood up straight and pushed back his hair as we approached. He was wearing braces over a plaid shirt, the way Abe Lincoln is depicted, splitting rails. The other man, in a cap, a little older, paused, leaning on his axe.

'You must be Cousin Polly,' the tall one said to me through the open window.

'*I* am Cousin Polly,' said Polly tartly.

'You're very tiny for one of us,' he said smiling, poised, pleased, and stuck out his hand. 'Cousin Arthur.'

'And this is Kate Preston.'

We shook hands through the window.

'H'llo, Ned.' Arthur greeted the taxi driver,

52

who shifted his cap.

'Tell the governor I'll be up in half an hour, will you?' he said to Polly. 'In time to change for lunch.'

Improbably, I took this for some sort of male governess, but soon learned it was his father to whom he had so archly referred.

As the house loomed, framed by gigantic cedars, its leaded casement windows, soft pink herringbone brick walls and fanciful Jacobean pepperpot chimneys seemed out of a novel. Suddenly I felt like Isabel Archer, Henry James's eager young heroine, visiting for the first time Lord Warburton's patrimonial estate. Playing a role and entering an imaginary life would help to hide my intimidation, which was mounting, and soon enough would have good reason to.

Lady Brydonne met us at the door. 'Now which of you is Polly? Let me guess,' she said, giving us a quick once-over. A thin woman, very tall: thin body, thin lips, a long thin nose, eyebrows plucked thin; unlike her son, she got it right. 'I see a vestige of the Brydonne nose on your little face,' she said in a high-pitched, condescending voice to Polly. Her tone declared the American branch's inferiority and Polly's surprising good fortune at having even a vestige of the primordial trunk.

England, I must add here, was a different place in many ways then from what it is now. Class permeated everything. Money being in such short supply, they fell back on it more heavily, I think, for status. Certainly class saturated Lady Brydonne's attitude that day, unless, looked at more closely, it in fact was, at the subtlest level, about money. But her entire conversation aimed to pin you down socially, rather than discover anything about you as a person.

'Kansas is the corn belt, isn't it?' she asked me, as we entered the elegant, oval drawing room. Her tone implied it was an insalubrious address.

'No,' I answered, with defensive pride. 'Kansas is America's breadbasket.'

'Then it's in the corn belt,' said Lady Brydonne shortly, giving me a peculiar stare.

'But Kansas isn't corn,' I persisted. 'It's wheat.'

'My dear child, corn *is* wheat,' declared Lady Brydonne with patronizing benevolence.

I shrugged. It was her house, and if she wanted to call sheep goats, or goats sheep, that was her affair. Then something occurred to me, a remote association I must have known in childhood but had never thought about since. 'Corn means Indian corn,' I added, in slender hope of clarification.

'Ah, you mean maize.'

'That's corn to us,' I said, apologizing. 'We call wheat and barley, wheat and barley. It's the reverse over here, I guess. Kansas is mainly wheat.'

'Wheat is the more desirable crop,' Lady Brydonne declared, conferring upon Kansas a clear if somewhat obscure award.

'*"Oh, everything's up to date in Kansas City. They've gone about as far as they can go!"*' Lord Brydonne had entered the room, singing the hit song from *Oklahoma* and transforming at a stroke the atmosphere, as he must have intended. A big man, red-faced, in a tweed jacket too small for him, his jovial easygoing manner was the opposite of his wife's. 'Now which is our American cousin: the short or the long matchstick?'

'Pick one,' said Polly, responding with ready mischief to his warmth.

But Lady Brydonne was already making introductions, so her husband proposed an attack on the sherry decanter. 'Where the devil is it?'

'Isn't the governor looking after you?' Arthur had turned up in a jacket and tie, a silk handkerchief bursting flamboyantly from the top pocket. 'Everybody's empty-handed. Ah, sherry,' he eyed the decanter with

55

disappointment. 'Wouldn't you rather have a whisky or a gin and tonic? No? I would. The latter, I think.'

From the start, Arthur Brydonne struck me as someone who, despite his easy-going poise, brimmed with contradictions. Friendly yet reserved, eager but reticent, his handsome, almost pretty face was over long, his aristocratic bearing verging on gawkiness. He had a job, he told us, in the City, London's financial district, something very junior in a bank, and he lived in London during the week. He didn't like it a bit. 'Country life is much to be preferred,' he announced good-humouredly, settling down with a whisky instead of a gin and tonic. 'Making money's awfully vulgar, but it must be done. So there it is and there also am I.'

Ambivalence about money was endemic, I would learn: the English spurned it at the same time as they dearly treasured it. But I think they knew its value well, since after the war even the better-off knew something of life without it. Where it came from mattered a great deal too: trade and industry weren't particularly respectable, though, oddly, finance was; while landed money was the best of all. But landed money was in retreat, according to Arthur: you couldn't give land away these days; nobody wanted it.

56

'Well, if you can't get rid of it and you don't like town life, why not stay here and run the farm?' said Polly. 'Make it more profitable.'

'This is the governor's patch,' Arthur merrily replied, giving his father a small salute with his glass.

'Besides,' Lord Brydonne took it up, 'what this family needs isn't another farmer but a financial wizard. Our hopes are pinned on the lad to make us a pile of lolly.'

'With income tax at 90 per cent, it's impossible to make real money in any legitimate way,' Arthur cheerfully insisted, implying that unless he revamped his morals the City was largely a waste of time.

'I should love to see the American South one day,' Lady Brydonne said to Polly, going in to lunch. 'You must tell your parents that.'

The American Brydonnes might be an inferior branch, but the American South at least had cachet; while Kansas, if no longer Red Indian country, was, to Lady Brydonne, indubitably redneck. She asked patronizing questions about square-dancing and drinking beer out of bottles, when she must have known better. And she stared unblinkingly as I shifted my fork from left to right hand between cutting slices of lamb. Polly, I noted for the first time, ate like the English did.

Lord Brydonne was of a different stamp, however, and, unlike his wife, fascinated by the great breadbasket that was Kansas. He asked questions about the crops, the soil, the land distribution and the farm machinery. He loved the big new American combines and longed to see one in operation. Suddenly Daddy's seemed almost an enviable business.

'Miles of maize, oceans of wheat, prairies teeming with game; now that's the big time for you,' he declared approvingly.

I suppose because I seemed knowledgeable about the new machinery and could talk about the latest John Deere threshing machine, he thought my family were farmers on a big scale — 'the big time' — and I confess I didn't disabuse him. I was clutching at anything to keep afloat in these formidable waters, with Lady Brydonne lying shark-like just below the surface, ready to strike (in order, as Polly later pointed out, to protect her boy's best interests).

'The governor wants to stamp his green thumb on the world,' said Arthur indulgently. 'An agricultural fief would suit him to a T. Why not sell up, Gov, hop it over to Kansas and stake out a farm? Be a pioneer,' he amiably teased.

'An excellent idea, my boy. If only selling up this old place could produce enough of the ready.' His eyes rolled dubiously over the magnificent plaster ceiling, while his wife, changing the subject, asked politely after our itinerary. It was clear she thought 'doing' Europe in a month incredibly silly and vulgar.

'Rome!' Arthur broke in. 'How very jolly. I'll be there in a fortnight myself, so if you're still around I'll look you up.' He was smiling warmly across the table at his pretty cousin, so warmly that I felt a little left out. 'I've nothing whatever to do there but see the sights,' he said. 'We could see them together.'

Polly promised to write with our dates and address, which caused Lady Brydonne to ask in more detail about our little group.

'*Ronald* Hartfield's daughter?' she exclaimed of Olivia, her thin lips opening in a surprisingly wide smile. 'We knew them in Paris. Peter, darling, you remember the Hartfields.'

Lord Brydonne screwed up his face reflectively. 'Everybody's going abroad,' he said, his large fists resting on the table, 'even though we can't take tuppence out of the country. How the devil do they manage it?'

'The black market helps,' said Arthur laconically.

'I read yesterday that your queen is abroad,' Polly looked blankly into space, 'with a big entourage in New Zealand. But I guess she's on an expense account.'

'Oh dear, she must be so exhausted,' said Lady Brydonne, with real compassion in her voice. 'Meeting all those natives. They're tattooed, you know: graffiti from head to foot. And they want to rub your nose when introduced. It must be such a trial for her, poor thing. My heart goes out to her!'

'Do you know her then?' asked Polly.

Lady Brydonne looked surprised. 'I've met her,' she responded stiffly. 'Several times.'

Wisely, Polly let it go. But later on, strolling about the grounds, she said to Arthur, 'You English are kind of peculiar.' We were being shown the flower garden and the ha-ha, a kind of moat separating garden from pasture, so that animals, though appearing to be within, were in fact without. Ha-ha. 'Why does your mother care so much about the queen's being tired or not, when they aren't even friends? Nobody cares about Mr Eisenhower's workload. He does his job, that's all.'

Arthur grinned. 'Mama would feel the same about a horse or dog, though not much in between, I should imagine.' His tone was wholly uncritical. 'That's the way we are.'

'Kind of peculiar,' Polly repeated.

'Oh no, not at all peculiar. Utterly predictable, in fact. Read P.G. Wodehouse and a bit of Trollope and you'll have us in a nutshell. We're very simple, really.'

'What about Henry James?' I asked.

'Never read him, I'm afraid. American, wasn't he?'

That succinctly disposed of Henry James.

At the end of the garden, in a tangle of weeds and honeysuckle, was a small fishpond, and our approach produced a scurry of diving frogs. On the far side, in a niche built into the garden wall, a stone figure was seated on a low plinth.

'Oh, look!' said Polly, ducking her head to see better. 'It's a Buddha — it's Siddhartha.' She had been reading Hermann Hesse's fictionalized life of the Buddha, which was becoming popular with college students, possibly as an antidote to existentialism. In Buddhism, man is never isolated by his freedom. Quite the reverse, since freedom means unity with the universe.

The Buddha sat cross-legged, facing the fishpond and smiling, patches of grey-green lichen spotting his flaccid body. 'He's a bit of a mystery,' said Arthur, pulling a handful of honeysuckle back the better to reveal the moss-encrusted statue. 'Great-Grandpa nicked him from some temple in Ceylon when he was governor there. He's supposed to be very old.'

'Stolen goods,' Polly declared in mild reproof. 'No wonder he's kept so covered up. That pond should have some water lilies in it — lotuses. Buddhas like that,' she added authoritatively.

'Great-Grandpa was a proper Victorian. He believed in pulling down false idols on behalf of Christianity — or so he said. I'll mention the water lilies to Mama,' Arthur added, pulling off a few of the enshrouding vines.

Polly and I exchanged a rapid glance. Were we being teased or patronized, or did Arthur really mean to give Lady Brydonne this impertinent advice? It was impossible to know.

Shortly before tea was served, Arthur and his father left to attend a local agricultural fair. Arthur, to our astonishment, was wearing a sandwich board that read in large print: VISIT BRYDONNE PARK. OPEN SUNDAYS, NOON TO 6PM. PRICE 2/6.

'See you in Rome,' he waved from inside his wooden carapace.

'Sure,' said Polly dubiously, but didn't wave back.

Arthur Brydonne would prove to be a more able and determined young man than he at first appeared. But that was later on, after Polly's accident, when, calmly and efficiently, he did everything he could to help.

★ ★ ★

'Poor as church mice,' Polly declared on the train going home, partly in self-defence. In this important department American Brydonnes held the stronger position.

'But what treasures, even if they don't have much of 'the ready'.' We giggled over that. 'The house is incredible,' I said. 'Did you see that marble bust in the hall? I'm almost sure it was Roman. And that portrait over the living-room fireplace — the one with the woman and baby — looked like a Gainsborough!'

'Well, the whole place is falling to pieces.'

'I'm not surprised, with taxes at 90 per cent. Why do they put up with it, I wonder? We revolted from Britain over high taxes,' I added proudly.

'Probably they feel guilty. They've exploited the poor for centuries, just ground them into the dust without a thought.'

'Well, your family had slaves and you don't feel guilty.' It had struck me that Southerners, generally speaking, seemed rather proud of the fact.

Polly looked wisely wry. 'I expect they're lying low,' she went on, 'waiting for the main chance.'

'You mean to get their hands on some 'ready'?'

'Yeah. They're a nefarious lot, if you ask me.'

I didn't agree. I was thoroughly entranced. Even Lady Brydonne's archness had, in the end, seemed picturesque. But as I've said, my whole life had been a preparation for this trip. Europe represented the high altar of culture, and bowing humbly down before it, I accepted every aspect as an obvious part of a superior world. On reflection, however, I might have heeded Henry James a little more.

'Arthur's nice,' I said.

'He's OK. His mother's hoping like hell he'll marry Olivia. Did you see that? Her face looked just like a cash register: dollar bills in both eyes, and when she opened her mouth I'm sure I heard a 'ping'.'

'Gollypolly, that's so *rude*. They were very nice to us.'

'Well, it's how the English get their money, they marry heiresses. I *have* read some Trollope,' she added with a superior little pout.

'You're calling your cousin Arthur a fortune-hunter, you know, like that boy over in Paris.'

'A gentleman fortune-hunter. There's a difference, if only in degree. England is full of them,' she added knowingly.

'Maybe Arthur *should* marry Olivia,' I said.

'Rockefeller millions would be well spent on that lovely old place, and Arthur isn't the type to run through money foolishly, like some ne'er-do-well.' I thought it a fine idea. 'Olivia's parents would approve of Arthur,' I said.

'You mean because of the title? Ping!'

We sat for a moment in mutually reflective silence. 'Lady Brydonne hasn't forgiven your family for those bars of soap, has she?' I said, referring to her very insistent superiority.

'Probably some of them had been used,' said Polly.

★ ★ ★

That night I wrote my first article for the *Kansas City Star*, mentioning the embryonic corn-on-the-cob and the young milord encased in a sandwich board, details which would make it a big success. Then I wrote to Mother. 'I wish we were seeing everything together,' I said, and I meant it too. It made me sad to think she must have been as eager and hopeful for life at my age as I was. Yet instead of expanding over the years, her life had shrivelled, owing, I was forced to conclude, to our pronounced lack of 'the ready'.

At dinner, Mary-Moore and Sally totted up

the day's spoils — tartans and Shetland sweaters from the Scotch House — after which I rapturously described our jaunt to Oxfordshire: the house, the setting, the putative Roman bust and probable Gainsborough.

Olivia sat silently listening, or not. If she knew of the English Brydonnes she didn't say so, and Polly was watching her intently for a response. 'What's your research about, Olivia?' she suddenly asked.

'The Pharaoh Akhenaten.'

We waited.

'He was a famous heretic. He threw out Egypt's traditional gods and ordered the worship of only one.'

'Sounds familiar.'

'Yes,' smiled Olivia, 'but in his case it didn't last. When he died the Egyptians went back to their old ways.'

'I'd like to visit Egypt one day,' said Polly. 'You make it sound really interesting.'

Olivia's eyes lit up with pleasure. 'I wish I could show it to you,' she said. 'I know you'd love it. Everybody does.'

'I bet you can buy some great scarabs there,' put in Sally. Scarab bracelets were all the rage at college. 'I'd love another bracelet. And a little blue faience hippopotamus, like that one in the Metropolitan. He's so cute.'

'I'd like to buy a camel's hair coat,' said Mary-Moore.

'*A camel's hair coat?*'

'Well, they have camels in Egypt. That's where they come from, isn't it?'

'Why are you researching Akhenaten, Olivia?' I pursued, even though something in her manner forbade direct questions, made them seem coarse and inappropriate.

'I hope to visit the new excavations at Amarna one day,' she said. 'That's where Akhenaten's palace was. He built a whole city in his lifetime, and when he died, it, like his religion, was abandoned for ever.'

'Would you like to live in Egypt, then?'

'Oh, I don't know about that. Part time would be nice, I think. But the summers are terribly hot and the people are so poor. They live as they've lived for centuries. Almost nothing has changed.'

'I like the idea of going back in time,' I said.

'Not me,' said Sally. 'But guess who's having the time of her life *right now*. Miss Grist. She's out on a date! We were in the revolving door, going in different directions, she out and me in. She had on a long dress and there was a man waiting on the sidewalk in a tuxedo, if he wasn't blown away. He looked so frail, she could have thrown him over her shoulder. Maybe she had to, it's so hard to find any taxis around here.'

'I'm glad she has a beau,' said Olivia.

Mary-Moore had begun to enthuse about the forthcoming sale at Woollands, which unfortunately they were going to miss because of Paris.

'You two are a shot in the arm for the British economy!' said Polly, irony scarcely clothing her fast-swelling irritation.

6

Two days later, stepping off the *wagon-lit* at Paris's Gare du Nord, even Polly's natural equanimity was mildly unhinged by curiosity. Europe's most elegant city lay underfoot and, thanks to Olivia, the promise of a romantic drama was added to its appeal. Probably all hell was going to break loose. Youthful enthusiasm prevented us from taking it very seriously, however. Instead, we felt ourselves part of an emerging detective story: Holmes and Watson with a riveting unsolved mystery on our hands — a mystery we alone eventually might unravel, since we alone knew of its existence and were, therefore, uniquely poised to monitor developments. A tearful passionate reunion, a blissful affirmation of undying love, even an elopement, might be on the cards — and if the last, and a hitch occurred, there might, symbolically speaking, even be a corpse. Such harebrained speculation added to the fun.

'If she's going to flit, it's now,' I whispered, walking through the crowded station behind Miss Grist. I'd picked the word 'flit' up in England. 'But she'll have to get hold of her passport first.'

'Not if she stays in France.'

'You can't even check into hotels without a passport over here,' I said.

'Well, she can tell Miss Grist she needs it to change money — and she's off.'

We had reached the taxi rank, where Miss Grist was busy instructing the porters, their trolleys piled high with sets of matching luggage. I'd babysat all one summer to buy my matching set. It was like the one in *Mademoiselle*'s full-page ad of a girl going off to college. Dressed in a sky-blue suit and hat, three white Samsonite cases stood in a serried rank beside her on the station platform. I'd wanted so desperately to be that girl.

But now another image was emerging, like a developing photograph: that of a young woman sitting bareheaded in a Parisian sidewalk café, surrounded by sunshine, cigarettes, a Cinzano ashtray, the *New York Herald Tribune* — in other words, an American in Paris. Hollywood provided endless such scenes to step into, for us to feel more interesting and, paradoxically, more real, as a result. For lacking self-knowledge, borrowed pastiche served instead, like a series of shifting mirrors, to give us views of ourselves. It was, too, a means of trying on new roles, even occasionally new personalities; and it was part of travel. And laying aside Olivia's absorbing drama, I prepared to give myself up wholeheartedly to its giddy intoxications.

The café Deux Magots, where I went that afternoon, perfectly fitted the bill. Like the Café Irunia in Pamplona (Hemingway's favourite haunt), the Deux Magots was an object of student pilgrimages, a sanctuary frequented by the worshipful, much as shrines like Compostela had been in the Middle Ages. The café's august habitués Jean-Paul Sartre and Simone de Beauvoir had long since moved on (as had Hemingway in Spain), escaping, no doubt, the continuous influx of ogling students; but their powerful ambience remained, the equivalent of invisible religious icons.

Sitting at an outdoor table, having paid my tribute to Sartre, I ordered a café au lait and began to look about me. All the correct ritual images were in place: louvre-shuttered buildings, smartly dressed women with little dogs on leashes, those extraordinary pavement *pissoirs*, and the capped metal cylinders, like small circus tents, on which advertisements were pasted. Everything was as it should be, by which I mean all the reassuring clichés were provided; and,

71

embracing this yearned-for if prefabricated Paris, I moved happily into another Hollywood dream-machine production. It was like a rebirth.

★   ★   ★

That night Olivia, to our mute astonishment, failed to turn up at dinner. Scarcely able to believe it, despite our earlier speculations and suspicions, Polly and I eyed the empty chair with a mix of awed acceptance and down-right incredulity. It was really happening, then: Act One had begun. Up to that moment it had been a sort of game.

But Mary-Moore said Olivia had gone to a dinner-dance at the American embassy. 'She had on a beautiful dress, a peach satin sheath, bias cut, backless. And little gold sandals on her feet. No jewellery at all.'

'Well, she'd hardly carry good jewellery to the dumps that we stay in,' said Sally, who felt herself deserving of the Ritz.

''Beauty is itself a jewel unsurpassed,'' offered Mary-Moore with a serious air. 'I think that's part of a Victorian poem.'

'A vicar's valentine, more likely,' answered Sally smartly.

Polly and I regarded each other in silence. Our own thoughts lay elsewhere, and though

72

greatly relieved by Mary-Moore's report, we admitted, back in our room, that we couldn't make head or tail of it. I remember our window looked down on a drab concrete courtyard where, as we were talking, a lame girl ironed, dreamily humming one of Edith Piaf's songs.

'Olivia's boyfriend won't be the sort to move in embassy circles, so I don't get it,' I said, half-listening to the humming girl.

Polly was washing her stockings in the basin. 'Family friends have asked her to a party, that's all.' But even Polly couldn't deny it showed a strange priority. And, frankly, we were a little disappointed in Olivia.

'Could be he does move in them,' I therefore suggested. 'Could be he's in the Arthur category of pickpockets. Lady Brydonne knew the Hartfields through the embassy here, so — '

'So, there are pickpockets and pickpockets.'

'It was never established he's a penniless student.'

'*Moi, je ne regrette rien, non, rien de rien,*' crooned the girl at her ironing board. I went over to the window and gazed down at her. The court was dimly lit by a couple of bare bulbs hanging on a wire. Till that moment, I had thought of Olivia chiefly as a victim of parental tyranny, but suddenly I began to see her as perhaps her parents did: the inevitable victim of her money. No matter how beautiful or interesting or nice she was, her huge inheritance outshone everything. She was like a fine automobile obscured by its dazzling headlights. The lame girl below was probably better off; she was ironing baby clothes and a man called out to her cheerfully from inside. But poor Olivia; who was going to see her as she really was and love her for herself, as she deserved? Someone with even more money seemed the only answer. It made for a very narrow field.

★ ★ ★

Next morning, when Polly and I went out, Olivia was sitting in the lobby staring at the front door, a book open in her lap — evidently waiting for *him*. When we returned that evening her key was in its pigeonhole, so she was out, and for the second night she did not appear at dinner. This time, though, no-one knew her whereabouts. But Mary-Moore and Sally had, as on most matters, their usual contrapuntal exchange.

'Maybe she just isn't hungry,' Mary-Moore timidly advanced.

'Maybe she *is* hungry, so she's gone to

Maxim's,' said Sally, picking distastefully at the mushrooms in her soggy quiche.

'Maybe we should warn Miss Grist,' I whispered to Polly. 'Maybe she *has* eloped or something.' For the first time I was frightened. The thing could become serious; it might even be calamitous. Two young people in love and wanting to be together was one thing, but what if Olivia's young man wasn't so young? He could be a sleazy con artist, a fortune-hunting predator who hung about American embassies, waiting to ensnare young heiresses. Olivia could have been Svengalied — people were — and, though she was under age, cleverly importuned into elopement. Such things happened. But if it happened now, Olivia's terrible plight aside, our whole trip would be smashed. The police would be called in, her parents would arrive, the newspapers would take it up and we ourselves, after questioning, would be sent packing — in other words, bundled straight back home.

Olivia had always had our sympathy and her growing vulnerability had, if anything, increased it. But the fact remained that without our knowledge or concurrence, we almost certainly were being used — our whole group was. We had become an innocent and largely unsuspecting front. And now, wilfully, callously, Olivia threatened to sabotage the whole trip. Suddenly I was furious.

'The bird is still in its cage, thank God,' Polly wryly observed next morning, peering at the empty pigeonhole behind the reception desk. Sally James was standing alongside. She and Mary-Moore were off to the flea market but planning to change their money on the black market first.

'They're crazy for dollars,' Sally laughed. 'They'll pay anything to get them. But would you believe it, Olivia insists on changing hers at the bank.' She shrugged dismissively, implying, Well, Rockefellers. What do you expect!

'Do you need to take your passport?' Polly asked, more po-faced than usual.

'Not us. Only if it's a bank.'

★ ★ ★

Polly and I took the bus out to Versailles. We meandered through gilded halls covered with magnificent tapestries and huge panoramic pictures, then strolled round the gardens, admiring the reflecting pools and spectacular fountains. But Olivia mostly occupied our thoughts. She would have her passport now.

'Maybe we should have followed her,' I

said. I was still angry, but I was worried about her too. 'He could be some kind of monster.'

'And you'd see it, even though she hasn't. Come on, love isn't all *that* blind.'

'But what if she gets kidnapped and held for ransom, when we might have prevented it?' I extravagantly proposed.

But Polly, whose head was well screwed on, opined that if France had posed a serious threat, Olivia's parents wouldn't have let her come. It only stood to reason. The implication being that if something did happen it wasn't going to be our fault, but theirs. 'It's none of our business, so let's just forget about it.'

★ ★ ★

Perching on the balustrade above the water gardens, we ate sandwiches and drank Coca-Colas bought in the café. The sky was bright blue, the air like crystal; June at its best, a glorious summer day.

'What a disgusting place!' Polly said of the vast colonnaded buildings spread out panoramically before us. 'Conspicuous consumption on a monstrous scale. This certainly puts Mary-Moore and Sally in the shade.'

But I thought it was superb. The world

needed a few grandiose thinkers, with their incredible vanity and the ability to operate on a monumental scale. 'Louis XIV is right up there with the Egyptian pharaohs,' I said.

'Did you know he made everyone stand up in his presence all the time, except duchesses, who sometimes sat on little stools?' Polly gazed disapprovingly over her sandwich at the palace, visible through a water jet spraying like a barely submerged whale. 'It's a wonder they stuck around.'

I said I had a theory about that. I'd been thinking about it, and I believed it was because of the hive. 'You remember your cousin worrying about the queen out in New Zealand?'

'She's not my cousin, he is.'

'OK, but you remember how solicitous she was? She was really concerned — as though the queen was a close friend or even a member of her family. You said so yourself. Well, that's because England is a hive,' I said. 'The queen is exactly like a queen bee: she's revered by everyone. They accept the hierarchy, just as people everywhere accept family hierarchies. Ditto Louis XIV's court.'

'The triumph of absolutism over free will,' said Polly. 'More fool them.'

'Yes, but the irony is civilization could

never have developed if everyone was equal,' I said. 'There had to be the privileged few who wanted its benefits and could pay for them, and workers to make it happen — make the honey. Democracy wouldn't have worked back then any more than it does in families now. There would have been no progress.'

'So?'

'So, the trouble is that even though that phase is over and rigid hierarchies are no more necessary than in a grown-up family, Europeans can't break the pattern so easily.'

'They could swarm.' Polly rolled the sandwich paper up and, stuffing it in her purse, slid down off the balustrade. 'You're quite the bluestocking, Kate,' she said. It sounded derisive, but I knew better, and Polly's compliments were rare.

'Maybe I'm not so brainwashed by Europe as you think,' I said. 'Or as Europeans are, anyhow.'

'Smallish hope of salvation.'

In the gaudy atmosphere of Versailles, Olivia's affairs had miraculously faded, and we returned to Paris thinking of other things. The fact remained, however, that if Olivia was going to flit it must happen now. We were off to Rome the next morning.

* ★ ★

To our mixed disappointment and relief, Olivia turned up at dinner; and what was more surprising, she seemed almost gay.

'I've had a letter from my brother,' she announced, looking about the table, trying to gauge our responses.

The Eiffel Tower was uppermost in my mind.

'He's in Rome, or will be when we get there.'

'I thought you said he was in Egypt.'

'He's coming from Egypt to attend a meeting.'

'What a coincidence.' Polly was desert dry. 'Have you had a letter from *my* brother?' she asked me.

'What's the meeting about, Olivia?'

'Oh . . . hieroglyphics, I think.'

Polly and I didn't need to exchange looks. It was impossible such a meeting should coincide with our brief stay in Rome. Moreover, we had had the brother dodge before. Now, however, we were obliged to admit its brilliance. Miss Grist could hardly object to a brother's presence, nor could she decently ask him for identification. It was, in short, a most ingenious façade.

'What about his accent?' I asked Polly later.

'It won't be American.'

'He'll say he's always lived abroad, hardly knows America.'

'He could put on an accent and say it's Egyptian; we wouldn't know. Miss Grist is no fool, mind.'

'Olivia could even have him up to her room and get away with it.'

Polly was visibly shocked. 'Well, you know, he could *be* her brother. People do fly to Europe from Egypt. It happens.' In a repeated show of loyalty, Polly invariably defended Olivia when the chips were down.

'You really like Olivia, don't you?' I said.

'I guess so.' She seemed to think about it. 'Yes, I like her. I think there might even be a considerable person tucked away in there. But she *is* deceitful.'

'Maybe she has no choice.'

'Maybe,' answered Polly, but it sounded flat.

7

Our hotel in Rome, small and old-fashioned, the lighting fixtures with low-watt bulbs, the bathroom down the corridor, was located in a narrow street off the Piazza Navona. I found then, and still do, that this great square — it's an oval, really, the site of the Emperor Domitian's stadium — is one of the loveliest urban spots on earth. Three magnificent Renaissance fountains stand in the centre, like grandiose candelabra adorning an ornate and monumental table. Encircled by terracotta-painted houses that rise above the unpretentious street cafés, a fine patina of dilapidation suggests Rome's ancient and multi-layered past — a treasure trove for those who, through their imaginations, wish to dig. But the piazza also blooms with ordinary life: children run about, lost in other, intensely imagined worlds; ubiquitous pigeons rise in dusty clouds, and a smattering of aspiring artists, planted before their easels, live out private visions of the artistic life. While local residents, inoculated by familiarity, sit in the cafés, impervious, their noses buried in the morning newspapers. On this illusion-bound and magnificent stage my adult life began.

★ ★ ★

The minute we had arrived in Rome I'd rushed off, map in hand, to imbibe the city's complex atmosphere, for Rome had embarked upon its celebrated *dolce vita* and even the poorer sections, I discovered, sang to an upbeat tune. Walking in the direction of the Pantheon, the narrow tenement-lined streets were abuzz with active, raucous life: neighbours shouted, young men sputtered past on Vespas, often with a girl behind, vendors bawled out their wares, and from the open-fronted workshops, craftsmen's hammers pealed out in lilting rhythms like carillon bells. For nearly everyone, life was looking up.

Entering the Pantheon's great rotunda, coming from sun to shade, noise to quietude, I gazed up, stupefied, at the vast coffered dome open to the sky — one of the most awesome sights of my young life. For two thousand years, people had been walking here, reduced to ant-like proportions by its immensity. *Memento mori*, its vastness seemed to whisper: life continues, but you yourself are a mere speck in time. Sobered, I sat down on a bench and pulled out the unopened letter in my pocketbook. It was from Billy. I read it through hurriedly, eager for the overall gist, and then more slowly, each word becoming a stepping stone in the direction of a happy and alluring future. As a result, my unease evaporated like a sun-drenched puddle, and my speck in time resumed again its seeming infinity.

When I got back to the hotel, Polly was in the lobby, also reading a letter. 'Arthur's here,' she said, without enthusiasm. 'He wants to show us the Roman Forum this afternoon and have dinner tonight. There's a trattoria — a sort of sub-restaurant — he knows about near here. Dutch treat, he says.'

Now even the poorest American male would have felt obliged to pay for girls that he invited out, so I was impressed, even if it was double-edged. 'It's nice of him to include me,' I said. 'But aren't you surprised he didn't ask us to bring Olivia along?'

'He'd hardly ask *her* to pay, though she's the most able to.' Polly said that Arthur was probably working up to something, saving his money to take Olivia somewhere nice, start the seduction. 'We're mere stalking horses.'

'Polly Brydonne, you've a very suspicious nature! Where's your faith in mankind?'

In a clown-like gesture, Polly pulled her

skirt pockets inside out and shrugged, smiling weakly.

'I've had a letter from Billy,' I told her. 'He's crazy about New York but says it's hot as hell.' Billy had also said he missed me, and that since we both were graduating next year there were serious things to talk about when I got home. He had thought a lot about the future and hoped that I had too. I didn't tell Polly any of that, of course, but an inner excitement glowed that was hard to keep under wraps. The future Mrs William Brydonne! I saw my mother's proud and beaming face; her family restored at last to rightful social prominence. But don't misunderstand me, please: I wanted it too. I wanted it very much! It was almost an answered prayer.

'He says to give you a kiss,' I teased.

Very pertly, Polly offered a cheek. 'They're always kissing over here,' she said. 'Judas should have been a European.'

Arthur's stock rose mightily that afternoon. Being at home in foreign surroundings and much more knowledgeable than ourselves gave him considerable elevation. Walking through the Roman Forum, a crumpled linen jacket slung over his shoulder, that silk handkerchief still blossoming in the breast pocket, and pushing back his shock of pale straw-coloured hair, he translated Latin inscriptions carved on lintels and blocks of fallen stone, and talked of Caesar and Augustus with ease and familiarity.

'Caesar was murdered just about there,' he said, as we entered the high-ceilinged former Roman Senate, one huge room, with low platforms flanking both sides. 'As soon as he sat down he was attacked, but he stood up again after the first blow, and seeing the daggers around him pulled the top of his gown over his head and ungirdled the lower part so it covered his legs, in order to die with dignity. After that he never once cried out. Twenty-three dagger wounds, according to Suetonius.'

We stood in awed silence. The scene, having been painted in such detail, produced that frisson of awe the past sometimes awards to history's devotees. Arthur felt it too, I thought, given the precision of his description. But as I've said, Arthur was full of contradictions. Years later I learned that Caesar had in fact been murdered not in this forum but in another one, called Pompey's Forum, which has completely disappeared. Arthur almost certainly knew that.

'But Caesar did so much for Rome,' I ventured. 'He built the Roman empire. He really put Rome on the map.' Shakespeare's play was about my only source, while Arthur had read Caesar's own works and in Latin. But I was a scholarship girl and trying foolishly to keep up.

'He was changing the republic into a dictatorship,' said Arthur. 'Caesar had been on stage too long and there was only one way to get him off.'

Was he a good guy or a bad guy, then, Polly wanted to know. She said that with power on that scale, even a bit of bad could outweigh what ordinary evil men could accomplish in a whole lifetime.

'People think of him as a 'good guy' now,' said Arthur, side-stepping this interesting question. 'And the Romans did too, once he stopped being a threat.'

I tried again. 'If someone's a threat, that person is in equal danger — because of reprisals — isn't he? Isn't that what happened to Caesar?' Hardly profound, it would be, I can tell you, a prophetic remark.

Arthur said that Caesar had misjudged his strength.

★ ★ ★

The restaurant Arthur had chosen was in the Piazza Navona, on the sidewalk opposite one of the fountains. It was charming and about

87

as simple as they come. Polly and I ordered spaghetti bolognese, that being the only spaghetti we knew anything about; while Arthur, by comparison a cosmopolite, ordered grilled scampi.

'Where is the rest of your group?' he asked, pouring wine into the tumblers that passed for wine glasses.

Assuming he meant Olivia, Polly answered perversely, leaving her out. She said Miss Grist was out on the town with the Cicero Society, and Mary-Moore and Sally had gone to see a movie: *Three Coins in the Fountain*. Evidently they preferred Hollywood's Rome to the real thing.

'It almost certainly will be dubbed,' said Arthur, unable to pursue his intended question further — if Olivia's whereabouts *was* his intended question. He just smiled at Polly instead, with real affection, I thought, and said that next morning we should visit the Palatine Hill; it was the most beautiful of the Roman hills. 'Splendidly bucolic,' was the phrase he used. He said sheep were grazing there, among the ruins.

That was when I kicked Polly hard under the table. She thought I was trying to get out of the trip, but in fact Olivia had just entered the piazza arm in arm with a young man. They were gazing into each other's eyes, holding one another close, and laughing. They looked so happy, as if just being together was everything in life.

'Oh look, there's Olivia,' I managed offhand, and to Arthur, 'She's with her brother. He's over here from Egypt — at some meeting.'

Arthur looked around, hurriedly for such a well-bred Englishman, and having of course no clue a labyrinthine mystery was attached. That could be useful, though.

If the pair were headed for our hotel they would almost certainly have to pass the restaurant; but they were taking their time. They stopped before the Palazzo Pamphili, then again in front of the central fountain, its Egyptian obelisk rising over an improbable stone grotto, fronted by an even more improbable carved, wind-blown palm. Perhaps you know it?

Beside the fountain stood a golden-haired little girl, holding a tin cup. Evidently enchanted, Olivia leaned down to speak to her and was shyly offered the brimming cup by hands that then covered her little laughing face. Olivia drank and, handing the cup back, gave the child a coin.

All this presented a chance to examine the young man who had inspired such avid speculation and suspicion. He was, quite simply, very beautiful — outstandingly so. No other word will do. He had, too, a sort of feline grace; I can't describe it accurately but it showed in every movement. He was a bit taller than Olivia and, unlike her, very dark-haired. It curled loosely all over his head at a time when Americans wore their hair cut very short — short back and sides. He reminded me of a bronze *ephebe* who'd stepped down from his pedestal in order to amuse himself for a spell amongst mankind. Oh, they were a stunning pair all right, no doubt about it — a couple to turn heads. And heads *were* turning. I think people were wondering whether they were film stars, and all around us smiles unconsciously ignited. One of them was, I noticed, Arthur's.

It would have been awkward to hail them, like breaking into a private conversation; and then too they mightn't wish to be seen. But as luck would have it, Olivia caught sight of us. She smiled and waved as they came forward, evidently explaining who we were, as one might on meeting old friends unexpectedly.

Arthur sprang to his feet like a jack-in-the-box. He even made a little bow, which caused Polly's short upper lip to curl.

'This is my brother, Hugo,' Olivia said. They were still arm in arm, beaming with kindly benevolence on the ordinary world.

'And this is my cousin, Arthur,' Polly returned with dry significance.

The pair unfastened so the young men could shake hands.

Hugo looked each one of us squarely in the eye. Like hers, his were blue, but a darker, indigo shade of blue, and more opaque; the pupils were very large. He had extraordinarily fair skin, I noticed, especially for someone supposed to be living in Egypt.

Arthur asked politely if they would join us, and without looking at each other they exchanged a subtle telegraphic communication — then said, no, they couldn't just then, but they would love to another time.

'Why not tomorrow?' Hugo affably suggested. He was looking at her, not us.

Polly and I strained like anything to get the accent.

'Why not tomorrow?' she repeated, as if these particular words couldn't possibly be bettered. 'And why not here? It's charming.'

So it was fixed: same restaurant, eight o'clock; and off they floated, re-entwined, their heads nodding together. Before they disappeared I saw her kiss him impetuously on the temple, or else it was his ear; after which he hugged her closer, if that were possible.

91

'Let me treat you to a sambuca,' Arthur offered when we'd settled the bill. It was, he said, *the* Italian liqueur. Evidently he wanted to celebrate — or else to thank us for something. 'What charming siblings,' he enthused. 'So fond of each other, too.'

Polly started choking. 'It's the sambuca,' she insisted, very red in the face. 'I swallowed the coffee bean in it.' But I knew she was laughing her head off.

We'd discovered almost nothing, except that they were going towards our hotel. Could they really be going up to Olivia's room? It would be a profoundly shocking and brazen thing to do. For though seemingly outside mortal reach, Olivia was nonetheless a Sweet Briar girl, and she was on her honour to obey the college rules. That meant that under no circumstances could a man enter your room, not even to carry a heavy suitcase, if he wasn't the porter. A brother would be different, of course, but Olivia hadn't pulled the wool over our eyes on that score for a minute. Unlike poor Arthur, we already knew too much.

Back at the hotel, Polly and I couldn't resist passing by Olivia's room on tiptoe. We could hear them whispering, then something fell off a table, it sounded like, and there was a lot of muffled laughter followed by 'sshhh', then giggling, followed by more laughter. We were so shocked that neither of us said a further word about it.

8

The Palatine hill was, as Arthur promised, gloriously pastoral — and it was virtually empty. It is not much changed today, except that sheep really were grazing among the fallen columns and massive palatial ruins, whose brick walls, shaded by umbrella pines and the black-green cypresses I call nature's church steeples, were remarkably intact. Arthur said the word 'palace' derived from Palatine, so many of the caesars having lived there. A few excavations were in progress, consisting of trenches topped by low corrugated-tin roofs; but the sites were empty and it was sorely tempting to climb down and pocket a souvenir or two. Which, I confess, I did: a small marble fragment of carved acanthus foliage. I've no idea what became of it.

We had brought some food and a bottle of wine along for a picnic, and shaded by an umbrella pine near what had been the Emperor Augustus's palace, a Corinthian capital for our table, and leaning against the stones that had built Rome, we poured the rough wine into paper cups and munched buns filled with pecorino and prosciutto. There wasn't a cloud in the sky and, being lunchtime, Rome's incessant traffic noise had given way to the humming of a single bumblebee. Miraculously, we seemed transported into an antique pastoral idyll — the habitués of a vast and surprisingly rural paradise garden, belonging exclusively to ourselves.

'It's exactly like a Piranesi,' said Arthur, obviously pleased.

I'd never heard of Piranesi, whose prints of antique ruins decorated many an educated wall, but I'd begun to notice that Arthur, though well informed, repeatedly saw things through others' eyes — Piranesi, Suetonius, etc. — instead of looking at what was in front of him. He had some sort of screening system worked out. But then, on reflection, I probably did too — for instance when exploring views of myself: an American in Paris, a girl going off to college, that sort of thing. But that was little more than theatre. Or was I mistaken? Perhaps it went much further.

Setting down my paper cup, I stared hard at Augustus's palace, a most extraordinary thought having entered my young head. The Palatine Hill pleased me, I suddenly realized, for much the same reason that sitting in that café had. Again, preconceived images had fallen kaleidoscopically into place, ritual clichés, derived this time not from magazines or Hollywood but from reading history, which for some reason cast over such scenes a mysterious and romantic gloss. In reality, Augustus's palace was a pile of rubble, while the Palatine Hill as a bucolic paradise — what on earth did that mean? Like a thunderbolt fittingly hurled at me by Jupiter, it struck me that everything I took pleasure in wasn't because of the thing itself, but because of associations I had invested in it. In fact, learning about something meant just that — making associations: giving a name to something, putting a frame round it and setting it in relation to something else. In other words, erecting a network of interconnection. It enlivened and opened the eyes, but whose eyes were they, and did no-one then, except an original artist, which was rare, see things as perhaps they really were? The discovery called into review my whole education.

But there wasn't time to think about it further. On the path below, two people had been climbing slowly in our direction. I hadn't noticed till, rounding one of the excavation sheds, they suddenly halted and, briefly conferring, turned round and, quick as jackrabbits, disappeared back down the path they had come up.

'Hey, wasn't that Olivia?' Polly had her hand to her brow, shielding her eyes against the sun.

The couple, having reached the steeper path below, were still walking fast, their backs to us.

'If it was,' I said, leaning over the hillside for a better look, 'that wasn't Hugo with her.' The man was much, much taller. His hair, seen from above, was a pale champagne colour and combed back over his head in the continental style. 'What did you think, Arthur?'

'I think whoever it was didn't wish to be seen or interrupted.' He was frowning slightly.

'By us.' Polly gave me a significant stare.

Arthur grinned at this, and I was laughing. 'It couldn't have been Olivia, and you know perfectly well why,' I said, alluding to Hugo. 'You're seeing things, that's all.'

'I certainly am!' said Polly with impish glee. 'I see things all the time. I really do.'

9

Dedicated Sherlock Holmeses, Polly and I had worked out a couple of sleuthing strategies to tease out Hugo's true identity over dinner: questions about Egypt and hieroglyphics, for instance, mentioning specifically Amarna, a name we had remembered and which would almost certainly trip him up. I planned to bring up the Sorbonne, since they must have met there, and see whether they tried to hide the fact. But Hugo, we agreed, didn't look like a fortune-hunter, or certainly not our idea of one. He looked like a young man any girl might very happily fall for. Evidently Olivia's parents wanted her to marry someone rich and famous and make a marriage to do them credit — circumstances that in part at least justified her deception.

Arthur, arriving at the trattoria before us, had secured the same table. It was separated from the piazza by a low hedge of potted shrubs, with a fine view, if you craned one way and then the other, of the entire piazza. The three of us had just sat down and Arthur had ordered a bottle of chianti when Hugo turned up, walking towards us across the

98

square, hands in his pockets, his gaze fixed reflectively on the pavement. Like Arthur, he was wearing a crumpled linen jacket, but without the flowering foulard.

He shook hands all round. 'I'm afraid Olivia isn't well,' he said. 'She sends her regrets. She drank some water from a fountain last night and it wasn't *potable*. She's been in bed all day.'

Deeply disappointed, we mouthed, if a little sullenly, our condolences. At least it proved she hadn't been on the Palatine Hill, so that much was cleared up, as my pert look smugly reminded Polly. But Olivia was our star and her non-appearance cancelled a performance we had looked forward eagerly to witnessing. Under our sharply honed powers of observation, mystery was to have been converted into the solid ground of fact. But instead, the bottom had fallen out of the evening. In addition to which, Hugo showing up on his own was so embarrassing. Ought we to treat him as a friend or foe? Not knowing was very awkward.

Arthur's easygoing approach soon did away with these uncertainties, however. Instantly, he removed a chair so as to make a cosy foursome where talk could flow more naturally, binding us into a congenial web. And that is exactly what happened. In no time we were thoroughly caught up in our own lively weave of words and youthful enthusiasms, finding much common ground. Olivia's absence, so quickly and unobtrusively filled, miraculously had left no trace, and after our initial disappointment she wasn't missed again that night — or certainly not by me: there was a new, diamond-sharp point of glittering fascination and intrigue.

Sticking, if half-heartedly, to our agenda, Polly still tried out a question or two about Egypt, which Hugo skilfully skirted.

'Egypt's politics are in an awful mess, the country doesn't bear talking about,' he cheerfully declared, examining the menu. 'But *carciofi alla romagna*, now that deserves attention. Do you know it?' He'd turned to me and I had to admit I didn't.

'Then may I persuade you? It's in season right now, and it's delicious.' He looked expectantly around the table. Mesmerized, Polly and I willingly complied; only Arthur chose something different. I don't remember what. But Hugo's accent was proving difficult to place. It wasn't French or Italian, though it might, I thought, conceivably be German. Or perhaps he didn't have an accent, if that was possible. His English at any rate was excellent and his Italian seemed to be too.

'Aren't you at a conference on hieroglyphics?' Polly patiently persevered.

'Finished today,' said Hugo lightly, 'and, like most conferences, accomplished practically nothing.' Academics were as combative as seasoned warriors, he said, but being engaged in brain battles instead of bodily ones, the results were often waspish and unnatural. He was glad to be shot of it. And, looking pleased, he poured himself another glass of chianti.

There was from the beginning something immensely likeable about Hugo. His extreme good looks and wonderfully warm and boyish smile were certainly part of it, but equally beguiling was a sunny, easygoing openness and an accessibility that appealed enormously. It was highly deceptive, of course, since he was party to a devious and calculated conspiracy, but that was surprisingly easy to forget.

'Hieroglyphics must take years to learn,' I suggested feebly, desperate for a topic of conversation, now that Polly and Arthur had begun exchanging family anecdotes.

'It does, and you have to read some awful rubbish: inventories, religious mumbo-jumbo, that sort of thing. But it's valuable in its way. Without a knowledge of the past, the present would most likely be a formless

101

blur: there'd be no context in which to see it.'

Instantly hooked, I said I had that very day been wondering whether anything could be taken in without some sort of mental preparation. Unless one was an original artist, of course. I said I remembered reading in a European history class that when Captain Cook's fleet first appeared off the Australian coast, the aborigines on the shore hadn't even looked up. I simply couldn't understand that at the time. It didn't make any sense to me at all. But now I thought it was because the people had never seen anything like those ships before, so they just blocked them out; they'd lacked a context.

Hugo seemed to like this. 'Are you fond of history?' he asked me.

'Oh yes,' I said. 'But if everything's been interpreted by others, then in a way it's censored; it could also be very inaccurate — deliberate propaganda, even.'

Hugo claimed that would still be better than nothing. He said uneducated people's lives were often narrow as a result of having narrow contexts. They therefore took in less. 'Like your aborigines, people can miss what's lying right under their noses if they haven't a prior reference.'

I smiled inwardly at this, because where he

102

and Olivia were concerned we did have prior references. It was they, not us, who couldn't see through the looking glass and who naively suspected nothing.

Hugo said archaeologists and historians continued to reread ancient texts as a checking device, and sometimes new interpretations arose because they suddenly saw things their predecessors couldn't have imagined.

'Has that happened to you?' I asked, but he shied off — hardly surprising — saying evolution was probably the best example. The animal kingdom's development, for instance, could be traced by looking at fossils, but it had taken people for ever to notice the connections and fit the pieces together; they were so blinkered by their religion. Once the connections had been made, however, and the pattern explicitly set out, it became obvious to any open and receptive mind.

'What I like about history,' I confided, 'is in fact something akin to evolution. It's the sense of continuity, of being part of a chain, part of a long-term social development and not just a flash in the pan. That's a kind of social evolution, isn't it?'

We were interrupted by the waiter setting down plates of tiny artichokes, reminiscent of that minute corn-on-the-cob in London.

Bonsai vegetables appeared to be fashionable in Europe.

'There's the romance of history, too. I love that,' I went on.

'Oh, *romance*,' Hugo retorted dismissively. 'Romance is merely a form of necrophilia.' A surprising and disconcerting response from an archaeologist, I thought — even from someone pretending to be one.

'So this is where you-all hang out!' Sally's self-confident Southern drawl slid smoothly across the murmurings around the table; and seeing the young men she gave Polly and me an approving look, as if to say, well, you *have* been busy. She had just enough time to join us for a drink, she said, her blond pageboy cut falling over one eye like Veronica Lake's, as Arthur, having produced a chair, eagerly lit her cigarette, grinning like a lunatic the while.

'Oh, so you-all aren't Italian,' she offered, relieved, when introductions had been made. She said she was glad; that Italian boys were such a nuisance, they wouldn't leave you alone. She and Mary-Moore had been to the Vatican that morning and they had been pestered the whole way on the bus. She didn't sound too cross about it, though.

'Mary-Moore's a Catholic and she was hoping to see the pope, but no such luck. It's an amazing place where he lives, though

— really ritzy. Have you-all been there yet? The Catholics have to pay for it, so it's no wonder they're the poorest countries. Even the queen of England doesn't live in a palace like that!'

Arthur looked amused and Hugo inscrutable. Sally was pretty and certainly no fool, and the company of two handsome young men had inspired an animated performance.

'Olivia's ill,' I suddenly volunteered. 'She drank some bad water from a fountain.'

'Was it over at the Vatican? Because you know Catholics never drink that holy water themselves. Oh no, they stick to wine; they just wash their hands in it.'

This piece of innocent iconoclasm caused both young men to smile.

'It was over there,' I nodded towards Bernini's grandiose concoction.

'Contaminated by too many coins,' Sally opined. 'Well, I thought it might be at the Vatican because we saw her there this morning. And we met her friend the prince. That was even better than meeting the pope, I thought. He's a real peach, isn't he!'

We all pretended that she hadn't said it; what else could we do? Even Hugo did, after an initial startled freeze, but I could see that he was badly shaken. And suddenly sparing Hugo hurt or embarrassment was uppermost

105

in our thoughts. Instinctively we were on his side, and Polly and I didn't even exchange the glance in which she could have succinctly telepathed, I told you so. We simply ignored Sally's surprising declaration, much as the aborigines had so studiously ignored the arrival of Captain Cook's unprecedented armada.

Sally said she had to run, she was meeting Mary-Moore for a nightcap at Harry's Bar. Of course, it didn't occur to her to pay since there were young men present. 'See ya'll later, I hope.' Addressed to Polly and me, her eyes swept significantly over Hugo and Arthur.

It was impossible after that to put the evening back together again. A vision of Olivia with her mysterious prince loomed over the table like Banquo's ghost, so Arthur called discreetly for the bill and, to our amazement, and in spite of Hugo's strong protests, very generously paid it.

Then, as we were leaving, Hugo, who understandably had become subdued, suddenly declared that the night was young and he for one was feeling restless. Would we like to visit the Colosseum? It was exquisite by moonlight.

'Not I,' said Arthur. 'I've seen it too many times.' And Polly, who suddenly seemed a little down, said she was going to bed.

So, to my acute astonishment, not two minutes later Hugo and I were strolling off together across the Piazza Navona. I could not believe it! There was I, going off *à deux* with the object of such long-debated curiosity and speculation; and suddenly I was tongue-tied. I didn't know how I ought to behave — I mean, what sort of line to take; whether I should pretend to go along with the brother story and risk looking foolishly duped later on, or whether I should try to find out more, or else just side-step for the time being the whole thing, and try, if indirectly, somehow to comfort Hugo for Olivia's incomprehensible behaviour.

I didn't dare look at my watch. We were supposed to be in by midnight, unless we got special permission, and it must have been after eleven. But I could hardly bolt, pick up my skirts and flee like Cinderella catching a late-night pumpkin. In any case, it was a silly rule, I reasoned, and one it made sense in the circumstances to ignore.

And that was when I remembered Daisy Miller.

'There's a novella by Henry James,' I said, as we walked along the empty, dimly lit streets. 'In it this American girl goes about sightseeing in Rome, unchaperoned, with a young Italian boy — a thing unheard of in

Europe — and everyone is shocked: they automatically think there's something going on, when there isn't at all. One night the pair visit the Colosseum by moonlight and Daisy Miller's American suitor happens to see them together and assumes the worst. So Daisy loses her young man; but worse, she also loses her life. She catches Roman fever and dies.'

'Malaria,' said Hugo. 'It was before the Pontine marshes were drained. The Colosseum would have been a dangerous place at night, especially for foreigners.'

'I'm glad they've been drained now,' I said. 'But I think James was really saying that unconventional behaviour is fine, if it's being true to oneself. But it's important also to know the reasons for any rule before it's rejected, and wise therefore to 'do as the Romans do', because people generally have pretty good reasons for their customs, even if it doesn't seem so at the time to others. I think that's why he set the story in Rome.'

Hugo stopped and lit a cigarette. The massive hulk of the Colosseum was visible in the distance. 'Customs are largely matters of fashion,' he said coldly, 'and most of them outlast need or reason.'

Midnight curfews were probably a good example, I decided; but the hitch was that I was on my honour, and insignificant as that may seem today, it was then a profoundly serious matter: honour was at the very crucible of virtue. But thinking it over quickly, I determined to report my infringement to Miss Grist the next day, claim I had forgotten what time it was, and pay the penalty. It would certainly be worth it.

'People who want to 'belong' have to be conventional,' Hugo went on. 'They can't afford not to be. But I don't want to belong, do you?'

I didn't know what to answer. The truth was I wanted desperately to belong. Where, exactly? Why, in the American South, as a well-to-do wife and mother, as Mrs William Brydonne. That would be a fine life and a big step up socially, which was the only career properly open to a woman. But I couldn't say so. It sounded trite, even calculating; so I said that conventions were often linked to morality, and surely morality had a fixed value.

'In my view, another sliding scale,' Hugo answered irritably. 'Muslims believe it's immoral to drink alcohol and OK to have four wives. Europeans the reverse. While Americans, unlike many Europeans, think communism is evil — public health care too, it seems.'

'But honour is universally admired, and

109

everyone thinks that it's immoral to lie,' I said. 'Surely you agree with that?'

Hugo shrugged. 'I endorse Thomas Jefferson's definition of a lie: false information given to someone who *deserves* to know the truth. As for honour, I'm not at all sure what it is.'

We had entered the dark and massive arches of the amphitheatre, and, threading our way forward among the rising tiers, I saw that the arena floor had disappeared, exposing the Colosseum's cellars, a honeycomb of corridors and cubicles — behind the scenes, as it were. The moon was out and there was no-one else around.

'Think of all the horrors that went on here!' I said, gazing into the labyrinth of open cellars. 'Gladiators fighting to the death, Christians being martyred, animals wantonly killed — and people loved it. The world has certainly improved.'

'You think so?' A taut thread of anger sounded in Hugo's voice, so different from the open boyishness previously seen. 'I think people are just the same. Fear and anger produce the same violence and cruelty as before. Look at our short lifetime — the war, concentration camps . . . '

'But this was entertainment!'

Hugo said we didn't know what people's

110

lives were like back then: how much stress and fear they suffered, how much catharsis they required. But frightened and unhappy people sought out scapegoats, and enjoyed seeing others in worse predicaments than their own. 'Peace and good fortune have lulled us into thinking that we're better than we are, but go too far against convention, become a threat, and they'll string you up, even in peacetime,' he said with surprising passion. 'Look at Senator McCarthy's witch hunt in America.'

And Julius Caesar's murder, I thought; but, changing the subject, I asked him why he had called romance a form of necrophilia.

At that he smiled again, and shoving his hands into his pockets, his head cocked, looked sideways at me. 'Why? Because it's a love of things, like the past, that are totally out of reach, and therefore as good as dead. For some people that makes them highly desirable, though.'

'Well, archaeology is about the past,' I protested, confused.

For a minute he said nothing. He was busy working it out, I think. 'It isn't love of the past that primarily interests archaeologists,' he said at last. 'It's a love of the truth.'

This time I didn't back down so easily. 'Still, romance is thoroughly delightful,' I insisted. 'We would lose a whole dimension of pleasure to reject it out of hand.'

'I wouldn't.'

'Well, what about romantic love? That's not about the unattainable — or I hope it's not.'

I remember his impatient dismissive gesture. 'American girls are fixated on romance because they're sexually asleep — like your Daisy Miller. That's the story's underlying theme, but Henry James missed it too, being himself a sexual innocent. Mind you, with luck innocence can take a young person pretty far, because it inspires in some people an instinctive protection. But that's something Europeans rarely count on, and why their precautions are often more exacting.

'American girls haven't changed,' he continued, almost rudely. 'They think relations between men and women are like what they see in the movies. And that *is* romance, not sex.'

'So American girls are naive, but not European girls?' Of course, Olivia would figure as a European.

'Indubitably. And on the whole remarkably empty-headed. Your friend who joined us is a good example. She's quick-witted, and I imagine she's shrewd, even quite perceptive. The animal brain works a treat but the frontal lobes are air chambers, unfurnished except by a few items she may have bought that day.'

Hugo was leaning against the low wall that separated the gangway from the seats above, his hands still in his pockets, his head tilted to one side. The pose was casual but the frown of annoyance on his young face belied it. 'When people meet, they enter each other's minds, much as they do each other's homes. So the furnishings must be congenial and in a style that gives pleasure. I don't find empty unlit rooms interesting or congenial.'

Utterly unused to this kind of talk, I didn't know what to say. Hugo seemed to have examined so much and thought so many things through — while I, used only to accruing information, had rarely examined it. I was like those pre-Darwinians stumbling about over piles of fossils and never seeing any connections.

'At the Sorbonne,' he went on, 'I met unusually well-furnished minds — some of them very unusually furnished. That was probably the most exciting aspect.'

So he *had* been there! 'Then you and Olivia were both at the Sorbonne,' I said, deliberately offhand, amazed he had admitted it.

'Yes indeed. We had some of the same classes. We both like history and archaeology, and we enjoy the same sort of people.'

Boldly I threw out my little net. 'You were lucky to find so much in common — right off the bat, I mean.'

Hugo looked perplexed. 'It could hardly be otherwise, I think.'

I went a step further. 'Brothers and sisters don't often share the same interests, let alone the same classes, do they?'

Seeing the expression on my face, something occurred to him. 'You mean they don't share the same classes unless one of them has fallen behind?'

That wasn't what I meant, but I nodded anyhow.

Hugo produced a small strange smile. He paused, looked at me more closely, his eyes narrowed, gauging a possible reaction to what he would say next. 'But Olivia and I *are* the same age.'

I pulled my net in fast. 'I thought you were brother and sister,' I said, unable to disguise the hint of accusation.

'Ah, had you begun to doubt it then?' If he was daring me to say what I really thought, he immediately relented. 'Olivia can be impossible!' he declared irritably. Then, following this surprising non sequitur, he paused, weighing the situation rapidly in his mind before reaching a decision, evidently toying with me and looking sceptically from beneath his brow, as if waiting, a little impatiently, for me to figure it out.

Well, I *had* figured it out, only I couldn't say so, even though I was sorely tempted to. 'Is this a $64,000 question? Because if so, I'd like to win it,' I began.

Hugo laughed and, after a pause, pulling his hands from his pockets, he opened both hands, the palms towards me, and shrugged. 'Give up?'

Reluctantly I nodded.

'It couldn't be simpler, really; the answer is perfectly obvious and I'm surprised you overlooked it.'

Exasperated, I was about to prove to him I hadn't.

'Olivia and I are twins,' he said.

Thank God I was spared a reply! It was impossible at short notice to fit any of the pieces together, but part of me felt taken for a very bumpy, patronizing and unpleasant ride.

'Didn't Olivia tell you?'

I shook my head. 'Not that you were twins.'

'Really, she can be impossible,' he repeated.

On the other side of the theatre, a reedy male voice had begun declaiming, becoming louder, after a mumbling start, the American intonation evident.

''I come to bury Caesar, not to praise

115

him,'' the shrill, high-pitched voice insisted. It went on for a bit and then a female voice took over.

''For Brutus is an honourable man. So are they all, all honourable men.''

Goofy laughter followed. ''Upon my honour, they are, your honour, all honourable men.''

As the moon slid from behind a cloud two figures came into view: Miss Grist and a male companion, both evidently in their cups and, thoroughly enjoying themselves, taking it in duet.

''He was my friend, faithful and just to me. Yet Brutus says he was — ambiguous.'' More laughter.

''And shure he is an honourable man,'' intoned Miss Grist, affecting an Irish accent. ''So are we all, all ambiguous.''

'Let's get out of here!' I whispered, hiding behind Hugo. 'That's our chaperone, and if she sees me I could be sent home. It's after one o'clock and we're supposed to be in by twelve!'

Hugo, quietly chuckling, shook his head as he conducted me outside. 'So Daisy Miller's world is still around,' he said.

An open, horse-drawn carriage was parked alongside the pavement. Hugo hailed it and we clambered in, me busy examining, like the

116

repeated shutterings of a camera lens, a flutter of images from the past few days. Was everything there? Had it been carefully looked at? Had it perhaps been misinterpreted? Was that possible? Was it conceivable that what Hugo said was true? Twins, as I knew, were famously close. They had their own wavelengths, sometimes they even spoke a private language, and it was said that they could read each other's thoughts. Separated, they would naturally be overjoyed to meet again, their enthusiasm and affection blatant and unconcealed. Moreover, if Olivia and Hugo really were twins, then the prince's presence made a lot more sense. But if not, Olivia's character still looked very black indeed. And Hugo's . . . I put that inconvenient thought aside.

A little breeze, having routed the sultry summer air, still puffed and floated about the carriage. Hugo's arm lay along the seat back, almost touching me, and we were sitting close together on the narrow, button-upholstered seat. The moon was out again and under a starred mantle of darkness, like a magician's cloak, Rome was once again surprisingly quiet. Only the horses' hooves sounded, pounding in a steady rhythm on the cobbles.

How glorious this is, I thought, how

sublime, to be riding in an open carriage, leisurely clip-clopping across Rome two thousand years after its foundation and in the company of a handsome, highly intelligent, even highly mysterious young man. How romantic, yes *romantic*, I thought defiantly. The right clichés were splendidly in place and I was overjoyed.

Rapturously I gazed up at the lopsided moon. ''Bliss it was that day to be alive, but to be young was very heaven,'' I quoted.

'You have some unusual qualities for an American girl,' said Hugo. 'You've got some curiosity and imagination. Europe should do you a world of good, provided you let it bring them out.

'And you're very pretty,' he said lightly at the hotel entrance. For a moment he hesitated. I saw him glance up at Olivia's room. The light was out. Then he took my chin in his hand and, looking solemn, kissed me lightly on the mouth.

Hugo had told the cab to wait, and as our porter was opening the front door I heard him tell the driver, 'Hotel Excelsior.' It was, according to Sally James, the best hotel in Rome.

Polly wasn't asleep and one eye, open like a baby Cyclops, strayed towards the clock then back to me. 'Well?'

118

I sat down on my bed. 'Well, we've been barking up the wrong tree, is what I think. Our detective work has suffered from misreading some important clues.' And picking up the telephone, I asked the sleepy desk clerk for the Hotel Excelsior. I remember I had to say the name three times.

'Is Mr Hartfield, Mr Hugo Hartfield, registered there?' I asked when we were finally connected.

There was a pause.

'*Grazie.*' I put down the receiver. Polly's other eye opened expectantly. I returned her look in silence, creating what I hoped was a dramatic pause. Then, 'Hugo *is* her brother,' I announced. 'He really is. And what's more — can you believe it — they're twins — actually *twins*!' I was grinning. 'No wonder he was in her room last night! No wonder they were laughing. I only hope it wasn't at us, because we've been pretty stupid, making up all that stuff, when it was all such *nonsense*.' I felt surprisingly light-hearted, though what I should have felt was a right fool, given our ridiculous speculation and the wasted time involved. I suppose the reason why I didn't is obvious, though it wasn't particularly so to me.

Polly sat up in bed. She too looked pleased.

'You were right about the Palatine Hill,' I

said. 'That must have been Olivia with Prince Charming.'

Polly smiled slyly. 'One gold-digger down and two to go: cousin Arthur and the prince. Calls for a celebration.'

Gaily, we dug out our duty-free bottle of Jack Daniel's and, collecting glasses from the washbasin, poured out a couple of whiskeys.

'To brothers and sisters,' toasted Polly, giving me a butter-wouldn't-melt-in-her-little-mouth look.

'And enter the prince,' I replied, taking evasive action and making a sweep with my glass to show the mystery hadn't entirely fizzled. On the contrary. For why on earth Olivia's parents wouldn't let her marry a prince was beyond all comprehension.

Polly said I was being naive. 'If he really is one,' she added sceptically.

'Miss Grist was at the Colosseum,' I said, quickly changing the subject. The charge of naivety, implying provinciality, had pulled me up. 'A man was with her, and they were both of them pretty tipsy. I think she's really kicking her heels up over here.'

'She shouldn't have lied to him, though.'

It took me a minute, and then I came quickly to Olivia's defence. 'If her family's dead-set against this so-called prince, then it's only natural she wants to avoid a family collision. Besides, Olivia didn't even know Hugo was going to be here till two days ago, so what on earth could she do? And brothers and sisters can't go everywhere together. You don't go everywhere with Billy and me.'

'Poor old Billy,' said Polly, in response to my still beaming face.

It brought me up short. The last thing I wanted was to endanger my delicately unfolding future, already budding to an extent that Polly couldn't possibly suspect. Only a fool would throw that up for a Roman holiday; and I, though innocent and inexperienced, was, I was pretty sure, no fool.

'You're dangerously romantic,' Polly observed. 'The grass is always greener. He may be her brother, but we still know nothing about him — in fact, no more than before.' She paused. 'He could even be registered at that hotel under a false name.' This was so improbable, however, that she quickly topped it. 'Maybe Olivia meant to pass the prince off as her brother, and Hugo's turning up has scuppered it.'

'Gollypolly,' I laughed, 'for heaven's sakes, cut it out and let's go to sleep!'

'Maybe — '

'Maybe nothing. *Go to sleep.*'

She flopped down under the covers and I turned out the light. My thoughts fizzed merrily on, however. I was in Rome and, unlike all the caesars, I was alive. That in itself was a kind of triumph. Moreover, I had youth and intelligence, I'd been told that I was pretty, and an intriguing young man had kissed me on the mouth — albeit perfunctorily. Marvellous things could happen in life; the world might indeed be one vast treasure house bursting with glorious possibilities, if only you endeavoured to search them out. Yes, I was romantic and damned glad of it too! Like the religious instinct, romance was something in the blood, something that enormously embellished life, so long as — as with any opiate — you didn't overdose.

Dawn had begun to outline the closed shutters before I fell reluctantly asleep, and without having given a second thought to my so recently perjured honour.

10

Rome was the first place we hadn't been on half board at our hotel, and as a result our little group, already marked by hairline cracks, began to split along the obvious fault lines. Mary-Moore and Sally went off together and Olivia had disappeared with her mysterious prince, I supposed into some glittering fairy-tale world. While, literally overnight, Hugo, Arthur, Polly and I erected a brand-new universe of our own. The young can do that, of course: reinvent themselves and, overnight, dive into sudden and profound friendships, or fall in love as quickly as the prospect enters their innocent heads. It's partly how young people discover who they are — by trial and error, wandering through new experiences like fledgling tourists and up any number of meandering garden paths — some of them pretty shady — before wandering home again, the wiser for it or not. But only a very few, I think, permanently lose their way; and conceivably I was one of them.

The morning after we had discovered (sufficiently) who Hugo really was, Arthur

123

hailed him from a café near the Spanish Steps and suggested we all have lunch together. Hugo was at a loose end after Olivia's defection, and this, I suppose, plus Arthur's aristocratic credentials, made it possible to pursue so glamorous a person. Then, too, Arthur and Hugo had right from the beginning hit it off. Both were well educated, with humour, a keen intelligence and that enviable confidence which 'background' usually produces. Both also had an unconventional streak that, in setting them apart from their contemporaries, contributed a maverick dimension.

But Polly and Arthur were getting on famously as well. Polly's cool irony had found an English counterpart, and the two of them had fallen into an affectionate sibling-like teasing. They volleyed their exchanges deadpan, either ragging each other or else using their parents' myriad eccentricities for shuttlecocks.

A routine was quickly established: morning visits to some site, either together or separately; meeting for lunch; a siesta in the searingly hot afternoons, followed by an evening promenade and dinner together at our trattoria in the Piazza Navona.

Hugo's presence, like his sister's, caused life to scintillate. But if Olivia's magic came

124

from a distant serenity, like the moon's, Hugo's brilliant smile, his ready warmth and good nature had, with rare exceptions, a solar dimension, so that we revolved, contented planets orbiting in his solid gravitational pull. Even Arthur did.

At first, whenever we met, no-one mentioned Olivia. It seemed indelicate to do so, since her continued absence implied some sort of rupture with her brother. Nor had Hugo mentioned her. By the fourth day, however, this self-imposed silence was getting awkward, so, waiting in the Caffè Greco for Polly and Arthur, I told Hugo I had knocked on Olivia's door that morning, hoping to take her shopping, but she was out. Had he seen her recently, I asked, lighting a cigarette.

Hugo shook his head. 'She has an attentive suitor.'

'You mean that man Sally met at the Vatican?' It was the first time the prince had been directly mentioned and I was purposefully vague. 'Do you know him, then?'

'I know him.' Hugo sounded a little bored. 'He's turned up unexpectedly; but he's off tomorrow, I believe.'

Poor Hugo, they really are pulling the wool, I thought. 'Does he live in Paris?' I asked, pleased by my accomplished tone of easy nonchalance.

'Effectively.' Scanning the menu, he had lost interest, but mine was climbing fast.

'And is he really — a prince?'

'That's a good question. The family's Russian, and Russian titles were abolished in the revolution. Therefore, is he a prince or not? I would say not.'

'So he's French — now, I mean?'

'He was born in France, so yes, he's a French citizen. He married a French girl after the war, but she died in childbirth, three or four years ago, I think. There's an heir, a little *principino*, but with precious little to inherit except a phoney title, as far as I can see.'

'Is he a lot older, then?' Age plus an heir could be stumbling blocks; so could religion, since Russians were some kind of Catholics, I recalled.

'Older than what?'

'Than Olivia.'

'He's . . . thirty-two.'

That did seem older. 'And he wants to marry Olivia?'

Hugo smiled strangely. 'I expect so.'

'And?'

'And I am not privy to her intentions.'

'*Ciao, amico.*' Arthur clapped Hugo genially on the shoulder and, sinking into a chair, poured himself a glass of wine. Then, taking his handkerchief out, he mopped his brow. 'When I think I might have been plodding around Rome on my own, soaking up culture and reading dreary novels during meals.' He raised his glass to us.

'And I,' Hugo grinned, 'continuing to read hieroglyphics in a badly lit conference room, without even the flashlight that one has in tombs.'

'Tombs are, I imagine, preferable to bank vaults, whether one is alive or dead,' said Arthur, whose undesired future cast a momentary shadow. It was quickly dispelled by Polly, however, who, joining us, drolly started what would become a diverting but callous and juvenile game: sighting Miss Grist.

'I saw Miss Grist at a shop in the Corso,' said Polly. 'She was trying on a mink coat, and there was a man with her. He was wearing a homburg and he had Charlie Chaplin feet, bulbous and sort of duck-like' (improbable details would be an important part of the game).

'As we're giving tourist reports,' said Hugo, 'I saw your two girlfriends in the Corso, and despite the Hollywood-obsessed beginning, they are blending beautifully into local culture. They were in a café with a couple of Italian fellows, eating spumoni while the boys read movie magazines.'

Naughtily, Arthur took up Polly's thread. 'I saw Miss Grist myself not half an hour ago. Turns out she's a devout numismatist. She was wading about in the Trevi fountain, collecting coins and putting them in her pocket. She threw me one.' He produced a 100-lire piece as evidence.

Truth and nonsense were scrambled together as our imaginations played adolescently on Miss Grist's vivacious private life. I readily joined in, never admitting Miss Grist had my real respect or that I'd recently confessed my violation of college rules to her. That little affair sounds trifling, but in those days girls could be expelled merely for smoking in their rooms or staying out too late.

Miss Grist had listened to me in perfect silence, then said matter-of-factly, 'Oh yes, I saw you there, just as you saw me.' She wasn't the least embarrassed, only she let me know that she'd been waiting for me. She thought curfews were ridiculous too, but honour — that was quite a different matter. She told me as punishment to go to the Capitoline Hill and stand on the top of the steps for ten minutes, taking the square in carefully, then to spend another twenty minutes walking about. 'Decide what is the pleasure and the greatness of it. You don't have to tell me about it later,' she added in apparent self-protection.

The result was I learned something that has never left me. The secret conveyed by that superb square, framed by Michelangelo's elegant buildings and approached by great marble steps, with Marcus Aurelius on horseback at the top, his hand outstretched in blessing, is harmony. The square embodies an entire philosophy and one that I myself subscribe to: everything in proportion, nothing to excess, a balanced life. Imprinted like a picture postcard in my mind, this visual synopsis of ancient classical values remains a treasured *aide-mémoire* to this day.

None of this, however, deterred my making fun of Miss Grist with the others, and it was my turn. 'Hugo and I saw Miss Grist at the Colosseum,' I uncharitably revealed to Arthur. 'Drunk as a skunk. She thought she was Mark Antony, or that the fellow with her was; they couldn't make up their minds, it was an identity crisis.'

Oh, I wanted to belong, all right!

★ ★ ★

That afternoon, coming downstairs to meet Hugo after my siesta, I spied him talking to Olivia at the hotel's front door. She was on

129

her way out, and seeing their two profiles face to face, almost in silhouette because of the light, the family resemblance was for the first time strikingly apparent: the same straight noses, high, delicately modelled foreheads and well-proportioned chins, the same pale skin and finely sculpted lips. Only the hair colour and to a degree the blue tint of their eyes was individual. Olivia, glancing hurriedly at her watch, had nodded agreement to something and, giving her brother a rapid peck on the cheek, disappeared out the door.

'Paying my fraternal respects,' Hugo said gaily a minute later, putting his hand affectionately on my shoulder. 'And delivering invitations.' He said he wanted us to be his guests that night for dinner at the Excelsior. Olivia and her friend were coming and he was going to telephone Arthur from the lobby.

I was delighted, both by the glamorous invitation and because evidently things were smoothed over between the twins. I longed to say so, but as Hugo had never mentioned that there was a rift, it seemed unwise for me to imply as much — and it was really none of my business.

Outside the hotel, Hugo put an arm around me and, squinting at the sky, suggested we visit Keats's house. 'Aren't you majoring in English, as Americans say?'

'You're American. What do you say?'

'Oh, I'm a man without a country. A shiftless fellow, footloose and all that.'

We had turned right, and on the sidewalk in front of us stood two Arabs in jellabas and cloth pillbox caps, looking at nothing in particular. They seemed to be enjoying the brilliant Roman sunshine. Hugo paused. 'On second thoughts, let's forget Keats's stuffy little house and go to see the Baths of Caracalla. They're spectacular.' And we turned sharply in the opposite direction.

'Were those two men Egyptians?' I asked him.

'Who? Those? Archaeologists from my conference, I believe. A boring lot and to be avoided.'

They had looked to me more like diggers than trained archaeologists, but I didn't say anything. Like a devoted puppy, I was happy to follow unquestioningly Hugo's any suggestion. I wasn't in love with him yet, or if I was I didn't know it. Certainly, we had become much closer over the past few days; we very much enjoyed each other's company and when Arthur and Polly affectionately paired off, so inevitably did we. But Cinderellas must be circumspect. They can't afford, given

131

their anomalous position, to fall for passing princes without some serious encouragement. Hugo's casual kiss had certainly turned my head, but it was not yet hopelessly unscrewed.

11

'Rome is delightful, is it not?' asked the prince in a tone of genial wonder. 'Of course, it is necessary to outwit the sun, but the Roman nights are, I find, impeccable, don't you? So many stars: in the skies, on the streets,' he nodded, amused, 'at that table over there.'

We were sitting in the Excelsior's quietly elegant dining room, and Arthur, ever the good-natured diplomat, said that for his money Rome had never been more agreeable. Good company made such a difference. It enlivened the present and, by association, the past.

'Rome is a little like Troy, I think,' the prince observed. 'So many levels. But, unlike Troy, here they are not buried, most are visible; that is the Italian way.' He smiled at Arthur, sitting opposite. 'With you English it is different. Everything is behind closed doors. You are very honest but also very private, and you do not say to others what you think. Perhaps you are right, it is none of their business; but it is an interesting combination.'

'Oh, we're notorious hypocrites,' laughed Arthur agreeably. 'Whether it's diffidence or smugness, I can't say. We're stuffed with both, I fear.'

'Perhaps it is simply your good manners. But it is the Russian not the English temperament that misleads. We laugh and cry and love and hate almost simultaneously, so that emotionally we never know quite where we are — or even less, where we will be one minute later. This confuses everyone, including ourselves.'

He looked benevolently at Polly and me. 'But it is Americans who are the best: honest, straightforward and above board. The door is always open and everyone is welcome to come in and look around. There is nothing to hide. That is very remarkable.'

I expect he thought Americans hopelessly naive as a result, and us, rightly, babes lost in the European woods.

Alexander Felix Golitsyn was a descendant of Catherine the Great's celebrated lover, Prince Potemkin, of whom I'd heard, through Eisenstein's great film, but only as a boat. Like his ancestor, Alexei too seemed to be larger than life, and from the beginning he towered easily above us. For a start, he was six and a half feet tall. He had a strong chin and a prominent, aquiline nose; his hair, that

134

champagne colour I'd noticed on the Palatine Hill, was combed straight back, and his eyes, pale arctic blue, had a wolfish slant, very appealing. He had, too, exceptionally beautiful hands, with incredibly long fingers, and his gestures, which were rare, swirled like Arab calligraphy. Outstandingly, though, Alexei had 'presence', and by comparison Arthur's gawky bouts and Hugo's natural exuberance were like the antics of two playful cubs. For if Hugo was an *ephebe* off a pedestal, Alexei was up there on Olympus with the best of them, in my opinion. Having been in the war made a difference, of course — that and being older. Moreover, unlike the boys in their crumpled linen (tonight they were wearing ties), Alexei was perfectly turned out, his immaculately tailored suit made of something that apparently never creased. But despite his ease of manner, as with Olivia, an impenetrable film of *politesse* fixed him securely behind a castle wall, although Alexei seemed sometimes to occupy both sides of it at once — the famous Russian duality of temperament, I supposed. Yet mercurial emotions, I felt pretty certain, we would never see: he would simply vault back over his well-constructed wall.

To a Kansas girl brought up on fairy tales, however, Alexei was first and foremost, magically and intoxicatingly, a prince. And becoming instantly reverential, I'd even hesitated to enter the dining room before him. He had smiled at that and produced a calligraphic sweep of encouragement, then took my arm so that we went towards the table together; I, red in the face but thrilled to bits, if a little embarrassed by so much thoughtful attention. But Alexei, as I began to see, was unusually considerate where other people's feelings were concerned.

Evidently we made a riveting table, because even though movie people were nearby, the waiters were all over us: Signore Hartfield this, Signore Hartfield that. For the first time, I was seeing Hugo's wealthy side and it changed significantly my perceptions — by which I probably mean my unarticulated hopes. Till then, Hugo had been part of the world's confederacy of students, even if a more glamorous and charismatic part. But this I now saw was superficial and of short duration. Hugo had much larger roles to play and more imposing stages on which to play them. And suddenly I began to lose heart. Sitting amongst these blue-blooded and superior-seeming aristocrats, I felt myself an interloper; for, unlike them, persons of consequence from the day they were born, I was comparatively nobody. The serenely beautiful Olivia, flanked by three handsome but very different men, all of whom were there because of her, formed our centrepiece; and Polly and I, sitting modestly in our little black dresses, were mere backcloths for these sparkling jewels.

They say homesickness depresses the whole psyche, but bouts of inferiority are much worse. They maim the soul outright, relentlessly grinding it flat as self-worth is mercilessly squeezed away. Thinking about it now, had I been introduced that night to, say, the Queen of England or Elizabeth Taylor, I would have been thrilled — over-awed, certainly, and probably rendered speechless, but not remotely swamped by feelings of inferiority. For that to happen you must be either in, or striving to be in, the same class or tribe. I was striving. And as the others talked, relaying no doubt subtle and unfathomable shades of meaning, my soul curled up and sank into my body like a grave.

Olivia had on a beautiful cream silk dress and high-heeled silver sandals. She wore a white chiffon scarf loosely draped about her neck, and her blond hair was piled up on her head, making her look more worldly and grown up, even more beautiful than usual. It was obvious that Alexei was completely in her thrall: he looked at her with such open, evident pleasure, and with a kind of wonder bordering on adoration. If money really was an issue, it must be tertiary, I decided.

But then who wouldn't look at her that way! Like a celebrated portrait in a gallery, she sat there so serene, so silent and composed, drawing the eye, and with it, as often as not, the heart; mysteriously magnetic and with that impenetrable Mona Lisa smile that, suggestive of so much, told one in fact so very little. But her affection for Alexei showed plain enough in her eyes and manner, and it was altogether different from the spontaneous, demonstrative attentions she had so publicly shown her brother, being at once more graceful and replete in dignity, and more suggestive of depth — a saraband as compared to a gavotte.

I was struggling hard to retrieve some tiny grain of self-worth. My self-respect, fragile at the best of times, generally derived from work, from swotting away, fuelled by the need to be thought equal to those around me — knowing deep down, however, that it wasn't true. At college this hadn't been difficult, but in Europe so much was hidden and had to be interpreted or figured out. But I was learning. Tonight I ordered antipasti followed by grilled scampi, addressing my order to Hugo, as host, but pitched so that the waiter could hear and write it down. My voice was lowered, mimicking Olivia's soft contralto, my Kansas r's softened; and I held my fork with my left hand throughout the meal.

Sensing my inner gloom, no doubt, Alexei, who was sitting beside me, generously sought to draw me out. 'Kansas wheat fields!' he marvelled, just as Lord Brydonne had done. 'How enviable that is. Nothing to my mind equals good productive land.'

Kansas, I was finding, had respectability in Europe, where land still retained its traditionally high status. Americans, by contrast, en route to the big cities, had hurriedly put their farming phase behind them, and looked back with contempt upon this up-and-coming period in their past.

'Russia's breadbasket is the Ukraine,' Alexei continued, 'but I am not allowed to see it. They are afraid I will gobble up all the bread myself.'

'Alexei's family had big estates in the Ukraine,' Olivia offered, smiling at him with affectionate pride, her elbow on the table, her chin resting on her hand.

'And as landlords I confess that we were not ideal,' Alexei said. 'But it is Stalin whose appetite has been insatiable. He was the worst sort of gobbler: an ogre, greedily gobbling up the peasants. He is not the first ogre that Russia has endured and probably he will not be the last; but in the meantime you Americans are our great white hope, because you are giving communism a hard time. In Europe it is fashionable to be communist, especially if one is young. Hugo, you are communist, are you not? Your Jean-Paul Sartre is communist. He is the students' spiritual leader — your Gregory Rasputin,' Alexei teased, raising his brow, assuming a direct hit.

'I am a socialist,' Hugo bluntly corrected him, ignoring Alexei's swipe at a most sacred student idol.

'While I myself am so unfashionable.' Alexei turned, mock-mournfully, to Polly and me. 'I would like the cold war to be won by the Americans. Equality such as America has is very good, but an imposed equality such as Russia has is mere pretence. Another man chooses your fate and strings you on a chain of matching beads. So, chains continue to imprison man, you see; and the Russian peasant is again a serf: he is a serf of the state instead of his former landlord. That is the only difference.'

'With respect, Alexei,' put in Arthur lightly, 'the czars were hopelessly medieval; it's extraordinary they lasted into the twentieth century.'

'It is extraordinary,' agreed the apparently imperturbable prince.

'It's true Russia, although communist, is a dictatorship,' said Hugo. 'But if there must be a dictatorship — and it seems that for the present there must be — it's far better to represent the people's interests than those of a few entrenched hereditaries.'

'But crushing the individual is so unfair,' I protested, thoughtlessly taking Alexei's side against Hugo — fickle and ingratiating toady that I was!

'Russia must modernize very quickly,' Hugo went on, oblivious. 'But once that is done, the reins can be relaxed towards socialism.'

'Ah, the tepid man's communism,' sighed Alexei. 'Such men never rule; always they confer — which is to say they compromise. A compact word, in that the passive tense describes with accuracy the active one's effect.'

Hugo had turned to Polly and myself. 'Alexei is a cousin of the late tsarina.' His tone carried the faintest hint of deprecation, implying, 'What else would you expect, therefore?'

Alexei smiled back cheerfully. 'That makes

me very very bad, for I carry the genes of terrible despots and tyrants. And who knows whether they may one day demand their hereditary pleasures? Tomorrow I will show you the Golden House, the palace of the Emperor Nero, which is not open to the public. It is magnificent, even though it is the product of tyranny. All is not bad in tyranny, you know, as Hugo now admits; though there is much — much too much — that is.'

'But you go to Paris tomorrow.' Hugo looked quickly at Olivia.

So did Alexei, but unlike Hugo he was smiling. 'A short postponement. Two days more and then I really must go back. But what about you? Your meeting is over. Do you not return to Egypt at once?'

They regarded each other affably, but a challenge had been laid down, a mutual interrogation undertaken. Who would be the first to leave the field?

'On that subject I've a proposal to make,' said Hugo. 'I'm afraid it won't interest you, Alexei, since you must return to Paris; but I've thought it through and for the rest of us I believe it's easily accomplished.' He looked about the table in a kind of calculated pause. 'I propose that the day after tomorrow we go to Egypt together. No, seriously. I mean it,' he declared, forestalling with a raised hand any immediate responses and capping the proposal with a boyish grin. He said a colleague's plane was returning to Cairo in two days; he would himself be on it, but there was plenty of room for us. The plane would return in four days to collect its owner, and so could bring us back. It would cost nothing and when we arrived it would cost nothing either: the Egyptians were a most hospitable people. 'I'm sorry you must go back to Paris, Alexei. By all means change your plans, if possible,' he added politely. 'But everyone else is still on holiday, so ... ' He made a broad open-handed gesture. 'Why not?'

Olivia, always pale, had turned as white as her scarf; and yet she never said one word, remaining instead curiously passive or indecisive, or else waiting to see what would happen next. And for the first time I sensed that for some reason she mistrusted her brother.

Arthur, with a week's holiday left, thought it was a brilliant idea, and an immensely generous one. 'Perfectly splendid, really.' That was how Arthur talked.

For Polly and myself, however, such a trip was out of the question. We would never be allowed to travel unchaperoned and we would miss seeing Florence, as I said feebly by way of an excuse. (Moreover, my mother would have died of disappointment.)

'But you can easily rejoin your group in Venice,' Hugo lightly returned. 'And Florence is always there, it changes less than any city I know.'

'We would never get permission,' I repeated sadly. 'It's just not possible. There's no way round it, I'm afraid.'

Polly said the same, so there it rested.

'Hugo, you are a most excellent host,' Alexei generously declared when the bill was brought. 'In return may I invite everyone to a party tonight? It compares thinly with this delicious meal or with an invitation to Egypt, but it is nearby and everyone will be welcome. My hosts enjoy meeting new people and, like Americans — they are Polish, in fact — their house is always open.'

Of course, we were easily persuaded, and, pretending to seek out the ladies' room, I telephoned Miss Grist to let her know.

One other thing: as we were leaving the hotel, a fat Arab in Western dress came up to Olivia in the foyer. 'You are very beautiful, madame,' he said, making a little bow. 'I think you are in the movies, yes? I would be most grateful if you would kindly give me your autograph, please,' and he held out a piece of paper with something written on it in Arabic.

'No, she will not!' answered Hugo sharply, putting his arm protectively around his sister.

'Go away!' And moving towards the open door, he hissed something in Arabic at the man. He sounded really angry.

'Another archaeologist?' I hazarded as we were piling into taxis. But Hugo, still furious for some reason, didn't answer.

12

The party was in a luxurious renaissance villa on a hillside overlooking the Tiber, surrounded by magnificent gardens. I never discovered who the hosts were, but from the moment of our arrival everything was magical — by which I mean totally unreal. The windows and doors were open and light streamed out seductively into gardens already subtly lit by hidden lamps and carefully placed flambeaux. Inside, the house sparkled with what was to me unprecedented opulence: gilded furniture, chandeliers, caviare and champagne, and a bevy of glittering guests, including Alexei's promised stars. Sophia Loren and her husband Carlo Ponti were there, also Federico Fellini (someone pointed him out), and maybe others whom I didn't recognize. A number of people had titles, so must have been in the same boat as Alexei. Pushed out by popular uprisings, their nobility, no longer legitimate, had remained valuable coinage, even though underwritten almost entirely by romance.

Every woman was glamorous, in a glossy, over-the-top sort of style; no plainness, no ugliness, except for some of the men, like Carlo Ponti, which meant of course that they were highly successful. Beauties and beasts, I thought, gazing about, intrigued: beauties with dancing bears on golden chains. Or did the bears have the beauties on golden chains, dancing to their tunes? It was hard to tell.

The gardens, where we soon retired to, were even at night a most marvellous sight. I've always loved gardens, and I had tended with great affection our little suburban plot in Wichita; so I knew a bit about flowers, even a smattering about garden design. But this was totally new and unexpected. Everywhere, a strong geometric formality prevailed: the flowering shrubs, the boxwood hedges lining precisely laid-out radiating paths, even the flower-laden parterres and dark stands of cypress, declared the triumphant and rational rule of man. Nature had been taken very firmly in hand, and had obediently knuckled under. At key focal points, antique statues, splashing fountains and scroll-like stone benches embellished and punctuated. A small Doric-columned rotunda that must have dated from ancient Rome stood on the hillside, which was itself divided by a paved terrace, its balustrade adorned with classical statues, and from where you could gaze down upon the Tiber, flowing in a silvery, moonlit ribbon below.

But just as extraordinary, when you went outside into the gardens you were given a long black cloak, with a pointed snood-like hood that fell to one side like a jester's cap; also a lacquered, ivory-coloured mask — a sculpted face on a stick, to hide your own face behind.

Donning robes and taking up masks, our drinks in the other hand, Polly, Arthur and I strolled out in rising wonder and intrigue. People were wandering about in twos and threes in a haunted world of meandering spectres, indiscernible from one another, whispering and laughing softly, exhilarated by the loss of their identities and its concomitant, a rare and heady freedom. That was a big part of the magic and, for me at least, a remarkable revelation: being nobody was thoroughly delightful — so long as everyone was.

Olivia and Alexei had disappeared on arrival, engulfed by welcoming friends. Hugo too, and searching for him was impossible, though I badly wanted his company. His announced return to Egypt, although inevitable, had been a shock. Living so completely in the present, with so much happening, I'd simply failed to think ahead. Now, suddenly, our gorgeous idyll was about to end.

'If only we *could* go to Egypt with Hugo on that plane,' I said. 'Wouldn't that be something!' We were standing on the balustraded terrace above the Tiber.

'I am ready to depart,' offered Arthur with a flourish. 'And it will cost us nothing.'

Polly, from behind her mask — I didn't need to see her face — said it was odd I was so ready to quit Europe, when I'd been so eager only recently to get there.

'You said the other day how much *you* wanted to see Egypt,' I countered childishly. 'You told Olivia at dinner.'

As we left the terrace, I noticed a couple standing nearby, down a short allée, and framed by a boxwood niche. They were kissing. Their masks, held to one side as a screen, loomed like pale countenances, one comic, one tragic — traditional symbols of theatre. And who knew what drama or frivolous entertainment lay behind? For a moment I even thought the woman was Olivia. It looked like her gold bracelet. But the man was far too short for Alexei. And suddenly it crossed my mind that Olivia might be promiscuous. Probably I thought this because I was myself guilty of a type of promiscuity. Polly had been right when she suggested I was fickle. Overnight, I had transferred my affectionate interests, lock, stock and barrel, easily and without a second thought. Mightn't I do it again?

'You're consistent in one respect, at least,' as Polly said later. 'Going in for brothers.' And when I thought about it, it did seem odd — even a kind of theft.

Just below the terrace, we encountered without any doubt Olivia and Alexei — his great height unmistakable — strolling arm in arm, their backs to us, her head against his shoulder. Putting his arm around her, he drew her to a nearby bench, where they sat down. Though we moved quickly on, Arthur must have seen how the land lay, if he hadn't previously, but he didn't seem disappointed, or if he was he didn't show it.

'Where has old Hugo got to?' he asked cheerfully. 'And more important, where are the waiters? Are they in disguise as well? Our drinks are in a parlous state.'

Obligingly, Arthur went in search of refills, leaving Polly and me settled at a table on the terrace. It was the first time we had talked since meeting Alexei and our view of fortune-hunters was modified, influenced I've no doubt by finding two whom we liked enormously. Their position, in Europe at least, had begun to seem respectable. In America, where nests were comparatively easy to feather, a man marrying for money smacked of laziness and cheap calculation. But Europe was different. Hereditary overheads needed capital up front. Such couples couldn't start their marriage in the local stork hollow, as we called it back home, and work their way up, eventually buying, when they could afford it, a substantial family house. On the contrary, they had big outlays right from the beginning: châteaux to keep up, land to cultivate, tenants to house and hospitality to dispense.

'Going after money makes more sense than going after bosoms or blond hair,' Polly sagely opined. 'And people must go after something, it seems.' She sounded disappointed.

When a man owned property or had a title, I now proposed, he almost *deserved* a contribution on the woman's part, in order to make a proper partnership. That wouldn't be fortune-hunting but a fair exchange — and it dovetailed very nicely too. This view helped considerably to reduce the initial sadness of Olivia as prey. Further, Alexei was such a kind man; he was intelligent and sensitive and obviously crazy about Olivia, while his title, if no longer exactly valid, still counted for something in the world, as our present surroundings proved. So the Hartfields' strong objections made no sense. Was Alexei jobless perhaps, a sort of continental playboy,

151

which at home was tantamount to being a layabout? The Hartfields might easily object to that, even a quasi-princely version; it was so utterly un-American. At any rate, it was becoming clear that Olivia must almost certainly marry a fortune-hunter, and the point therefore was to choose the best one. On this score Arthur, we agreed, had the most to offer. He would inherit a substantial country estate; there was an empty cradle for his heir; nor was he a displaced person — and his title when inherited would be legitimate. But Alexei was more mature, he was a man of the world and Olivia was in love with him. So that was that, or should be. The Hartfields were wrong to push their desires and values on their daughter, and once they'd been persuaded to supply 'the ready', surely everything would be hunky-dory. As to fortune-hunters, well, Mr Hartfield had married a Rockefeller, hadn't he?

'Maybe they hate each other,' Gollypolly opined.

A moment later Arthur reappeared, together with a waiter carrying a tray of drinks, and to my great delight he had Hugo in tow. 'I found the fellow lurking in the bar,' he said, pretending disapproval. 'Losing his own fizz in a champagne bottle.'

Ignoring this, Hugo sat down heavily,

sprawling in his chair and throwing his mask so carelessly on the table that it fell on the terrace. 'Venetian frippery,' he exclaimed contemptuously of the costumes, and 'continental riff-raff', of the guests. He lit a cigarette. 'What are we doing here?'

'Oh, come now, a little decadence is a delightful thing, a little folly,' insisted Arthur, the traditionally repressed Englishman. 'It's all a tremendous lark.'

'Europe's redundant nobility — ignobility, if you ask me,' Hugo insisted. 'Flotsam and jetsam; every one of them rotten to the core.'

Picking up Hugo's mask, I put it back on the table. His ill humour, sparked for some reason by that Arab in the hotel, had remained, and drink had probably contributed to it.

'Well, shall we wander?' he said irritably. 'Isn't that the point? Wander and wonder.'

But Polly said she was tired of being a ghost and wanted to get a closer look at Sophia Loren.

'Then I'll accompany you, dear cousin,' said Arthur gallantly. 'And we can resume our Brydonne identities. I expect they're hanging on a peg somewhere, unless they've been made off with, raffish looking though they are.'

Polly gave him a really sweet smile.

153

Well, cousins marry, I thought, as Hugo and I strolled aimlessly off, he sullen and I increasingly uneasy.

Olivia and Alexei were still tête-à-tête on the bench, their masks lying forgotten on their laps. Alexei had Olivia's hands in his and she was listening hard. Perhaps they were discussing an elopement. But no, Olivia disinherited wouldn't do; bringing her parents around was a more likely topic. If only Hugo could be persuaded to help. But so far there was no sign of it; inexplicably he had sided with their parents. Could there be perhaps something in Alexei's past — something untoward? It was impossible to believe so.

Hugo, taking my arm, had turned quickly down another boxwood allée, and towards a little fountain. I remember it had a stone cherub standing in the centre, hugging an oversized fish whose mouth spouted a steady stream of water. The effect was that the cherub was squeezing the fish too hard.

'You don't like Alexei, do you?' I ventured, suddenly seizing my chance.

'Oh, he's all right.' Hugo smiled down at me. 'I wasn't avoiding them just now, only I wanted very much to be alone with you.'

I lowered my mask, gazing at him in wonder. My heart was pounding hard. But not knowing what to say in reply, I shyly kept to my topic. 'Does he have a job, I mean a career of some sort?'

'Oh, something; I forget what. He doesn't drive a taxi like most of them, anyhow.'

'Then why won't your parents let her marry him?' It came out with more force than I'd intended.

Hugo stopped and looked at me hard. 'Did Olivia tell you that?'

'Oh, no,' I said, 'and forgive me for asking. It's none of my business, really. Only Olivia is . . . vulnerable, and you seem anxious to keep her away from Alexei too . . . ' I trailed off.

Hugo brushed his hood back in exasperation, like shooing off a nagging mosquito. 'Oh, to hell with Olivia!' he said irritably. 'She can do as she likes.' And taking me in his arms, he kissed me, my whole being swirling in a heady, gloriously new-found euphoria. 'I've been wanting to do that all night.'

He still sounded angry, or else very impatient, one thing spilling over into another; but that didn't matter. What mattered was he had declared his interest, announced in a single positive gesture that he cared for me. In that instant, most wondrously, a new relationship was created, and one that carried with it certain well-established rights and freedoms. I was ecstatic, engulfed by a happiness unlike anything I'd ever felt — a happiness so complete, so right and so euphoric, that all my layers of accumulated self-protection instantly dissolved, and, undergoing an alchemical change, miraculously recomposed as gold. From that moment, I loved Hugo unreservedly.

'You look very pretty peeking out like a geisha from behind that mask,' he said, kissing me again before we continued languorously our meandering promenade. Good God, how quickly life can change in youth! You can leap from mountain top to mountain top, and each time it's as though you've never been anywhere else. There's never so much as a backward glance, or a forward-looking one either. As to pitfalls in between: the unhappy valleys and depressing, dark-veiled forests, the rivers of sorrow to drown in; you don't see them. Later on, however, we see them far too clearly to go foolishly leaping about, and we stick where possible to the familiar grassy slopes.

'Did you mean what you said about Egypt?' I asked, hoping to revive in talk at least that captivating offer, which now held a precious modicum of commitment.

'Of course I meant it.' Thrusting his mask into the robe's patch pocket, Hugo looked at me closely. 'I do wish you'd come!' The intensity was brand new and there was no mistaking that he meant it.

'Oh, I want to! Polly and Arthur do too,' I hurriedly tacked on. 'But how on earth can we? It's just not possible. I'm *so* sorry.'

'Is it the Daisy Miller world?' he asked drily, lighting a cigarette. But he was smiling slightly; he'd seen a wedge under the door.

We continued our aimless stroll, broken now by kisses and whisperings of sweet everythings, as we floated among other free spirits in a world enticingly devoid of burdensome identities, and as intoxicating as the inhalation of pure oxygen.

'Americans *are* the best people,' said Hugo. 'Alexei was right about that, but for the wrong reasons. They're the best people when they combine the best of both worlds, old and new; the traditions and wisdom of the continent, without its cynicism and crushing caste systems, with the refreshing, open-minded directness and optimism of America. You're on your way to that.' It was, he said, what he searched for in a woman and damned hard to find. It took the right surroundings and proper guidance to develop, so it was very rare. Suddenly Hugo stood stock still, arrested on the spot by an idea, seemingly transfixed by it. 'Shall I

157

mould you, then, make you my Galatea?' he proposed. 'How would you like that?'

It sounded marvellous to me — exactly like *Be My Valentine*. Used to mentors and wild for self-improvement, I was ready clay, as well as being head over heels in love with Hugo. Moreover, transformed under his loving tutelage, becoming polished, perfected, poised and better informed, even tenderly wise, I would emerge, like Venus on her half shell, as Hugo's ideal woman. At last I too would be *somebody*!

Today an offer like that, a Pygmalion offer, would irritate, even alarm most girls; but it wasn't an unusual proposition then, except perhaps in its explicitness. Indeed it was perfectly normal, as I'm sure you know, for girls to lay aside their personalities, subverting them to the main oeuvre and remoulding themselves to suit their husband's tastes and interests. Whither you go I will go, and all that. And hidden from view, Galatea, I suspect, lives on today, secretly worshipped at subliminal altars — a goddess high up in the libidinous pantheon of male fantasy.

Hugo said that to abandon the promise our relationship held would be a kind of death; that now and then life offered something rare — he compared it to an exotic fruit appearing overnight on an ordinary-looking tree. You

158

reached out for it, or you were too frightened or unimaginative and so fell back into the conventional mould — and stayed there all your life.

But the conventional mould was what I had long aspired to fill — Mrs William Brydonne with all the trappings: a good husband, children, money, social position. I too was a fortune-hunter, in a discreetly acceptable form. But isn't every woman one to some degree? It's requisite to successful nest-building, or it used to be.

Now, however, like good wine souring to vinegar, this carefully cherished idea had in an instant become unpalatable, as dull as dishwater, even in its way alarming. Instead of a desirable mould from which to arise newly made, a custom-built coffin loomed. Mould had revealed its double meaning.

Hugo said that he must go to Egypt, he had no choice; he had commitments there. But parting now would be calamitous and we must think of something. Our relationship must be given a chance. Suddenly his voice was laced with purpose, and, his mind working full out in the effort to evolve a plan, his ebullience returned. Arthur would go to Egypt like a shot, he said, and surely Polly would too — they got on so well, almost like brother and sister. While Olivia almost certainly would say yes. She loved Egypt and their parents would readily consent, especially if they knew Alexei was in Rome. They had their reasons for that, and so I must accept them.

'But *my* parents will never agree!' I cried in deep dismay. I explained that they had made sacrifices so I could visit Europe and I couldn't possibly let them down, and appear so shilly-shallying and ungrateful. It was the first time I had alluded, if indirectly, to our impoverishment; but Hugo was unperturbed.

He took me in his arms again. 'All tertiary concerns,' he murmured soothingly. 'We must look first to the primary ones and deal with everything in its proper order. That produces results.'

And we walked on, wrapped in a thoughtful and unembarrassed silence, mulling over our situation, till, approaching the brightly lit villa, Hugo stopped again and, rooted to the spot, appeared to be mesmerized by the dazzling scene before us. In fact his thoughts ran very differently, and, smiling suddenly, his mood entirely changed, he turned and took my hands, casting my mask aside and holding me at arm's length and under careful scrutiny. There was no mistaking he had made a decision about something, and was preparing to act on it.

Embarrassed and uneasy, I dropped my eyes. My mask, lying on the grass, stared back mockingly. 'What is it?' I asked shyly, afraid he was about to make fun of me again, as he had that night at the Colosseum, calling me a Daisy Miller, inferring I was naive and a thoroughgoing provincial.

But he didn't. Far from it, in fact.

'Why not tell your parents that we're engaged?' he calmly proposed. 'We practically are, aren't we?' He said it so gently and with such self-assurance, but out of the blue, just like that, still holding my hands and beaming at me with such sweetness and warmth, clearly delighted.

I stood there dumbfounded! I simply couldn't believe my ears or utter a single word in response. Joy and incredulity danced insanely in my muddled, half-comprehending head. Could this really be happening? It was a piece of luck beyond my wildest hopes!

'Well, I suppose it is sensible to get to know each other a little better first,' he went on, seeing my astonished face. 'Before making it official, I mean. Your parents will at any rate see the wisdom of that, so it might even work to our advantage.' He gripped my hands more tightly. 'You don't have to say anything right now. Come to think of it, I'd rather you didn't: I want you to know me better first, and I want you to know and to like Egypt, and, just as important, to know and like me in it. I'm not the same person there as here, I warn you.' His laughter rose up suddenly, full of pleasure and much amused, I think, by my bewildered face. He told me later I looked as if I'd seen a ghost. 'In Egypt I'm a different person,' he went on gaily. 'Just you wait and see!'

'However you are, you are,' I answered softly and wholeheartedly, throwing my life in one magnificent sweep upon the fickle winds of chance, without another thought. Well, we all have to do it.

But we needed to act fast. Arthur's agreement was instantaneous, of course, but Polly, on being pressed, regarded me strangely. 'OK, so long as we all go,' she said gloomily. 'Olivia too.' Getting parental consent wasn't a difficulty for Polly. Arthur, being her cousin, made a suitable escort; added to which the connection between the two families would be further soldered by the trip — something the American Brydonnes were almost certain to approve.

'Ping,' said Polly, gimlet-eyed.

Hugo planned to square it with Olivia next morning. With Alexei off to Paris it would be a cinch, he said. In the meantime he would wire their parents, so as to oil the wheels. 'I'm

162

going to tell them about us,' he promised, obviously pleased. He had removed his cloak and, taking two glasses of champagne from a tray, handed me one. 'So there it is, you see: it's really going to happen.' He raised his glass. His optimism was so contagious that I too finally began to believe that we might bring it off.

★ ★ ★

Next day, almost shouting to be heard across the ocean — it was my first transatlantic call — I told Mother straight out that there was a young man and it was serious; in fact we were practically engaged, only we needed to know each other a little better first. I inferred this was my own highly sensible idea. The problem was he had to return to Egypt, but if I could go with him for four days, Polly and Olivia would go with me. It wouldn't cost anything: travel and lodging were free, and we could join the others in Venice. 'Oh, Mother, it's what I want, more than anything in this world!'

'Good heavens, Kate!' Her voice was shrill with regret for letting me go abroad. 'An Egyptian!'

When I said it was Olivia's brother, her tone, still edged with worry, softened some.

But Mother knew a big gamble was involved. My mother was a realist; life had made her one, and in real life princes, as she believed, never married Cinderellas; they seduced them and left them sitting forlornly among the ashes, where they rightly belonged, in Mother's view, for having given in.

'What about Billy?' she wanted to know.

'Billy's fine,' I yelled. A buzz had started on the line. 'I had a letter from him this week. *So don't worry!*' I'd callously implied he was on hold; moreover, that what he didn't know wouldn't hurt him. I knew Polly wouldn't say a word. 'Mother,' I cried, 'my life depends on it! I love him that much — and going to Egypt will make all the difference!'

I was right about that, at any rate.

So Mother caved in. 'I'll tell your father you're definitely engaged; he would never approve otherwise. Going off without a chaperone — it isn't right.'

Miss Grist, whose reactions were always surprising, declared it a fine opportunity. 'You will see something of an ancient civilization predating Europe's, and by comparison what European enlightenment has contributed. It will give you a valuable perspective.' She said we mustn't expect reimbursement from our hotel in Florence, booked in advance, though she would do what she could about the meals.

'She's a good old stick,' Arthur acknowledged, embarrassed he had been making fun of her.

'Oh, I'm going to miss you all so much!' Mary-Moore cried with real feeling the next day, throwing her arms around me. Mary-Moore was a very nice person and I'm sure she made Billy a much better wife than I'd have done. But I won't dwell on that.

'It's only for four days,' I said, giving her a hug, and turning to Sally promised, cross-my-heart-and-hope-to-die, to bring her back enough scarabs for two more bracelets.

That night Miss Grist received three telegrams giving permission for the trip. I didn't see the Hartfields', but only Polly's family, I suspect, mentioned a deserved rebate.

★ ★ ★

A big surprise came the following day at lunch. Olivia and Alexei had joined us before making the promised trip to Nero's Golden House.

'I have been all this morning on the telephone,' Alexei declared, showing mild exasperation. 'It has not been easy, but at last

165

everything has been sorted out. Hugo, your generous offer is irresistible and I am able to accept your invitation with the greatest pleasure.'

Polly and I stared, inscrutable as those party masks, while Olivia smiled encouragingly at Alexei and never once looked at her brother, whom she'd so skilfully outwitted, even securing their parents' permission with his assistance. Quietly, passively, she had got exactly what she wanted. It was either ingenious or else extremely lucky.

Hugo handled Alexei's bombshell with aplomb. 'What good news,' he said evenly. 'I'd better telephone to make sure there's a seat left on the plane.'

Alexei said that if not he would meet us there and come on a commercial flight. So Hugo was roundly defeated, but I was glad for Olivia. Probably Hugo was used to exerting a strong influence on his sister, even a dictatorial one. Twins were so tightly bound up together, so intricately entwined that letting go now probably wasn't easy. Yet growing apart was part of growing up, and sooner or later something that must be faced. Besides, very soon I would myself be everything Hugo wanted, a top-of-the-class, award-winning Galatea, dedicated to his every need and expectation. For I was nothing if not ambitious, and getting top marks was by this time second nature.

Polly, on the other hand, smelled a rat. 'There's something odd about all this,' she said. 'Whose plane is it anyhow — do you know?'

I couldn't have cared less. 'People at that archaeological meeting, I suppose. There's nothing odd in that.'

'Hugo's not telling the truth; he's got something up his sleeve.'

'I expect you're right,' I said slowly, and sitting down beside her on the bed, I confided proudly and in a conspiratorial whisper our virtual engagement.

Polly didn't exactly leap forward with congratulations. 'But you hardly know him,' she insisted, looking vexed. 'Why, only last week you thought he was someone else.'

'I love him!' I answered gently. 'That's all that matters.'

Polly, with no experience of being in love, couldn't possibly understand; and of course there was her loyalty to Billy. 'I've told my mother,' I added by way of formal confirmation. 'And Hugo has told his.'

At that moment, Hugo knocked on our door. The plane was leaving in one hour, he said.

'Darling,' I cried, throwing open the door

167

and giving him a kiss. 'We'll be down in exactly two minutes.'

★ ★ ★

And so we left Europe, not having been there very long. England, France, ancient Rome, and now this older, more exotic world, organized along different lines and built according to other, largely alien, values. I was going forward in my life but backwards, it would seem, in time — unless it proved to be some kind of circle.

A twin-engine Bonanza stood on the tarmac, the pilot and co-pilot standing alongside to greet us. They looked to me like those two Arabs in the street opposite our hotel, except that they were wearing uniforms. But what could I say?

Everyone shook hands and smiled.

This is a high point, I thought, mounting the metal steps the co-pilot had pulled down. Can life ever be better than this? I am in love, travelling to exotic places and in some style; I have no burdens or cares; I am young and intelligent and the world really and truly is my oyster.

I can't say it ever did get any better.

13

Is any story really new, I wonder? probably not, since what can happen in life is limited, both in its disastrous pitfalls and its heady and intoxicating summits. Soon enough, therefore, we get to know the available plots, life's basic themes and actions, if you will, and the prime ingredients of stories. One theme that figures unavoidably here, of course, is innocence abroad. That old chestnut, you're probably thinking; Henry James roasted it to a cinder a hundred years ago. In fact, James only explored one aspect of this seminal topic: the effect of a shocking piece of reality on innocent minds, which must then cope with it as a rite of passage to maturity. And James's characters cope; they grow through suffering. Henry James came to believe in suffering. It was a preferred catalytic tonic of his generation: it was good for you, decidedly therapeutic. My own view is, however, very different. I believe a little suffering goes a long way towards useful metamorphosis, while a big dose can inflict irreparable harm — that suffering in fact can kill.

But what about innocence that atrophies into ignorance? Is the line between the two simply a matter of age, after which anyone who remains innocent is branded ignorant — a coward or an oaf who can't or won't look truth in the face or call a spade a spade, and in not facing up to reality, can't grow? If so, what is that age? Ignorance is a highly pejorative word. And where is religious faith in all this: the armour that holds reality at bay and lets people get on with it, regardless? Why should that be an acceptable means of ducking out — if it still is?

But certainly Polly and I were innocents — cliché innocents — about to be hit by a big double-fisted blow of reality. And I won't pretend it was a nourishing experience, not remotely so; in fact, quite the reverse. Let's look at it like this. Here you and I are, sitting comfortably in our closed railway carriage, as it were, watching endless birch-tree-covered steppes slide by, as on a movie screen. But mercifully, as in the movies, it is someone else's world; we are ourselves preserved from it — unless of course our train should suddenly crash. Well, at the time of which I speak, I was in a similar compartment, metaphorically speaking, and the train did crash, hurling us into a desert that must be painfully crossed — not in order to mature by suffering, but because the crash wasn't sufficiently brutal to permanently stop the heart. Or not in my case, anyhow.

Yet people claim that travel broadens, and it's true there is always much to learn, and that in new surroundings all of us are comparatively innocent or comparatively ignorant. Which is why some people categorically refuse to travel. They may wish to learn but they don't want, even remotely, to be out of control. They don't think it will do them any good to feel at sea, it will only make them seasick, which it does. So travel is for optimists, I think; and I was one, gliding along on polished silver tracks and gazing at the stars, the desert stretching out ominous and unseen below.

But innocence abroad isn't remotely my theme, merely a coincidental aspect of the story; nor am I interested in 'themes'. But if I were, after this last and very recent encounter with Olivia, and discovering my innocence intact (which at my age makes me, certifiably, an ignoramus), a plausible theme might be *delayed* innocence abroad, and the limbo life led in between as a result. But I'm jumping ahead. I must tell you first about that disastrous trip to Egypt and the commencement of my years of stunted growth.

Our hotel in Luxor, the Winter Palace, was a far cry from the embarrassingly opulent gem it is today. In the 1950s it was a rather austere colonial hotel and, the British having recently left, already a bit run down. But the rooms were high ceilinged and huge; there was a lovely garden at the back, full of bougainvillaea, and a splendid view of the Nile running parallel to the road in front.

'Who's paying for all this?' Polly wanted to know, gazing suspiciously around the cavernous lobby.

A discreet question put to the receptionist, who wore a fez, brought the reply that Mr Hartfield's friends were always welcome at the Winter Palace; the Hartfield name was revered in Egypt. Which didn't tell us much. Our porter was, however, more forthcoming. He said the hotel was normally closed in summer, but part of it had been reopened for an important meeting, and we had the rooms left over.

'Archaeologists,' I told Polly. 'You needn't dig any further.' I wasn't surprised they got top treatment. In addition to important academic discoveries, they kept on finding more things for tourists to come and see. 'Tourism must be on a par, economically speaking, with the Nile,' I suggested as we unpacked — or rather as I unpacked. Polly never properly unpacked; she improvised. 'And archaeology is responsible for it.'

'People don't look very prosperous to me from either,' said Polly, making a face at the dress she was putting on a hanger. 'Everything's pretty primitive, like Olivia said.'

'Things haven't moved along because there wasn't the need,' I loyally declared. 'But tourism creates foreign currency, and people can use that to buy things abroad.'

'You've been talking to Arthur,' said Polly, 'but I doubt these people have ever seen a nickel, so where does it go?'

Of course, I couldn't answer that.

The hotel's main floor, the first floor up, was the only part of the building that was open. The lobby was in the centre, the rooms opening off a corridor at each end. Polly's and my room overlooked the gardens, as did Arthur's, while Hugo's and Olivia's, opposite ours, overlooked the Nile. Alexei's room was on the far side of the lobby — because it was booked later, Hugo said. But Polly insisted Hugo was playing chaperon and that it impugned Olivia's honour. What's more, he was in cahoots with their parents and busy conspiring against Olivia's happiness.

'That's so unfair,' I told her. 'You don't

know anything about it, so why pretend you do, and why on earth take sides? It doesn't concern you, anyhow.' It was the sharpest I had ever spoken to her.

'I don't like seeing people misused, that's all,' she muttered, chastened.

'And I don't like to see them slandered,' I retorted.

The tension between us was new, our friendship showing for the first time a perceptibly jagged edge. And ours wasn't the only one. Other relationships were beginning to shift. Polly, for instance, had begun openly to back Olivia, who, faithful to Alexei, viewed her brother with a growing unease. This threw Polly and Olivia more solidly together, and marginally, it seemed to me, at Alexei's expense; while Hugo and Alexei, mutually suspicious, eyed each other like a pair of mastiffs pretending ease on either side of a medieval fireplace.

Youth, however, quickly accommodates rapid change; or so I believed, unaware that life's most afflicting events happen in a trice: accidents, illness, deaths, falling in love; and the years are spent not in experiencing such momentous things, but recovering from them. An interesting word, 'recovery': instead of a cure it suggests a temporary burial or covering over — like an encysted disease that, dormant for years, wakes up to kill you stone dead later on.

But all of this was in its infancy.

Slipping quietly out at dawn that first morning, I discovered to my surprise that Hugo was up, too. He was sitting in a little parlour off the lobby, his back to me, talking to three Egyptians in Western dress. They were drinking coffee and speaking in low, serious voices. The cadences sounded English and I paused to listen, surprised to find archaeology of such intense concern.

At that, a porter stepped swiftly in front of the parlour entrance, like a guard, to block it. I wasn't going in anyhow, but it was interesting he'd done that, and I did overhear one thing: 'He was arrested on Friday,' followed by what sounded like, 'We don't know.'

This was my first hint that Hugo might, even remotely, be involved in politics. I knew nothing of Egypt's politics myself — I'd vaguely heard the prime minister kept on changing — but hearing someone had been arrested sounded serious. I'd read that European students got mixed up in political movements: the Sorbonne was, according to *Newsweek*, a hotbed of communists (and communism was illegal in America). That Hugo might be politically involved was

175

therefore pretty alarming, though conceivably admirable too, and I determined to find out more — although discreetly, for there was an air of secrecy about that little meeting from which I'd been so pointedly kept out.

Outside the hotel, a grandiose staircase descended to the street. I could imagine Fred Astaire and Ginger Rogers dancing down it to the Nile, singing away just as I felt like doing. The sky, a duck-egg blue, was edged in pink, and on the glittering river red lateen-sailed feluccas swept by like flurries of autumnal leaves. A veranda-encrusted tourist boat, something like a Mississippi riverboat, was moored alongside the bank, and several horse-drawn carriages stood nearby, even at that early hour. Unfortunately, Luxor's merchants and urchins were up too, and in Egypt they never leave you in peace. The children fluttered about like starlings. 'Give me money, Miss. You want buy antique, this really old.' Perhaps it was, but needing nothing I walked on, beyond all irritation, the palm trees making a graceful canopy of plumed umbrellas overhead. Sketchily, I began to imagine a future in Egypt, wondering vaguely too about our marriage; when and where — provided all went well — it would take place. Should I return to America and finish college first? I didn't want to. And since my parents couldn't afford the sort of wedding Rockefellers expected, why not marry abroad and have an American reception later? Though nice to think about, such things were part of a distant and hazy future. The present, so full of pleasure and new experiences, had completely captured my attention, each moment linked in an exquisite mental chain that I imagined myself in old age going over and over, like a rosary, each link marking a moment of special happiness.

★   ★   ★

Later that same morning, we paid a visit to Karnak temple. I won't bog you down in travelogue; suffice to say that Rome's Pantheon compared to Karnak is a shepherd's hut, and the temple's great hall a forest of stone columns that gives our sequoias more than a run for their money. My head only reached the columns' bases, and every inch of their gigantic shafts was engraved and had originally been painted. Hugo explained some of the history, which I now forget, except that the temple was built over generations, with different pharaohs, especially Rameses II, adding very big bits.

But Karnak is significant for another reason too, because it was there that, like a barometer's sudden plunge, I first caught Olivia's changed attitude to me. Till then she'd been so considerate, and so kind and conscientiously polite. Moreover, I'd assumed that Hugo's declared attachment conferred, to some degree, a rightful niche among these golden young people.

I had asked Olivia if the temple we were going to visit that afternoon was as big as Karnak. A stupid question, I know, but strolling along beside her I had to say something, and talking to her was never easy. Anyhow, that's what came out.

'Hugo,' she called out softly, 'aren't we going to call on Khadija this afternoon?'

Hugo, busy explaining to Arthur what some symbols meant, looked at her strangely, then back at the engraved column. 'We are indeed,' he said. 'Arthur can be dragoman this afternoon. His Baedeker will tell you what I would and probably edit it better.' Khadija, he explained, was their old ayah.

And we strolled on. Olivia hadn't answered my question, but she *had* let me know that she was taking Hugo off; and suddenly I realized she hadn't addressed one word to me since Rome, when, shortly before we left, Hugo had told her about our virtual engagement.

178

'Is your ayah expecting you, Olivia?' I asked, sitting over coffee at a little kiosk beside the temple's sacred lake. (If Alexei was surprised by her plan, he didn't show it.)

Again Olivia directed her response at Hugo. 'She's always expecting us, wouldn't you say?' she asked dreamily, looking almost through me at her twin. This was repeated, as we walked along the corniche before dinner, when I asked about the visit.

'It *was* a success, wasn't it, Huggie? Wouldn't you say it was?' I'd never heard his nickname before. No doubt the old ayah had revived it; or had Olivia never addressed Hugo directly in my presence? For a minute I wasn't sure. But at any rate, her manner had shut me out, as it so obviously was meant to do.

Sensing his sister's rudeness, however, Hugo put his arm protectively around me and, walking ahead of the others, began to ask about our visit to Luxor temple. So, for the moment at least, it all blew over. Arthur and Polly, following behind us, were enthusing about the temple's avenue of sphinxes, and Olivia and Alexei, now arm in arm, brought up the rear, Alexei comparing the industrialized Volga to the Nile. Alexei had never set foot in Russia and it was unlikely that he ever would, but he felt a touching

179

responsibility for the country. It paralleled his real existence in a sort of alter-life.

Clear as anything, I can see this very minute the picture that we made: the Nile running in a dark ribbon beside the pavement, the hills visible across the river, rose tipped in the sunset and concealing a honey-combed labyrinth of luxurious tombs, the palms arching in delicate green parasols overhead. I had on a blue print dress, with white high heels and dark glasses, like Grace Kelly wore in that Hitchcock film; and Hugo looked so handsome in his open-necked white shirt and khaki trousers, his eyes, deep and opaque, gazing thoughtfully at those hills, whose inner secrets he knew so intimately.

Well, I won't go on, except to say that a blot no bigger than a pinprick marred this pristine image of happy, blossoming youth; and it was spreading, creeping like ink across heavy absorbent paper and indelibly seeping in. Everyone saw it, but like the Rorschach test so popular then, each of us saw something different. Not good enough for Rockefellers or an adored twin brother was the blot I saw. No money, no breeding, very little polish or sophistication — in short, a thoroughgoing social pauper; someone to befriend but certainly not to marry; someone to be blotted out. What others saw would become clear later on, and maybe each interpretation was in its way correct, and everybody's truth was different. It is possible, of course.

Alexei had offered to take us out to dinner, but Hugo said the hotel was the only place safe to eat in, because of parasites, so Alexei good-humouredly relented. The restaurant was about a quarter full when we arrived. We were, I noticed at once, the only party that included women and, more remarkable, the only Westerners. The men with whom Hugo had been in conversation that morning were at a table in the corner and nodded solemnly as we came in. At another table, where there was a lot of laughter, everyone wore army uniforms. There wasn't a jellaba in sight.

We talked at first about the day's marvels. How ancient people could have constructed buildings on such a scale was to me mind-boggling. But Alexei disagreed. 'You have left the key out of the padlock, Katherine,' he said (he always called me by my proper name). 'You have omitted the power of autocracy, of absolute rule.' Autocracy was, he said, the equal of steam, of electricity, even of atomic power. People forgot that today because it was so rare. But

181

Russia had it and it made the country a superpower to a degree the West had failed to comprehend. 'A dangerous oversight,' declared Alexei. He looked archly at Hugo. 'While the poor Egyptians, bereft of autocratic kings and searching for an alternative, so we are told, have only the water wheel for power.'

Naively perhaps, Hugo took the bait. 'On the contrary, Alexei, Egypt has failed to progress *because* of autocratic rulers, not the lack of them, I assure you.'

'I daresay that includes the British,' Arthur offered, looking pleased. 'We like to think we're being helpful, bringing our modernity and culture to the needy, which is how we look at anyone who is without it.'

'Alexei,' said Hugo gently, ignoring this, 'I don't believe you read the newspapers. Egypt is in the midst of colossal change. In two years they've thrown out British rule, got rid of King Farouk and divided the arable land among the people. They even plan to build a huge dam on a super-pharaonic scale, to regulate the Nile. It will stop famines and provide massive hydroelectricity for industry. Having their affairs in their own hands has given the people tremendous motivation!'

'With respect, Hugo, their affairs are not, I think, in their own hands, but in the hands of a military junta — in the hands of those gentlemen over there.' Alexei nodded towards the table of uniformed officers, who, nodding back, smiled at us in a friendly manner; so we all smiled and nodded back.

'Friends of yours?'

'Acquaintances,' said Hugo.

'I understand your 'acquaintances' removed Naguib as prime minister because he wants a constitution, and that his replacement Colonel Nasser does not. Nor does Colonel Nasser approve of parties, neither political parties nor, like King Farouk, non-political parties. He doesn't care for either. He prefers that they should all be banned.'

'You're right about the junta,' Hugo answered, lowering his voice, surprised, I think, by Alexei's knowledge of Egyptian politics. 'But many people, including many in the army, still support Naguib and a return to civil government. One must be patient, that's all.'

'You refer to the Muslim Brotherhood, I think?'

Here was my chance to learn something of Hugo's involvement. What was the Muslim Brotherhood, I asked.

Alexei, not Hugo, answered. 'An improbable association of political idealists and religious maniacs.' He was looking quizzically at Hugo. 'And, like all idealists, crypto-autocrats who believe they are doing the people a big favour. The religious faction comes to the same thing: the Muslims want a religious oligarchy, perhaps a state religion. They too are sure of what is good for people. But which of these two certainties will win? Your Brotherhood is a doomed combination, because there will have to be a fight.'

'The Muslim Brotherhood,' said Hugo in answer to my question, but really addressing Alexei, 'want a return to civil government and a constitution. That's what binds them together, a desire for democracy.'

'An old-fashioned pharaoh would be preferable,' Alexei wickedly suggested, 'dreaming every day of his afterlife. There would be less interference. With militants there is always interference. And where is this democracy to come from? Who will give up their power?'

'With Naguib back in and a constitution, the necessary compromises will be made. The people will insist on it, and there will be elections.'

'You are active in these affairs, I think,' pursued Alexei, looking with narrowed eyes about the room. 'Is it for politics you are in Luxor now and why you were in Paris during the winter? You were in the riots at Cairo

University, were you not — and had to leave the country? Dear boy, be careful. The son of an ambassador has considerable protection. The son of a former ambassador has almost none.'

Hugo, to my astonishment, didn't deny he'd been in Paris. Yet if it was true, Olivia's letter must have been exactly what she'd said: from her brother who lived in Egypt, but who, forced to leave, would very naturally have written to tell her that he was in Paris. Polly's and my imaginations, absurdly over-heated, had concocted a silly cover-up worthy of a mawkish Hollywood romance. And now Alexei inferred we were ourselves providing Hugo with some sort of front.

'So, we are in a political cell?' Alexei continued, unchallenged, looking about the room again. 'But whose cell is it, and who exactly are our hosts? Their generosity, perhaps even their propinquity, requires acknowledgement.'

'*Propinquity!*' Having dropped her knife and fork, Olivia was staring blindly at her plate. 'Propinquity is responsible for every-thing!' she suddenly cried. I was astonished, even a little frightened. I'd never seen her so intense, and from the way she spoke you would have thought some sort of Greek tragedy was being acted out. It was so unlike her that even Alexei registered perceptible surprise. And how could mere proximity be responsible for something? It was true, of course, that if Hugo hadn't returned to Egypt he wouldn't be mixed up in their politics, which were becoming dangerous. But Olivia had said propinquity was responsible for *everything*, so I knew that, whatever else she meant, she also must mean me: that if Hugo and I had never met he wouldn't have made this hideous mistake, becoming engaged to a provincial nobody. Well, it was she who had introduced us, so she as much as propinquity was to blame, I decided, muffling my alarm.

In thinking about it now, however, I see a third possibility, another angle that was impossible to guess at then. So you never really know, do you, what people mean or whether they themselves do either, really and truly? Suffice to say that Olivia, looking at that spreading inkblot, as she saw it, was, Cassandra-like, rightly inferring doom.

Just then, more men in military dress arrived, producing a sudden hush before the soldiers in the room jumped to attention as one body, their chairs rattling like a fanfare behind them.

Hugo froze, staring intently.

'Who is it?' I whispered.

His eyes stayed on the party. 'Colonel Nasser.'

'What sort of a conference is this?' Polly whispered to me. 'Archaeology my foot! That plane belonged to those Brothers, I bet you anything.'

Hurriedly, Arthur tried to bring our talk round to something general, but Hugo wasn't having it. 'This is a birthday celebration,' he announced quietly, raising his glass and smiling thinly. 'The coup that toppled King Farouk occurred two years ago today, so everyone, except perhaps Alexei, wishes to celebrate. And thank you for your counsel, Alexei, but I do tread carefully.' He lowered his voice. 'At present there is, however, some advantage to Colonel Nasser: since he alone can remove Britain's troops from the Canal, he is of use to everyone right now.'

It was a big room, but such talk did seem unwise and probably was, because at that moment a man from Nasser's table approached ours. He was wearing an army uniform with lots of decorations on his chest.

Hugo stood up, looking grave.

'Our prime minister welcomes you back to Egypt and sends his personal greetings, Mr Hartfield,' the officer smoothly declared. 'He hopes your archaeological work will keep you fully occupied while you are here. He is an admirer of your father, who used diplomacy so skilfully to avoid undue intrusion in our affairs, and wishes to be remembered to him.'

'Please thank the prime minister for his kindness,' said Hugo formally, then turned to acknowledge directly Nasser's interest. But Nasser, concentrating on his dinner, had his eyes on his plate. 'I will gladly give my father the prime minister's message, and will you please say to Colonel Nasser that I wish him well in his negotiations with the British? Word has it that he has them on the run.'

'Let us hope that this time word has it correctly,' said the officer, and they both bowed slightly.

Hugo had received a firm but avuncular warning. It was good of Nasser, I thought, especially when Hugo told me later that evening that the Canal negotiations were being hindered by the Brotherhood's activities. They were in fact foolishly risking suppression. He admitted to having been in student protests at the university, and he had briefly gone to Paris; but he refused to talk about it further.

'As you see, I'm a different person in Egypt,' he said, almost airily. 'I warned you. I wanted you to know it.' He said it lightly, his arm around me; and walking along the narrow Luxor streets, he began to explain the current power struggle. Nasser and Naguib kept on alternating as prime ministers, bouncing back and forth like shuttlecocks; but Naguib had recently been seriously outmanoeuvred, losing a lot of support as a result. The future was uncertain.

'But darling, isn't it dangerous taking sides?' I cried. 'It could threaten your whole career, especially if you back the wrong horse. You could be banned from Egypt, and what would happen to your work?'

'It's certainly possible,' he answered evenly, gazing towards the darkened mortuary hills across the river. 'But the living are infinitely more important than the dead, and one must never forget that. It's a mistake these people made for centuries, and many archaeologists make it now.' He said some of them opposed the new dam in the south because important ruins faced inundation there.

'I hope Egypt pleases you,' he said, kissing me goodnight outside my room. 'Its surface is remarkably deceptive, especially to a romantic,' he chided gently. 'It's best to look as deeply as possible and find the solid bedrock of reality.'

Was that a hint? It could have been. I don't know. Unheeding, I put my arms around his neck. 'Egypt pleases me enormously,' I said, 'and you in it.'

Olivia was coming down the corridor, and I was glad she saw us. When a person turns against you, I'm afraid you reciprocate. It's a natural defence, isn't it? And how enemies are made.

'Oh, Huggie, have you got a minute?' She gave me a pale smile.

'One minute only,' he said significantly, looking at his watch. 'We have an early day tomorrow.' And giving me a light kiss, indicated his door.

14

The next day would prove fateful, although unfortunately I would be the last to find it out. Oh, I sensed the shifting sands all right, but not the deep movement of tectonic plates. That would have taken a finer sensibility and greater knowledge of the world than my mere twenty years provided. Besides which, everything began so pleasantly.

It started with an early morning ferry ride across the Nile, from a dock opposite our hotel, en route to visit the royal tombs. The little boat was packed with local people bent on immemorial routines, their dress, chores, religion and way of life unchanged in a thousand years. Boxes of melons, a few chickens, even a goat accompanied us, and of course the children hounded us for tips, or baksheesh as they called it. A canvas awning was stretched overhead to protect against the sun and standing outside it, in the bow, were almost certainly those two men I'd seen in Rome — although my saying so made Hugo laugh. 'All Arabs look alike right now,' he said. 'But you'll soon be in focus.' He suggested I concentrate on one physical

191

feature at a time and study it. Noses were a good beginning: unlike Europeans, Arabs had charismatic noses.

I meekly agreed, convinced, however, that Hugo was being watched and possibly was even in some danger. Used to enjoying unusual freedom in Egypt, he may have believed, as Alexei had suggested, that being his father's son would get him off any unsavoury hooks. Nasser, after all, had merely shaken his finger at a naughty boy. Nonetheless, a serious power struggle was under way, arrests were being made, and reportedly some brutal reprisals had been taken. And what if Naguib lost? Olivia, I noted, looked uneasy too, watching those two Arabs. She was unconsciously biting the inner edge of her lip. And she knew more of Egypt and what was happening than I did.

At the dock, a turbaned guide met us with a string of tiny donkeys about the size of Mexican burros. He and Hugo knew each other, and warm greetings were exchanged in Arabic before we mounted, Olivia joining in. Donkeys are notoriously stubborn but these were an exception: like wind-up toys, they scooted along in a stiff-legged running walk, never once pausing to snatch a blade of grass — not that there was any after we began to climb. The route took us through two biblical-looking villages before ascending the steep hillside which rose like a rubble wall along the narrow strip of alluvial plain. The two mysterious Arabs followed at a distance, also on donkeys, and this time Hugo, looking over his shoulder, questioned our dragoman, who merely shrugged. Then Hugo did too. I looked back questioningly at Olivia, but she was talking to Polly and paid no attention.

Though not yet eight o'clock it was already hot, the sun, bouncing off the rocks, intensifying the heat by its reflection. I thought of Moses leading the Jewish people out of Egypt. They would have crossed a similar terrain, escaping from many decades of enslavement. My own position was, I mused, exactly the reverse: I had arrived in Egypt a willing thrall, happy to stay and to do Hugo's bidding. I could imagine Polly's cool response to that: I was a right fool. But she and Olivia were still talking, and suddenly Olivia reached over and patted Polly's arm. A unique gesture. I couldn't help wondering whether they were ganging up, trying, for different reasons, to separate Hugo and myself — Polly for my own good, as she saw it, and Olivia for Hugo's. An overreaction, I expect, but the kaleidoscope was turning, the patterns shifting and re-forming, as I've said, click click click, inescapably. One shift was

193

that Hugo and Olivia hardly spoke to each other. Whatever she had said the night before must have gone down very badly. Probably it was about politics and the dangers involved. But whatever it had been about, I was delighted by the result.

With Olivia continuing to keep Polly's company, however, another shift emerged, in that Olivia seemed subtly to be avoiding Alexei. Dear Alexei, a model of poise, good sense and maturity compared to us, and immaculate as ever in a white linen jacket and broad-brimmed panama fedora, was beginning to look a trifle out of place. He felt the heat tremendously, his marble complexion had turned fiery pink, and astride that tiny donkey he resembled a giant carried on the shoulders of a feeble dwarf. It was a little pathetic. Moreover, as Hugo's guest Alexei was to my mind obscurely diminished. A silly prejudice, I know, but an older man accepting hospitality from a young one struck me as improper; and they weren't exactly friends. But was it Hugo's hospitality we were in fact accepting? Alexei had implied that it was not, and Hugo had been vague, possibly out of politeness, not wanting us to feel indebted. In any case, I felt certain he would never allow a political faction to pay, as it might implicate us in some way, and he would never do that.

Hugo was riding up front with the donkey man, so I trotted along beside Arthur, who was wearing a big straw hat, his ever-present foulard coming magnificently into its own. 'Mad dogs and Englishmen,' he quipped, squinting at the sky and re-pocketing his handkerchief. The sun's reflection off the rocky hillside was blinding, whether you looked up or down.

'I've never been on a donkey before,' I said. 'It's fun, isn't it?'

'Fun-ish.' He said we could switch to horses in Cairo. You could hire them and ride across the desert from one group of pyramids to another. And they weren't plugs either, but plucky Arab steeds. 'As you see, I've been boning up,' he confirmed with a big smile.

But a donkey was about my speed, even though the tack was primitive: the bridle a rope halter and the reins two strips of frazzled cotton cloth. Polly was the one for horses, I said; she had even won some prizes at Virginia horse shows.

'That scarf is very becoming,' said Arthur a moment later, changing the subject.

I'd bought it in the souk. Red and white checks, it looked like a tablecloth, but men wore them as head-dresses, like Arafat does. I'd wrapped mine around my head and shoulders, however, biblical fashion, even

195

pretending I was the Virgin Mary going towards Bethlehem to give the waiting world a new messiah.

'It's becoming the headdress of the Arab nation,' Arthur said.

'Oh dear, I hope they won't be offended.'

'Not at all. T.E. Lawrence set a fashion, I believe.'

Arthur continued alongside as we climbed the steep hillside, the donkeys scrambling agilely over loose rocks, till finally we reached the backbone of the ridge. A desolate lunar surface spread before us in every direction: a desert of rocks, a no man's land beneath which lay the royal tombs, mysterious caverns of opulence and death.

The two Arabs were now some distance in front of us. They must have taken a short cut.

* * *

We visited two royal tombs, I think. Shafts cut hundreds of feet into the rock, with tricky angular feints to confuse potential robbers, but without success. The walls were splendidly decorated with murals depicting men and gods, framed by columns of carefully written hieroglyphics. The main topic, Hugo said, was helping the dead to the other side and past a lot of horrors. Apparently, gaining immortality was no picnic but required a journey replete with the hazardous trials typical of epic poems. Suffering continued, even in death it seemed, to be a proving ground.

Osiris appeared repeatedly, swathed in linen, holding a crook and flail and wearing his high-hat royal crown. It was his world we were in, the kingdom of the dead, literally an underworld; and Osiris, vividly painted, sat in magisterial splendour, doling out final judgments — first- or third-class tickets, one-way only and no cancellations. Doom, foreboding and a depressing inevitability permeated everything. It made my young flesh creep.

But Hugo said Osiris was credited with making the afterlife accessible to ordinary mortals. Originally it had been the exclusive preserve of kings. 'Osiris became the enabler — a sort of Jesus figure in a way,' he said.

'Surely Isis was the enabler,' Olivia retorted coolly, gazing around the painted burial chamber. 'She resurrected Osiris.'

'I said the enabler for *mankind*,' Hugo answered sharply and turned abruptly away.

'But isn't Isis and Osiris supposed to be about fertility?' I ventured banally, hoping a re-focus would help to smooth things over. We were emerging from the tomb; the sunlight blinded and the heat hit you like a fist.

'It is indeed. But fertility involves rebirth as well as birth,' said Hugo with some enthusiasm. 'A tree dies in winter and comes back to life in spring. If trees could do it, people reasoned, why couldn't they, who after all were superior beings? It must be that they popped up somewhere else — conceivably in another world. It was the only logical explanation.'

This made us laugh, as it was meant to do.

'A reasoned argument for immortality at last,' said Arthur, adding what a brilliant wheeze burying people with all their possessions was. New artefacts would be needed and the economy less inclined to stagnate. 'Jolly forward-looking chaps, always with an eye on the future, you could say,' he merrily observed.

'Wasn't Osiris a pharaoh before he was a god?' I asked, trying to keep up my diversion — and Hugo in a good mood.

'Supposedly the first pharaoh, but he was born a god.'

Hugo said the family had a grisly history. Osiris was the eldest of four siblings and heir to Egypt's throne. He married his sister Isis and their other brother and sister married each other, they being the only gods of marriageable age around. It had solved the marital problem, but having only one throne exacerbated the hierarchical one. It was an old story, the fight for dominance: Cain and Abel. But unlike Cain, Osiris proved indestructible, and after Isis had resurrected him they even had a child, named Horus. Horus dispatched the usurping brother and became pharaoh, while Osiris reigned forever-after in the underworld.

'What a superb melodrama; they should make it for television,' said Arthur. We were walking in the direction of a concrete pavilion where we were to eat our lunch. Alexei, waving his panama hat like a fan, said the pharaohs probably deigned to share immortality with the lower orders because they needed an entourage. A pharaoh without minions would be a nobody, a mere pharaoh among other pharaohs; that would be hell indeed.

'Well, they may have agreed to share the afterlife,' said Arthur, 'but not the royal blood. They kept that solidly in the family, marrying their nearest relations.'

'More self-interest,' said Hugo, laughing. 'Inheritance was through the female line and the men weren't about to lose out because of it. The gods had set a convenient precedent, so they used it.'

'That must have produced a lot of idiots,' declared Polly. But Hugo said inbreeding wasn't as devastating as people thought — except socially, perhaps, or in the case of a defective gene; then it was more likely to show up, to be dominant.

'Like Akhenaten,' answered Olivia, a challenge of bell-like clarity in her voice. Akhenaten and his family, she told us, had distorted bodies: fat pear-shaped hips, weird elongated faces and overall flabbiness. 'Obviously something went wrong.'

'That's complete nonsense!' retorted Hugo. He said Akhenaten's dynasty had produced some of Egypt's greatest pharaohs, and the Amarna representations were symbolic, linked to Akhenaten's radical religious beliefs. That was the informed archaeological view, and Tutankamun, Akhenaten's son, certainly hadn't been deformed.

'Still, nobody really knows,' Olivia stubbornly persisted.

The antagonism between them was ballooning fast, with Olivia determined to challenge her brother at every turn. And Hugo naturally didn't care for it one bit. He was, I rather suspected, used to having her under his thumb, and might well have got the upper hand very early on. With twins, I'd read, it could even happen in the womb.

*   *   *

We ate our picnic sitting at a table in the concrete pavilion, where they sold deliciously ice-cold beer. It was an oven outside and the few tourists had disappeared back to their hotels. Squatting nearby under a rush matting, together with a guard, the two Arabs pretended to ignore us; but Hugo gave them the once-over, I noted with some relief.

'Hot as hell' said Polly, holding her frosted beer glass against her cheek. 'Egypt's underworld is the reverse of ours: so much cooler. No wonder Osiris preferred it.'

'A troglodyte existence does suit the climate,' Arthur agreed, opening a packet of sandwiches and passing them around.

We ate in silence till Alexei, his face still very pink, his brow beaded with sweat, remarked how childishly the ancient gods behaved: jealousy, vanity, petulance and eternal squabbling had governed their existence.

'Inventing them, man could only build on the familiar,' Arthur offered, smiling at Polly who was dubiously admiring an insect in her glass.

'Gods of any sort must have been an improvement over uncertainty,' I suggested. 'For some reason our brains insist on having answers to things.'

Hugo nodded emphatically. 'We're estranged from the animal kingdom by a single word, 'Why,'' he said.

'Why?' Polly pertly queried.

'Why? Because, unlike animals, everything isn't programmed.'

'We had it well worked out for quite a while, though,' Arthur jauntily observed. 'Imagination supplied the necessary answers and faith stepped smartly in and backed them up. Science has made that successful partnership redundant.'

'Enter truth at last,' declared Hugo approvingly, lighting a cigarette and leaning back comfortably in his chair. 'The brain has finally come into its own.'

'You mean it's been sitting there all this time waiting for science to catch up?' Polly sounded dry to the point of rudeness.

'Maybe we have a new task,' I hurriedly injected. 'Faith and imagination got people so far, but with reason we can go further, and work things out scientifically.'

Alexei smiled at this. 'Reason could prove an equally insufficient tool,' he said, 'merely peeling another layer from an onion of infinite dimensions.'

'Anyhow, we still make up answers for what we don't know,' Polly observed, 'and pompously call them theories. So faith and imagination still fill in the gaps.'

'I hope so,' Olivia answered with conviction. 'I hope they continue to shroud harsh truths and spare people unnecessary sorrow and unhappiness.'

'That's ridiculous, Olivia. Truth doesn't need a shroud.' Hugo glared furiously at his rebellious sister. 'Only those who can't face reality do, and they live false lives as a result.'

'Falling in love is a work of the imagination,' said Polly, cutting me a sideways glance. 'I read that somewhere.'

'And is it so very beneficial?' asked Olivia, shifting smoothly to the side of reason.

'It is to the unborn,' said Arthur.

Olivia was about to reply when Hugo, to our astonishment, slammed his fist down on the table. 'Olivia, for God's sake, *stop doing that!*'

Dumbfounded, and caught inexplicably in a family row, we didn't know where to look. Olivia had been collecting bottle caps and, without paying much attention, idly lining them up along her forearm. They did look like a row of warts or scabs, but Hugo's burst of anger was wildly out of place and all proportion, and I was embarrassed for him.

'A most godlike reaction.' Alexei was icily

ironic. 'Best suited to the ancient world, I think.'

He was right, of course. Hugo was behaving childishly and Alexei's rebuke was or should have been a direct hit: man triumphing over boy, Goliath over David. And Hugo would, I felt sure, have apologized, given half a chance. But Olivia's tears welled, and brushing the bottle caps off in one sweep, like banishing an attack of wasps, she jumped up, knocking over her chair, and hurried towards the blinding furnace outside.

Hugo caught her arm as she went by, and quick as a flash she slapped him hard with her free hand, a stinging blow, right across the face. 'Leave me alone! Just leave me alone, will you?' she cried. 'You've caused enough trouble. I hate you, Hugo! I really do!' And breaking free, Olivia started to run off in the direction of the tombs.

Refusing to be outmanoeuvred, Hugo rose like a shot to go after her, but amazingly the two Arabs, together with the guard who held a stick, stood and blocked his way. Maybe they thought he was assaulting her. It all happened so quickly. A heated exchange in Arabic followed. I don't know what was said, but probably Hugo explained that she was his sister, which in the Arab world made things like that OK. At any rate the men desisted, as did Hugo, who must have seen it was by now too late; and Alexei, who had also stood up, was encouraging him in a reasonable voice to sit back down.

During all this commotion, Polly had quietly slipped out the back; everyone's attention, understandably, had been on Hugo. I was terrified he would be arrested or something. He'd given those men a pretty solid pretext, so when they finally sloped off I was hugely relieved.

'Who are they?' I whispered anxiously when Hugo came back, his head down, clearly preoccupied.

'Who are they? They're nobody. A couple of nobodies!' But he looked worried; it had even displaced his anger, or what should by now have been his mortification.

Alexei, watching him coolly, said nothing, but his face was stern and reproving, and my heart went out to Hugo for behaving so foolishly.

★   ★   ★

Polly and Olivia took shelter in one of the maintenance huts, as I later learned. Olivia was crying, but Polly, when she told me the story that afternoon, simply glowed. Olivia had said Hugo was being intolerable; he was trying to dominate her life and make all her decisions for her. He'd done so since childhood and now he couldn't stop. He was convinced he knew best, and of course he didn't. I didn't point out that the reverse was true as well, because Polly went on to say that in fact it was Alexei, not Hugo, that Olivia was most concerned about. Things looked different in Egypt and she felt so guilty and confused, Alexei having come all that way to be with her. She didn't know what to do.

It hadn't cost him anything was Polly's view, but she didn't say that.

Polly and I were stretched out on our hotel beds, Polly propped up on two pillows, a straw fan lying in her lap, an odd sense of triumph suffusing her little face. I was listening hard, amazed at Olivia's sudden disclosure of her feelings. Though when thought about, she hadn't in fact confided very much, only that she was confused. Still, for Olivia that was a colossal give-away; while her outburst at lunch was even more extraordinary — almost as if another person was emerging. Maybe she was having a nervous breakdown or something. 'She's been wild about Alexei for ages!' I said. 'He's what brought her to Europe. So what's happened, I wonder?'

Polly drew a blank. She thought Hugo

might be about to involve the Hartfields, who didn't know Alexei was in Egypt, and that might have frightened Olivia. Their parents were fierce, Olivia had said, and very remote. As children she and Hugo had seen very little of them. She said that Hugo had been her only friend, challenging their imaginary enemies and always looking out for her. He'd even killed a poisonous snake once in her room, beaten it to death with a broom handle. The trouble was that now he couldn't let go, and worse, he was becoming so despotic.

'She's certainly nicer than her brother,' Polly finished up.

'There's no reason to say that! None at all. What have you got against Hugo? He's only trying to help. Even if it's a little misguided, he means well by it.'

'I haven't got anything against him, but he behaved abominably this morning.' Polly was sitting up, fanning herself. 'I only said his sister was nicer. I meant *even* nicer, if you prefer. Don't be so defensive.' She gave the fan a few quick sweeps. 'Mind you, if Hugo really *was* some sort of gruesome monster, you'd be the last to know. Your state of mind is certifiable, or should be.'

I shut up. It had dawned on me that Polly was probably defending Billy's interests, and that over the past few days she had shown a remarkable and courteous forbearance.

'The nicest of them all is Alexei,' Polly went on. 'Olivia thinks so too. But this is the ridiculous part: she's worried because she hasn't completely lost her head over him, like you have over Hugo, and she wants to. That's what's so absurd. She can still admire him objectively, but she doesn't want to do that, she *wants* to lose her head. And given that, it sounds like in another way maybe she's beginning to.'

That was when we heard the shouting. It was incredible! Their voices came right across the hall, through two closed doors. They were in Olivia's room and she was screaming at him and he at her, like two children suddenly gone berserk in an angry battle of wills, and finally having a showdown.

'I don't care! I just don't care!' she cried out hysterically. 'I know what I'm doing and you don't. You're going to ruin your life, for God's sake!'

I will never forget those words. Desperately wounded, I looked over at Polly who was clearly very taken aback as well. 'Olivia is under a lot of pressure,' she said feebly.

'You're a fine one to talk,' Hugo was shouting. 'You're such a coward, Olivia! Face the facts and grow up, will you? You've brought all this on yourself. All of it's your doing. Every bit of it. And don't you ever forget it!'

They must have come to their senses after that, or else realized where they were, because the shouting, if not the haranguing, suddenly ceased. But I was scared stiff. Olivia had a lot of influence, even if Hugo pretended otherwise — or didn't know how much, which was more dangerous. What if he listened to her?

Things having quietened down, Polly retreated into a catnap, or pretended to, so I tiptoed over to the door, opened it slowly and hung my head out into the corridor. I could hear their voices, if not the words, and it was just possible to catch the tone. Evidently an intense discussion was under way, so they must still be thrashing it out, but in a lower key — or, conceivably, as the voices sounded more reasonable, some sort of bargaining was going on. But if that were so, given what I'd overheard, it almost certainly would involve Alexei and myself. They might even be making decisions that directly affected us, making them over our heads and without either consultation or any acknowledgement. A horrifying thought. I felt powerless, and so desperately thwarted.

Closing the door, I sat down on the floor,

then after a bit peeked out again. At first I thought I heard giggling, but that couldn't be right; they couldn't possibly have changed moods so quickly, I decided. Yet how wrong I was! A second later, a burst of pellucid laughter rippled across the corridor, and then another one. 'Huggie, you look so silly! Now put it down! *Huggie!*' More laughter. They sounded like a pair of riotous and unruly children, who, noisily pushing aside obstructing furniture, make room for some new, raucous game. And Alexei and I were the furniture! It was chilling, I can tell you.

I shut the door and sat down again — just sat there — till eventually I heard Olivia's door open. Then after a second I peeped out: Hugo was entering his room.

'Darling,' I called out in a whisper, and on pure impulse rushed forward. 'Is everything all right?'

He looked really astonished — as if he'd no idea what I was talking about.

'You were shouting.'

'Good Lord, could you hear us?' He seemed to think back. 'We were behaving like children, I'm afraid. There was a silly row.'

'But it's all right now? Things are OK, I mean?'

'Oh, fine,' he said, a little vaguely.

'You've made it up then?'

'Yes, we made it up.' He smiled in a way that did not encourage confidence. 'Terminally.'

'Olivia doesn't like me,' I blurted in a whisper, rapidly mounting a defensive action.

Hugo looked at me straight. 'How wrong you are,' he said with great firmness. 'She likes you very much, very much indeed.'

It was almost convincing. 'But she doesn't like me for you' hovered unsaid, because suddenly I took a very different tack, surprising even myself. 'Shall I come in?' I offered lightly; it sounded almost nonchalant.

Hugo, who knew Sweet Briar's rules well by now, responded with equal aplomb. 'What a lovely suggestion,' he said, not looking in the least surprised; and, smiling warmly, gave me a kiss. 'But sadly I've a meeting in exactly two minutes,' he added, nodding towards the lobby. 'Politics, not archaeology, in case you're wondering. Nothing serious, though; I won't get shot.' And tilting my chin up, he kissed me once again lightly on the lips. He seemed happy. 'But thank you for that, dear Galatea.'

It was the first time he'd called me that, and I was so pleased that for a moment it outshone everything else.

But why on earth, you may be wondering, had I made what for me was such an extraordinary offer, at that precise moment, and so easily? Why, for instance, hadn't I made it earlier? Perhaps one answer is because at that precise moment I became a woman. My swaddling clothes miraculously unwound and fell away like mummy wrappings, as desire rushed over me in a powerful and unexpected wave. I was as limp as a rag doll. Indeed, I'd almost melted at his feet, dissolved into a concupiscent dew. Lunatic, I know, but it can happen like that — in a flash; like losing your religion or loving or hating someone. A feeling wells up and a taboo collapses, making forbidden territory perfectly right and normal; and as a result conventions can go to the devil. But thinking about it now, a more interesting question is: why hadn't I felt like that before? I don't know, but what I do know is I wanted desperately to bind Hugo securely to me, and I needed every bit of ammunition I could muster just then to do it. The mind is a superb communicator to the body.

Seconds later, however, as Hugo disappeared down the corridor, my worries bounced back multiplied, because when looked at straight Hugo had very flatly turned me down. No two ways about it. He ought to have cancelled that meeting on the spot, given such a momentous and significant event! That would have been the gentlemanly thing to do, and I swelled with righteous indignation — and not a little mortification.

Equally disconcerting, however, was the feeling that something ominous had resulted from the twins' extraordinary confrontation. Alexei's and my fates really could have been decided, a treaty drawn up and for all I knew signed in blood, those two were so disastrously stuck in childhood — Peter Pan and Wendy, inhabiting some fantastic never-never land, unable to free themselves. My happy, hopeful world could any second now explode like a rotten egg.

But why shouldn't Alexei and I unite? We could form a common front and resist becoming pawns in a trade-off designed to satisfy naively misconceived priorities. Alexei was a man of wisdom and considerable resource. He would be able to retrieve the situation, build a viable strategy and put everything right.

Minutes later, knocking hesitantly at his door, I still had no plan — only a need for action — and greeted by Alexei's benignly curious gaze I could only ask feebly if he cared to join me for a coffee. If he was surprised by that he didn't show it.

'Will you be coming to Venice, Alexei?' I began politely as we sat down. It was the parlour where I'd seen Hugo tête-à-tête only the day before. Yet what a long time ago it seemed.

Alexei looked at me closely. 'Such charming company would be irresistible,' he said, 'but I have as yet received no invitation.' Would Hugo be joining *me* in Venice? he asked.

'I believe Hugo has work to do,' I said vaguely; but it pulled me up. As so often recently, I'd let each day take care of itself, believing things would work out in the end, if only because in the movies happy endings were inevitable.

'I too have my work,' Alexei matter-of-factly announced.

'Oh, what is that, Alexei?' We were getting off the point.

'Diplomacy.' He smiled at me a little tiredly. Not the usual sort of diplomacy, he said, not the sort practised between feuding nations, but diplomacy between large corporations, which in their way were also modern nations.

So, Alexei had a public-relations company.

'But it is private relations that are in difficulty just now,' he volunteered with a surprising openness.

'Alexei, what's going on? Everything's changing, and I don't know what to do.' I was

214

a child appealing for guidance to an older relation.

Staring thoughtfully, Alexei sipped his tiny Turkish coffee. 'Perhaps Egypt was a mistake,' he said reflectively. 'Perhaps it has pulled us back into the past instead of pushing us forward, towards the future.'

This was too vague. I needed something practical that I could act on, or at the least some positive encouragement. 'Alexei, I'm scared,' was what came out.

He looked at me so kindly then, but a little sadly too. 'You are very young, my dear, and unfortunately have been swept up in a current that, conceivably, cannot just now be channelled. You must brace up, dear Katherine, consider your roots and who you are, and then, if possible, find an environment where you can develop fully and into your best self. Don't become a foreigner in life, avoid that if you can.'

In other words, go back to Kansas. 'But Hugo and Olivia — '

'Hugo and Olivia, like myself, grew up on foreign soil. It has given them a different reality: the reality of outsiders, of strangers, exiles even. And it is an isolating position.' He was holding his cup between two graceful fingers, as delicately as a tiny flower. 'Family ties can sometimes be the strongest ties of all, you know, and Hugo and Olivia, twins brought up away from home and thrown together from infancy, are, even as families go, unusually interdependent. They are also very young. They are trying hard to break apart and set up separate lives, but to do so it is necessary that they fight each other. It will be a hard fight, even though their goal is precisely the same; their lives are knitted so very intricately together.' He paused. 'And you and I,' he added very gently, 'may be casualties of the first campaign.'

I had no time either to protest against or to digest this dire surmise, because Alexei's gaze had gone immediately over my shoulder, and turning around I saw Olivia entering the parlour. Alexei and I stood up, he looking pleased and I guilty at being caught red-handed in an attempted conspiracy. But Olivia looked at me so warmly and in such a friendly way that my embarrassment was instantly dispelled. She smiled even more warmly and affectionately at Alexei, although I noticed she didn't quite look him in the eye. But then who does when you are bent on sending someone who loves you to his execution?

★ ★ ★

The guillotine fell either that afternoon before we left for Cairo, or else shortly after we arrived at Shepheard's Hotel, because even though it was very late Alexei and Olivia headed solemnly for the bar. Evidently they had things to talk about.

By morning at any rate it was over, even though there wasn't as yet the slightest sign: citadels of fine manners prevailed, and if Alexei was suffering, as he must have been, it certainly never showed; he had vaulted neatly back over his solid castle wall. A telegram had been awaiting him was what he said. Urgent business, he must return to Paris at once. 'It has been a memorable trip,' he told us, smiling urbanely, 'and Hugo a memorable host, so generous and such an informative guide.'

We were at breakfast and all the right noises were being made, Alexei's departure unfolding as smoothly as an elegantly choreographed dance — a dance of death, you could say, and one in which a useless and unnecessary sacrifice was being made. Nor could I help but feel that Hugo was largely to blame. Olivia may have had her doubts, but Hugo, I felt pretty sure, had goaded her into action. And if that were true, a deeply alarming question hovered, intensified by Alexei's baneful prediction. If Olivia had done her brother's bidding, as apparently she had, was Hugo obliged then to do hers? Was it a trade-off? The idea was absurd, grotesque, insane — and horribly possible.

When Alexei's taxi arrived, he and Olivia kissed on both cheeks like casual friends and looked each other mournfully in the eye. Or he did; I couldn't see her face. Then she just stood there, watching the taxi move away. She didn't wave; nor did Alexei, I think, look back. They would doubtless have found that overly sentimental and undignified.

Watching them, despite my own growing apprehensions involving Olivia's muddled intentions, I felt really sorry for her. Alexei was right. Olivia was too young and inexperienced to know what she was doing, while his own hands were tied: as a gentleman, he must do her bidding.

It was all so *futile*.

When Olivia came inside, I stopped her in the lobby and said how sorry I was Alexei had gone, how much I liked him and that I would miss him — all noises within the prescribed boundaries of good manners.

Olivia, genuinely touched, I think, answered with sudden feeling, 'Yes, he's wonderful, isn't he? I believe he's the finest person I've ever known.'

Then for God's sake don't let him go! I

longed to say. But I too was obliged to keep up the dance. 'Perhaps he can join us in Venice,' I ventured with a new and surprising smoothness.

'Yes, that would be so nice, wouldn't it?' she warmly agreed, completing with dignity a final graceful bow, before the inevitable curtain fell.

15

After that, things went forward ostensibly as if nothing had happened. A plan was under way, as Arthur had predicted, to hire horses and ride across the desert from the great pyramids at Giza to the older step-pyramid at Saqqara, visiting en route some ruins that tourists rarely saw. Occupied with these arrangements, Hugo became very elated and said with enthusiasm how much I was going to like the desert: there was nothing else like it on earth. Unfortunately, it hadn't occurred to him I couldn't ride.

'I'd like to learn sometime,' I said, showing myself willing and offering in compensation to meet them at Saqqara by taxi, with a picnic lunch from the hotel. This was roundly welcomed. 'You're an angel!' Hugo put his arm around me, pleased by my making the best of a disability. He said there was a rest house at Saqqara where we could meet, and in the meantime I could visit Cairo's archaeological museum, which was magnificent.

Arthur, who clearly thought it rude to leave a young woman on her own, generously offered to go with me. It was a particularly gallant gesture, as I knew he would have enjoyed that desert ride and had looked forward to it. I still ask myself today whether things might have come out differently had he gone.

We saw them off at Giza, Lilliputian equestrians beneath the mountainous pyramids and inscrutable fixed gaze of the Sphinx. They were wearing Arab headscarves as protection against the sun, and Arthur had been right about the horses. Small and beautiful, with great dewy eyes, they sprang about like kittens. The dragoman's was the only plug.

Everybody waved and grinned, buoyed up on a current of imminent adventure. Polly, cantering slowly around in a little circle, very collected, was obviously pleased with her horse, and even Olivia appeared, with remarkable resilience, to have recovered her good spirits. She said goodbye to me with the sweetest smile, and I lit up with pleasure like a Christmas tree. Despite everything, I still yearned for her good graces, and I was delighted to see her happy again. I wanted us all to be happy.

'Don't forget the palette of Narmer,' Hugo called over his shoulder as they rode off. He'd said it was one of the finest things in the museum and absolutely must be seen.

Waving, I threw him a happy kiss. Miraculously, everything seemed solidly back in place, everyone in high good spirits, friendly and full of enthusiasm, and my own earlier fears ludicrously out of place. Very likely Olivia had acted on her own. Her doubts about the relationship had been growing, even Alexei had been aware of it, and Hugo's influence, if existent, was probably minimal. I had foolishly over-reacted.

Before they left, I had photographed Hugo on horse-back in front of the Sphinx. The picture never came out, but thinking about it now, recalling Hugo standing there so poised and confident between the Sphinx's enormous paws, an image of cat and mouse comes to mind, symbolic of the capricious paws of fate, about to toy so wilfully and so perversely with us all.

* * *

Arthur made good company in that dusty old museum. A film of fine sand covered everything, and inside the glass display cases, faded typewritten labels curled like dead worms; but at least they were in English. While all around, chock-a-block and seemingly disorganized, lay the most extraordinary treasure: vast granite and basalt statues; tomb furniture, gilded and finely carved, that looked brand new; intricate beaded collars, golden masks and elaborately painted coffins; even some handkerchief linen 2,000 years old. Arthur and I pretended we were archaeologists stumbling like Lord Carnarvon upon a previously undiscovered tomb, marvelling at the richness of our find and anticipating our celebrity. It was an easy game, as we were the museum's only visitors.

Dutifully I examined the palette of Narmer, a polished flat slate like a giant arrowhead, two entwined heads of dinosaur-like creatures making a shallow pot for unguents or something. It was, Hugo had said, the earliest sign of Egypt's unification. Well, I was interested in unification, but far more exciting to me then was looking the great Rameses II in the face. His mummy lay in one of the display cases, the face uncovered — a surprisingly delicate face for one of history's most celebrated and imperious rulers. Rameses had lived to a great age and had expected to go on like that, living the life of Riley, housed in his palatially furnished tomb, his spirit flitting in and out at will and hobnobbing with god-kings of the past, many of them his relations, of course. Instead, he was preserved like a rare butterfly, under glass. A kind of immortality, I suppose, but not remotely what he had had in mind.

'At least he never knew he got it wrong,' I said, gazing at the long thin figure wrapped in stained brown linen.

'Lucky chap,' said Arthur. 'He was embalmed in life as well, by his illusions. His self-confidence must have been immense.'

'You think the truth is unimportant, then?'

'I don't think people should be wantonly deceived, but in the end we mostly live by our illusions, I suspect; like old Rameses here.'

'Oh dear, I hope not.' Instinctively I sided with Hugo, for whom, as far as I could see, truth largely meant self-knowledge, coming to terms with oneself and therefore with one's life, or something like that.

★ ★ ★

Saqqara was only twenty minutes by taxi, and shortly after collecting our picnic we could see the great step-pyramid rising in the distance. The heat was so intense, however, that the air shimmered like water rippling in a pond, throwing our vision out of focus, so that even from a distance the pyramid looked as though it had begun to melt. As we got closer, oddly enough, the blurring actually increased, even though a strong breeze had

224

begun to whip the air. I removed my sunglasses and peered hard, wondering if my eyes were being affected by the light, when suddenly Arthur called out hoarsely, 'Good God! Roll up the windows!'

I looked round in surprise.

'Hurry up — it's sand!'

Instantly, visibility was non-existent. A parchment screen had descended, masking the quickly rolled-up window my face was now so anxiously pressed against. 'They could get lost out there — and die of thirst!' I cried.

But Arthur, sitting back comfortably now, said sand-storms were frequent in the desert. People were used to them and the dragomen knew how to cope; the horses did too. It happened all the time and generally it happened very quickly. He'd seen them himself in the Yemen.

Our driver's apparent lack of concern confirmed this view. He merely slowed down to a crawl, turned on the windscreen wipers and hunched more closely, if that were possible, over the steering wheel; so that we continued to creep along but at a snail-like pace, until, God knows how, the car eventually inched up to the rest house, a sort of adobe hut, the outline of a veranda running the length of it, supported by poles.

Grabbing the picnic basket and shielding our faces, we rushed inside, where Arthur ordered two well-deserved cold beers. About ten minutes later, the pyramid surprisingly came back into focus and we were able to take our chairs out onto the porch. Except for little piles of shifted sand it was as if nothing had happened; everything was so peaceful, and so beautifully still.

Leaning back, his chair tilted against the wall, Arthur read aloud from his guidebook about the pyramid's history. A little later, caught looking at his watch, he claimed it wasn't because he was worried, only that he was getting hungry — 'peckish', as he called it.

Hugo had said the trip would take about three hours, yet nearly four had passed. Hardly surprising, said Arthur; they would have taken shelter during the storm, stopping and putting headscarves over their faces; or they might have sheltered in one of the ruins Hugo had mentioned.

I was busy brushing sand off the picnic basket and making sure the food inside was OK, when, squinting against the glare, Arthur made out a wavering black speck on the horizon. 'Here they come!' he cried, standing up, his chair tumbling back into place.

We stood on the veranda like a pair of

statues, watching intently, our eyes narrowed, our hands protecting our vision, as, slowly, over minutes, the image metamorphosed from a black speck into a spinning top, then transformed itself into a swirling spectre, a sheikh's speeding limousine and, finally, a horse flying towards us across the desert at full tilt. But there was only one.

'Is it somebody else? Where are the others?' Silly rhetorical questions, but nonetheless soothingly cathartic.

Arthur was the first to see that it was Hugo. 'The others will be coming along more slowly, with the guide,' he said, still mesmerized by the galloping animal.

When, at last, the horse halted abruptly in front of the hitching post, Hugo had already dismounted. I rushed forward, but he hardly saw me. 'There's been an accident,' he said, the tightness in his voice betraying urgency. And pulling his headscarf off he went inside, where an animated exchange took place in Arabic. The bartender got on the telephone, then Hugo did. He wanted a doctor, an ambulance and, alarmingly, a search party. While he was waiting on the phone, Hugo sketched out the story for us. Polly had had an accident — or so he believed; nothing was certain. He didn't know what had happened exactly, but when the storm was over they discovered that she had disappeared. Hugo said her horse had probably bolted in the storm and she hadn't been able to stop him.

'But she's such a good horsewoman,' I answered feebly, thoroughly bewildered.

The owners often raced their horses in the desert, Hugo said, so sometimes, when urged forward, the animals thought it was a race, making it almost impossible to stop them.

'In a sandstorm?' I murmured, surprised. It seemed so improbable.

Hugo said Olivia and the guide had stayed on at the ruins where it had happened, just in case; but that normally a horse would head for home. He had alerted the stables back at Giza.

As there was nothing to do but wait, we retreated to the veranda and sat down. But something really frightening entered my head. 'Those two Arabs,' I asked Hugo hesitantly, 'were they out there too?'

He looked at me in surprise. 'They were to start with, but we gave them the slip.' He said it almost proudly. 'Don't bother about them, though. It isn't relevant.'

Wasn't it? How could he be so sure?

Having time to kill, I opened the picnic basket and urged them to eat something, taking some cheese myself. But Hugo wouldn't, though Arthur accepted a sandwich and a hard-boiled egg.

'It must have been tricky to get here without the guide,' I said, trying to fill the silence; but Hugo said that once the storm was over, you could see the pyramid from a long way off.

More silence.

'I bet Polly is on that horse and headed for Giza,' I insisted brightly.

'Yesss,' said Arthur, slowly.

He had only eaten half his sandwich when a lot of shouting issued from behind the rest house and, in a cloud of dust and sand, half a dozen rough-looking men appeared, unshaven, wearing Arab dress and mounted on scraggly, hee-hawing, tassel-bedizened camels. It was the search party. At the same time, the ambulance siren could be heard, eerily wailing away like a banshee. We all jumped hurriedly up.

Hugo quickly remounted, without another word. The camels were jawing and shoving, the men herding the recalcitrant animals into a shambling formation and beginning to whip them forward, till, suddenly, with a raucous whoop, their whips waving in the air, the whole party galloped off hell for leather into the desert. It was a dramatic sight. The camels' necks were stretched out in front of them like rudders, the men's robes billowing sail-like in their wake, and those myriad tassels bobbing up and down like multicoloured corks; until, becoming smaller and smaller, the whole party disappeared, like so many grains of sand thrown back into the oceanic desert. This time the archaic element wasn't in the least romantic; rather it increased alarm.

The ambulance team had gone inside for beers.

16

They found Polly late that afternoon, her horse having returned riderless to Giza hours earlier. Polly was unconscious. In falling, she had hit her head on a rock, rare enough in a desert full of sand and probably part of a ruin they'd visited. Her leg was broken, but mercifully she hadn't been covered up during the storm. She was carried out by stretcher, still unconscious, and taken to a hospital in Cairo.

Olivia, who had joined the search party, returned completely exhausted. She went straight to the hotel and fell asleep. They'd had some water with them but nothing to eat. Hugo too, after helping to sort things out at the hospital, went back to the hotel. He was deeply distressed. It was his expedition and he felt responsible. My heart ached for him. Accidents happened, and there was nothing anyone could do. They were outside human control, a matter of chance or, more mysteriously, fate.

Arthur and I stayed on at the hospital. I'd seen Polly briefly after they set her leg, when she was still unconscious. It was a bad break, in the femur, they said. She was dehydrated and probably had suffered mild sunstroke. Her skin was very red and flaky, her face badly swollen, having been exposed for hours to the sun, and there was a drip in her arm. But she looked so young, like a little child, really. There had always been a special innocence about Polly behind that dry scepticism, and now it seemed to possess her entirely.

At about eight o'clock that evening I was allowed in, but the doctor said not to stay long; she was very weak and her system had suffered a considerable shock.

Poor Polly! She looked so miserable, just staring into space, her face swollen up like that.

I took her hand. 'Are you in pain, Polly dear?'

'Kate . . . ' It came from a great distance. She didn't turn towards me, but continued staring at the ceiling. 'Go away. Go away now.'

'I'm not going to leave you, dear. You don't *want* me to leave you, do you? The doctor says you're going to be just fine.'

'Go away from Hugo.'

Despite the circumstances, I had to fight my anger. 'Hugo couldn't help what happened. It wasn't his fault, it was that awful storm,' I said, patting her hand.

Still looking at the ceiling, suddenly Polly smiled. 'She kissed me!'

'Did she?'

'Yes, *kissed* me. And I kissed her.'

'You did?'

The look of dismay returned. 'I thought she liked me, Kate.'

'Who, Polly dear? Olivia? Of course she likes you. It's me she doesn't like so much.'

'They aren't brother and sister, you know. They aren't even twins.'

'You think so?' The doctor hadn't warned me she might be confused, but of course concussion did that.

She was trying to sit up. 'I saw ... I couldn't see ... the sand, and ... oh, Kate — sandman! Sandman!' she cried out shrilly. 'I was so scared, I ran off. I don't remember ... '

'There, there.' I had pulled my chair forward and, bending round the drip bottles, smoothed her hair, trying to comfort her, as one does a child waking up from a bad dream. 'It's all right,' I crooned. 'Of course you couldn't see. Nobody could. It was the storm, that's all.' The hallucination was unnerving, though.

Closing her eyes a moment, Polly seemed to relax, almost to smile.

'I had a rough ride, didn't I?' A glimmer of the old ironic Polly.

'You sure did, a very rough ride.'

Again the subject changed. 'She wants to get away. She told me so. She *is* beautiful, isn't she?' It was tacked on like a coda, full of wonder and pleasure.

'Yes, indeed,' I said. 'Now you must get some rest, dear. I mustn't tire you.' A nurse had appeared in the doorway and I stood up, feeling relieved. 'The others want to see you too, you know.'

'Not them,' she whispered, turning her head for the first time in my direction, searching my eyes.

'Yes, they do!'

'Not those two.'

'Well . . . but Arthur's here; he just wants to say hello, see you're all right. He'll only stay a minute.'

'We're lousy detectives, Kate.'

'We weren't very smart, I guess.'

'Kate — '

I stopped at the door, half-turned. Polly was looking at the ceiling again. 'Hugo doesn't love you, Kate.'

Stop it! Stop it right now! I wanted to say, but I said instead, 'Now try and get some rest; that's the main thing. Tomorrow everything will be fine.'

'They're not even kin,' she murmured. 'That's the plot.'

* ★ ★

I warned Arthur that she was very confused, and, waiting for him outside the room, tried hard to address the most pressing practicalities. Miss Grist must be notified at once, and of course I must stay with Polly until she could travel, so Venice was out. But how long would Polly be in hospital, and what if we missed the boat at Southampton; how would we get home? I doubted Olivia would go to Venice now either.

When we returned to the hotel, Hugo and Olivia were sitting in a corner of the lobby, clearly very upset. They looked so isolated and so vulnerable, like two lost children, their gilded, grown-up exteriors having been laid aside like theatrical finery. Peter Pan and Wendy, I thought again, but this time I felt almost sorry for them; they looked so helpless. It put Hugo in a different light, of course, but one that, in another way, moved me equally, because I immediately felt so protective towards him.

We stopped and brought them briefly up to date. Polly was badly confused, I said, but definitely on the mend. She needed rest,

235

though, and it was probably a good idea not to visit until she was stronger.

What had she said about the accident, Hugo wanted to know. Could Polly recall what had happened? His voice was tense and he looked exhausted.

She hadn't said much, I answered, and even that hadn't made a lot of sense. It was the concussion, but tomorrow she would probably be OK.

We went upstairs together in a wilted clump, everyone mumbling their goodnights. I was so tired I fell asleep fully dressed on top of the bed, a thing I'd never done before. I would have slept like that all night, I expect, if a strange noise hadn't suddenly woken me up. Somewhere a bell was tolling. At first I thought I must have dreamt it, everything was so quiet. But then a muezzin began to chant, his voice, whining and highpitched, carrying across the rooftops from his needle-pointed minaret and calling the faithful to prayers. Allah is great. Allah is good.

I envisaged the entire Egyptian nation prostrate beside their beds and deep in prayer, united by a single action, everyone sharing the same thought: Allah is great; Allah is good. It didn't matter in the least if it were true; it was so profoundly comforting. Life, it suddenly appeared, was divided into two distinct and discrete modes of being: separate and together, group and individual — polar opposites that gave existence its abiding tensions and its satisfactions. This was a perfected moment of togetherness.

Marvellously comforted, I undressed and quickly got into bed. But lying there, staring into the dark, my tranquillity was short-lived: Polly's accident began to loom in full traumatic glare, the way things do at night with nothing to balance or give any perspective. We were marooned in a primitive country with no grownups to advise or help us. Miss Grist had been out, but I had left a message. Ought I to call Billy? If Polly felt up to it, maybe she could call him, or else Miss Grist could call Polly's parents. Much the best.

Piecemeal, I went over what Polly had said. It made no more sense than a bad dream, but nonetheless I felt ashamed at having, if unavoidably, eavesdropped. Was Polly, in fact, too fond of Olivia? It had sounded like a girlish infatuation, an adolescent schoolroom crush. Olivia couldn't possibly have kissed Polly: they were on horseback in the middle of a sandstorm. But was Polly suppressing something she was largely unaware of, which had inadvertently bubbled up? If so, it helped explain her growing dislike of Hugo, who had such a strong hold on his sister; and Polly's wishing, deciding even, that they weren't kin. But to say Hugo didn't love me was so cruel! Almost vindictive. Still, people said all sorts of things when they were off their heads. It didn't bear thinking about; and, pulling the sheet around me in the dark, I let the matter drop. Tomorrow things would be cleared up. Very likely Polly wouldn't remember what she'd said, but if she did then we could talk about it sensibly. And if she didn't, well, that was fine with me.

★ ★ ★

I went very early to the hospital the next morning, and taking the elevator to Polly's floor, announced myself at reception. The nurse said to wait, so I sat down. After about ten minutes Polly's doctor appeared and I stood up, but he asked me to sit down again; then he sat down beside me. His English wasn't very good and the accent hard to understand. He had a little moustache, like a misplaced eyebrow, that he kept on touching. He said he deeply regretted what he was about to tell me but that sadly, most unfortunately, there was no way round it: Polly had died, quite suddenly, during the night. It was totally unexpected. He said it occasionally happened after a serious fracture; no-one knew why, but it was most unusual when the patient was so young.

Stunned and incredulous, I just sat there, mesmerized by his pink, well-washed finger touching so reassuringly that little brown moustache. Then, beyond speech, I jumped up and, rushing down the corridor to Polly's room, pushed open the door. Her bed was empty.

'It's a hot climate,' the doctor said gently a few minutes later, steering me outside.

The nurse brought me a coffee. There would be papers to sign. Was I the nearest relation?

I don't remember answering. Only that I stood up and, paying no attention to anything, wandered off down the corridor. There was nothing real or sensible in my head, only foreboding, the disquieting intimation of a nightmare hovering at the edges of consciousness. And I told myself I had to stay awake.

The corridor was empty until, eventually rounding a corner, I spied a hospital attendant coming towards me, pushing a trolley. To my utter horror a body lay on it, covered by a sheet. I froze — just stood there, my back against the wall, waiting. As the trolley neared I saw something protruding at the end. It was a pair of bare feet — but a man's bare feet, the soles strangely pale against the darker skin of his body. Despite my horror, I felt such relief!

Following behind the trolley, a woman shrouded in a robe, her face covered up, was moaning gently. She had a little boy by the hand, five or six years old, in a tattered blue shirt, none too clean. As the trolley came alongside, the little boy's eyes suddenly skewered mine. His expression was desperate, filled with such pitiful confusion and an unfathomable despair. It was terrifying.

Whispering something, the boy's mother had let go of his hand. He looked so startled, his black eyes instantly vacant, like the recoil of a camera lens. They could have been two holes.

I had to get away. Something was welling up inside, nightmarish and dreadful and threatening to overwhelm. I moved on, walking very quickly down the corridor. But a second later the little boy was beside me, tugging at my skirt, not looking at me, not looking anywhere. 'Baksheesh,' he whispered plaintively, '*baksheesh*,' in a voice you would have thought was asking for the moon.

Frantically I reached for my bag, but it wasn't there. I'd no idea where it was. I must have left it in reception or somewhere. I didn't have it with me, anyhow. 'Oh dear, I have no money,' I cried.

'Baksheesh!' He repeated it in a high pathetic voice, laced with urgency.

'But I have no money!' I cried again in dismay. 'No money. Look.' I opened my empty hands, holding them out.

He stared uncomprehending, disbelieving perhaps; such despair — such world-weariness in his little aged face.

'I'm sorry, I'm so sorry! Oh, I'm so so sorry!' I wailed, stooping down to embrace him. It was all I could do. Suddenly everything was breaking into pieces, the fragments crashing into my consciousness like meteors. But as I stooped the child backed away in terror, flattening himself against the wall. 'Baksheesh,' he kept on gibbering in a tearful voice. And flinging an arm across that harrowed little face, knowing so much more about the world than I did, he ran off.

'Wait!' I cried out. 'I have money. I can get it.' And then, I can't explain it, 'Polly! Polly!' I was calling out.

The little boy kept on running. He never once turned round.

Shortly afterwards, the nurse appeared. She looked so silly, I thought, in her white dress and bandanna, with my handbag on her arm — as if she was going out shopping. 'Won't you come and rest?' she urged.

I was sitting on the corridor floor, weeping unrestrainedly. 'Polly, Polly, Polly,' I kept on repeating mindlessly. I don't believe I made a scene, but they gave me a sedative anyhow, just in case.

After that, things happened in a curious limbo. It may have been the sedative, or more likely it was shock, but reality seemed to be suspended. There was this empty hole and I went round and round the edges, bewildered, staring into the void. How, I kept on wondering, could Polly so mysteriously disappear? She could have been kidnapped, or poisoned — given the wrong medicine — and they had hidden her away till she was better. Who knew what went on in Cairo's hospitals? But above all, I could not take it in that she had *ceased to be*, had literally disappeared from life. Rather it was like the end of term, a familiar interval of separation, after which things were always much the same again. That must be it! Something like that.

★ ★ ★

Reality began its drear imprint when I telephoned Miss Grist from the hospital. Miss Grist listened to my rambling, tearful

242

account in complete silence. It was an accident, I sobbed, the cause of death unknown, even the doctor didn't know what had really happened. 'Oh, Miss Grist, I can't believe it — it's so terrible! I don't know what to do!'

Miss Grist, a practical-minded woman, understood well the importance of activity as a defence against brooding or excessive grief. 'There's a great deal to do,' she promptly replied. 'And it will be of tremendous help to everyone.' Then she explained what arrangements must be made, at the hospital and elsewhere. There would be papers to sign, a death certificate, the consulate must be informed. Finally, Polly's body must be flown to England and taken to Southampton.

Polly's cousin Arthur was arranging that, I said. His mother would call Polly's parents.

'No, I'll do that,' Miss Grist answered with great firmness, clearly believing it was an obligation she herself must shoulder. Then she asked solicitously after Olivia and me. She said we bore a heavy load on our young shoulders. 'But on no account must you blame yourselves,' she declared with energy. People unaccountably did and there was no good in it. 'Horses are treacherous beasts,' she added, inferring perhaps that blame might be laid there, must it be laid at all.

243

'Polly was a wonderful rider,' I offered in tearful tribute. 'She couldn't see, and the horse must have stumbled.'

Poor Miss Grist. What could be more dreadful than informing parents that their child was dead? Technically, Polly was in Miss Grist's care, and even though she herself wasn't there, her responsibility remained pre-eminent.

I would go to England with Polly and wait for them, I said forlornly, staying with Polly's cousins. I imagined Olivia would too.

What about money? Did we have enough?

This hadn't occurred to me. I said I would have to see. Suddenly there was, as Miss Grist rightly said, a very great deal to do, and for that at least I felt immensely grateful.

★ ★ ★

Hugo had gone straight to the hospital with Arthur, to make arrangements. Tired and tense, he held me, at first silently, in his arms. 'I'm so sorry!' he murmured with passion. 'I've been an incompetent fool, in every possible way.'

'No, no, you mustn't think that. It was an accident,' I insisted, reining in my own feelings before his obvious distress. Bravely, he had taken more on board than I as yet

244

was prepared to do.

We were in the visitors' room, waiting for the release papers, and sitting down I took his hand. 'It's dreadful, dreadful, but you mustn't blame yourself. There was absolutely nothing you could do.'

Instantly Hugo demurred. 'Accidents don't just happen. They carry and imply blame; so does mishandling,' he declared morosely. 'It's all interconnected.'

Again I protested strongly. 'It was fate and outside anyone's control.'

Rejecting fate outright, Hugo shook his head. 'There's something I must tell you,' he went on, evidently agitated, but holding it in check. 'Those two men, the ones you asked about, were bodyguards. They were there to look after us. I found out at the tombs, when there was that trouble with Olivia and they stopped me. They told me then. Whether they were Nasser's or Naguib's men, I don't know. I was so angry, because I'd rather have been watched than nannied like that. It was so stupid of me! So incredibly stupid and childish!' His lips tightened in self-disgust. 'If I hadn't given them the slip, they would have found Polly, because one of them almost certainly would have trailed her — and then none of this would have happened!'

'You couldn't know!' I said, and putting

this extraordinary news aside, holding his hand tight, I asked him to tell me what exactly had happened in the desert. Polly had been delirious and she hadn't made much sense.

Hugo said they had stopped briefly at a temple ruin. He'd wanted to show them something — I forget what, or if he even said — but Polly wasn't interested in seeing another ruin, 'the epitome of a ruin', she'd called it, 'a pile of rocks'. So, dismounting, they'd left their horses with her and the dragoman. But when the sandstorm came up, Polly began to worry. The dragoman told her it was OK, but either she didn't believe him or she couldn't understand him. So she gave him Olivia's horse and began skirting the ruins on hers, maybe even calling out. Visibility was hopeless, of course, though horses saw better than humans in a storm. But pressing the animal forward may have given the wrong signal, or else something scared it and it had bolted. When Polly didn't come back, the dragoman assumed she'd found them and they had taken shelter together. It was only after the storm that they discovered she had disappeared. 'Probably the horse stumbled or she lost her balance, not being able to see.' It was becoming a sort of litany.

'She hit her head,' I offered redundantly. 'But you never saw her — looking for you, I mean?'

'Of course not,' he answered indignantly.

'Darling, I must go back to England with her.'

'It's all arranged.' He said there was a flight the following morning at eleven o'clock.

The news whizzed down like an avalanche.

'Everything's taken care of. It's the very least I can do,' he insisted, abolishing my worry over fares.

'Olivia and I can stay at Brydonne Park,' I said, pulling myself together, trying to sound responsible. 'Arthur's mother is expecting us.'

Hugo didn't look up. 'Olivia isn't going back yet,' he answered, staring at the linoleum floor. I remember it was yellow, with a lot of black scratches on it.

'But she's coming with us on the boat!'

'You'd best ask her; I've no idea what she wants to do.'

Suddenly the only thing that mattered was *my own life* — saving it! At that moment it overreached everything else; and I was scared stiff, my newly constructed world teetering wildly, hovering dangerously on the edge of collapse.

'Oh Hugo, this awful void!' I cried. 'We mustn't allow it to swallow us up, destroy everything that's good. It's worked so well, hasn't it? Except for this dreadful accident. We've been so happy and I've loved every minute.'

He pulled himself upright, as if on strings. 'It's going to be OK,' he said calmly. 'But we need to regain equilibrium.' He said that once a degree of perspective was restored, he would be able to think things through and form a plan. Then he would write or telephone. Egypt was becoming increasingly unstable, and that too must be considered. 'But for God's sake, don't worry! You have enough on your plate right now.'

'I'll go anywhere,' I said. 'Anywhere — I only want to be with you and make you happy. Oh, I can if you will let me, Hugo!'

'It's what I want too, more than anything,' he said, and, still staring at the floor, he continued absently to stroke my hand, the way one does a favourite cat. I just sat there, passive, grief-stricken, and now horribly afraid, till finally the administrator arrived, bearing a sheaf of papers.

17

There followed the sad ordeal of packing Polly's few (mostly unpacked) things. The little black dress she'd worn in Rome hung in the closet; she must have meant to wear it in Cairo, for Olivia. The thought was heart-rending, and, folding the dress up carefully, I wondered if it was in Rome that we'd begun to quarrel, or was it Luxor — and what had it really been about? Either I couldn't remember or I never knew, but I kept on apologizing in my mind.

Closing that suitcase was like a burial, and though it was only six o'clock, I immediately swallowed two sleeping pills the doctor had prescribed and was able to spend the next twelve hours in blissful unconsciousness. It helped a lot.

In the morning, a thoughtful note from Hugo lay on my breakfast tray. He and Arthur had gone to the hospital; he would call for me later, in plenty of time. 'Please don't worry,' he had written. 'Everything is being taken care of.'

I was busy packing my own things, trying hard to focus on the task at hand, when, earlier than expected, there was a knock at the door. When I opened it, Olivia stood there instead of Hugo. She looked extraordinarily fresh and cool in a yellow shirtwaist dress, a little gold-winged scarab pinned to the collar. I kept staring at it, expecting it to crawl onto her shoulder or something.

'Scarabs symbolize eternal life,' she said, seeing my interest. 'But they're really only glorified dung beetles.'

We had met briefly in hospital the day before, but now Olivia had come to offer her condolences formally. It was a ritual we must both go through — painful, awkward, but unavoidable — and I dreaded it. But Polly must be spoken of and praised and kept alive, by whatever means and for as long as possible.

'It's been the saddest time,' Olivia began. She sat down on Polly's bed, her hands folded in her lap, and I sat opposite. A photo-image of our Luxor promenade swirled across my mind. Already another world. That black spot had spread as quickly and virulently as plague.

'Such a terrible accident,' I murmured vacantly. Eloquence at such times may be fine in plays, but in real life it's platitudes that safely float one through. 'You're not coming with us to London, Hugo said.'

Olivia said she couldn't face staying with strangers just then. Moreover, she was reluctant to leave Hugo on his own; he was very depressed. She would fly to London a little later, in time for the boat.

'Poor Polly; she was such a wonderful person. I can't believe it,' Olivia said, returning to her purpose. 'Such a terrible accident.' She'd repeated my own futile-sounding words. Had Polly said anything in hospital about what happened? Were there no clues?

'She was concussed,' I said shortly, 'even hallucinating a bit.'

'Oh, it's so difficult to take on board,' Olivia went on. 'It's all so tragic. Something has happened that can never be changed or undone. That's the awful thing about death, isn't it? In life things can almost always change: decisions can be reversed, mistakes rectified. Life is fluid, but death is unequivocally solid — a forever frozen moment.'

'Yes,' I answered vaguely. Talking about Polly was proving impossible. The words trivialized, at the same time bringing reality much too close. Polly's death was too recent and my own feelings too raw. But in addition, something else hovered that urgently needed sorting out, and in this respect at least,

251

Olivia's presence presented a rare opportunity. It was a chance I couldn't afford to miss.

'Mistakes can certainly be rectified, like you say,' I began, taking up her thread, the tension producing a shrill, metallic quality in my voice. 'Forgive me, Olivia, it's none of my business, but speaking of mistakes ... ' My eyes pleaded as I leaned towards her. 'Your letting Alexei go like that, when you said yourself he was the finest person that you'd ever known — and when you had waited for so long to be together. Was that necessary? Is it necessary? Because it's not too late. It isn't a real death; it can be rectified! Oh, I know Hugo disapproved,' I hurried on, 'urged you to give Alexei up, and you're very close — used to agreeing, and all — but I'm sorry you didn't stand up to him this time. I think you should have; you still can. And families nearly always come round in the end.'

I was afraid she'd jib, claim she didn't know what I was talking about, but instead she listened quietly. Polly's death may have brought her feelings to the surface, made her more communicative. She even smiled slightly; such a sad smile, directed towards those folded hands. I imagined them in white gloves.

'I can't stand up to Hugo, I never could!' she said with sudden intensity. 'Besides, this time I'm afraid he's right. He knew I wasn't in love with Alexei. He knew it before I did. Oh, I wanted to love him, and in ways I did. Does being *in* love really matter so much, I asked myself. Hugo thinks it does and that it's wrong to settle for less; but I felt Alexei and I could have a wonderful life together — probably the only normal one I'll ever find.'

Deeply touched by this unexpected and distressing confidence, I tried to respond in kind, show I understood by admitting my own position had been similar. Did she remember Polly's brother? They had met at Sweet Briar once. 'We were sort of engaged,' I said, and explained that I hadn't really been in love either. Oh, I had thought I was; I was very fond of Billy, admired him and so on; and like Alexei he too had offered a normal and happy life. 'So it's the same, I guess; but now that's over too.'

Instead of signalling her rapport, Olivia, turning the tables, stared at me in alarm. 'But it could be revived?'

'Falling in love changes everything,' I answered quietly. But suddenly I was on my guard.

'Yes, maybe it does,' she solemnly agreed, 'but it's no guarantee of happiness.' She was looking vaguely around, and I could see she was about to leave.

'Polly was very fond of you,' I said.

Olivia smiled again. 'She had such an affectionate nature, even a passionate one, I think — and so lonely behind that droll little mask. It was tremendously touching.'

Is that why you kissed her, I wanted to say, but something far more urgent pressed. 'You don't like me, though, do you?' I baldly declared.

Olivia, looking surprised, retreated into her fortress of acquired politeness, and, banging down the portcullis, continued to gaze at me suspiciously through the grille. 'Why, of course I do, and I admire you. You're much the cleverest of us, and probably the most solid too.'

'But you don't think I'm good enough for Hugo.' At last the cat was out of the bag!

'That's not it at all.' She stood up and, retrieving her handbag from the writing table — I thought she was leaving — hurriedly lit a cigarette. Then, after gazing for a moment out of the window, she turned towards me. 'But it's true, Kate, I don't think that you're *right* for Hugo, or that he's right for you. I believed there was a chance at first and I was really pleased. I hoped so much that it would work.'

'Surely that's for us to decide!' It was none of her damned business, but remembering her uncommon influence, I collected myself pretty quickly. 'Olivia, I can make him happy. I know I can, given half a chance. Won't you help me, please? Let me try?'

'Whatever you can give him, Kate, and I know it would be considerable, he could never give you in return what you want and need. He couldn't do it! And in the end it has to be reciprocal.'

'You are much mistaken,' I said tersely, barely masking my offended pride. 'He's given me a very great deal already; so it is reciprocal.'

Extinguishing her cigarette after only a few puffs, Olivia sat down again, fiddling with that scarab on her collar. Then, folding her hands, she leaned forward slightly. To my surprise a screen of unshed tears bathed her azure eyes. 'Hugo and I are not the cosmopolitans people take us for,' she began haltingly. 'Far from it. In fact, the truth is very different: the truth is we're a pair of shipwrecks facing slow starvation on a desert island, and as I've recently come to see, beyond rescue — every attempt having ended in failure and unhappiness all round.'

'They haven't *all* ended in failure!' I remonstrated. After all, Hugo and I were still together.

'It's hard to understand,' she went on,

ignoring this outburst, 'but we grew up in such peculiar circumstances.' She said they had been very isolated, living abroad and with no other children around, or none who were remotely like them. Their parents were busy people, so she and Hugo were always together and, being twins, shared things children of different ages wouldn't have: the same lessons, the same games, the same nonsense and confidences. They never talked much: there was no need, because they always knew what each other was thinking. And they always agreed.

'We felt — ' she paused, trying to find the right words. 'We felt we were a single being, that each of us was part of the same person — an indissoluble unit. And that seemed to us perfectly natural.' She said that by the time it was taken note of and strenuous efforts were being made to separate them — make them more independent and self-reliant — it already was too late, because apart they simply wilted.

'We've tried so hard — you can't imagine how hard — to get on with our respective lives. But separated we feel that half our self is missing, or dead. We might as well be Siamese twins, I often think; and it means others can't get close enough to make a difference — a real difference. That's the saddest part. We just squeeze them out. We can't help it. Our closeness is a sort of curse, it blocks out so much. And now we're becoming each other's albatross. We have no independent future, we don't belong anywhere and we can't go anywhere without being chained together. Exiles, that's what it amounts to. Alexei understood that, and he tried so hard to make a difference, to rescue me and give me a new life. I badly wanted him to, but it just didn't work.' Her hands fluttered up like birds, then came to rest again in her lap.

Touching, yes; it was certainly that. But I wasn't going to be diverted, got round again by the demands of sympathy — not for anyone. This time I stuck to my guns. 'It's a trade-off, isn't it?' I blurted. 'That's what you're really saying. You gave up Alexei and now Hugo is supposed to give me up. It's crazy, Olivia.'

Seeing her expression, I tried to modulate my tone and sound more reasonable. 'Close family ties may be indissoluble, but people still leave their families and begin to start their own. It may not be easy, but as you said yourself, outside death anything can change. Besides, Olivia, it's part of growing up; it *is* growing up. *People have to do it.*

'I know you have enormous influence over

him,' I went on. 'Won't you use it to give us a fair chance? That's all I ask. Don't make him give me up because of some childish, cabalistic pact. Can't you see how wrong that is? I know I can make him happy. I know I can; only let me have that chance. Please! Let me prove that I can do it.'

'We've all been trying so hard,' she said. 'Everyone has. And we've failed. It's been a bad time. We've made some huge mistakes, hoped so foolishly for impossible results, and it's caused nothing but grief.' Sighing, she reached for her bag.

'Just agree not to interfere, to leave it between Hugo and myself. Will you do that?' I asked.

'I must let you get on with your packing,' she said, standing up. 'I'll be at the airport.'

'Olivia, *please*!'

For a moment she was silent, then she relented. 'I'll say nothing,' she promised. At the doorway she half-turned. 'I'm dreadfully sorry about Polly, Kate. That's what I came to say.'

★ ★ ★

This was our longest and only frank conversation, until the extraordinary revelations yesterday at Château Carrielle. It isn't

258

verbatim, of course, but it's pretty close. You don't forget much when you're fighting for your life. Even when it's shadow boxing, the details get imprinted. Olivia's story, poignant and unexpected, had bordered on the tragic, and for a moment, given both our predicaments, even the dreadful calamity of Polly's death had been obscured. Olivia had described with such an anguished bitterness a barren life of unrelenting isolation, a doomed future in which her closest tie would also be her mortal enemy. And I'm sure she believed it. She was young and had so little experience and no knowledge of the effect time has on any relationship. I had no experience either, but loving Hugo I longed to rescue him, which meant, I see now, having him exclusively to myself. If I succeeded, I generously reasoned, their claustrophobic little circle would be broken and Olivia's own chance at normality could begin as well. Everyone would be happy. Absurdly, I had cast myself as a rescuing knight, innocently setting forth and determined to produce a happy Hollywood ending for us all. The tragedy and the essential unfairness of life, its innate hazards and sad insoluble ambiguities, had still to register.

18

'Isn't Olivia Hartfield with you?' Lady Brydonne's dismay, even in the circumstances, was brazenly unconcealed. 'I thought she was coming with you.'

I explained that she had stayed in Egypt to comfort her brother.

'A spiffing chap,' Arthur volunteered.

Lady Brydonne waited patiently, but no word followed about Olivia, so, shaking her head in exasperation, she gave up. Later, however, taking me round the overgrown garden, she asked for details of Polly's accident and why we were in Egypt. Were the Hartfields there? Had Arthur been nice to Olivia and vice versa? She said she had spoken to Polly's parents, who were bearing up well. 'Showing considerable dignity,' Lady Brydonne benevolently allowed. Then she gave me some writing paper with *Brydonne Park* embossed on it in blue, so I could write home and of course to Billy — after which she left me pretty much alone, as the English tend to do on visits.

Arthur stayed on for a day before going up to London. We were by now easy if not intimate friends, our talk, out of necessity perhaps, confined to everyday things. Arthur had loved Polly and beneath his light-hearted banter he mourned her silently, as was his way — something which I too preferred. It made his presence the more comforting, and as a result I felt badly let down when he left.

'I'll be in touch,' he promised, pushing back that shock of pale hair. 'I'll ring up or something before you sail.' (Lord Brydonne was going to drive me to Southampton.) Arthur and I knew we were unlikely to meet again, or not for a very long time, and forcing smiles, formally shaking hands, we made our parting noises.

'Cheerio,' said Arthur. 'Chin up.'

'Goodbye,' I murmured in a gloomy whisper. The words seemed all wrong though.

'Now, come and see my new combine harvester,' Lord Brydonne urged, trying to distract me as one does a child. 'I expect your father's got one of these,' he said of the huge grasshopper-green contraption, JOHN DEERE emblazoned on it in bright yellow. A boyish sense of competition laced his voice.

I nodded absently.

'Buck up now, it's not the end of the world. That's a girl. Come along, I'll introduce you to Henry. He won a prize last week.' Henry was a large fuzzy-looking Suffolk ram. 'His

261

offspring will salt the countryside — white specks everywhere,' Lord Brydonne proudly declared. 'Just look at those horns. Quite a fellow, isn't he?'

The weather was mostly mild and I wandered about outside, my mind refusing to focus on anything much. Strolling beside the ha-ha, I watched the sheep methodically mowing the park, serving so innocently their useful purpose. That would be the story of their lives — from our viewpoint, at least — and it made me think of Sartre. Man wasn't useful automatically; he had to make it up, and he was alone. How fortunate I was then to have found my life's purpose so quickly, and to have embraced it with the ardour of a true vocation. Making Hugo happy would be sure to make me so. Nor would I be alone.

Sitting at a table beside the fishpond, I wrote to Billy, keeping strictly to the topic of Polly's death. It was a hard letter to write, the words clichéd and inadequate, and, because of our relationship, much of the content necessarily evasive. Moreover, my thoughts kept on straying — ricocheting repeatedly back to Hugo and the future. Once I had heard from him, I told myself, a new life would begin. It would be like a rebirth. Right now everything was on hold, as of necessity it must be. But soon all that would change. A kind of curtain had descended, but I was standing in the wings, and waiting eagerly to go on stage — waiting to give quite literally the performance of my life. I vowed that I would make it a brilliant one.

Opposite me, across the fishpond and wreathed in honeysuckle, the Buddha smiled inscrutably.

Miss Grist telephoned that night to say she had my ticket and where to meet them in Southampton. She said Olivia was going to fly home. She wanted to celebrate her twenty-first birthday with her brother. Taken aback, part of me greeted this news with relief. I hadn't been looking forward to incarceration with Olivia for ten days on that boat. We had little to say to one another at the best of times, and considerably less, it seemed to me, right now.

* * *

The boat was Dutch, entirely tourist class and therefore, it being summer, predictably full of students. When I went on board, Mary-Moore, standing beside the gangplank, hugged me tight and burst into tears. 'Oh, I can't believe it!' she cried. 'It's so awful! I'm so sorry! It's just unbelievable!' Sally said

263

more or less the same, but without the emotional underpinnings, and pretty quickly asked about the scarabs. When I said I hadn't got them she didn't make a fuss about it, though.

We were a miserably reduced group, the table laid for four not six; and as I lay in bed that night I thought woefully of Polly, who should have been lying opposite but who was instead lying somewhere below, permanently asleep. The thought was terrifying, non-existence incomprehensible. Now you see me, now you don't. I simply could not take it in. Moreover, I felt so vulnerable now myself. But above all I missed her, and I felt such anguish that she'd been so cheated — deprived so inexplicably of her intrinsic right to live. That morning I had seen the unmistakable shape of a coffin carried up one of the gangways, and very likely it was Polly's. Others too had watched, as at a shadow passing, and had abruptly turned away. Strike up the band, they probably thought. Roll out the barrel, and let's have a barrel of fun. Yes, yes, yes. For tomorrow we too may die! Desperately I clung to visions of my future life with Hugo.

★ ★ ★

At breakfast, Miss Grist said the purser was looking for me, but when I stopped by his office it was closed. It was a beautiful morning, and feeling better I went out on deck. Leaning over the rail and enjoying the sunshine, I began to review the events of the past month. Europe had made an indelible impression, but not, I reflected, along the culturally refining lines anticipated. Much bigger things had happened. Love and death had made themselves known, and what was more important than that? Acquainted with such new and fundamental experiences, I thought of myself almost as a different person. Henry James's Americans abroad, I grandly concluded, had enjoyed by comparison exceptionally sheltered lives. A school of silver flying fish were leaping along in the wash of our propeller, and as I inhaled the crisp fresh air, suddenly my spirits spiralled miraculously upwards on a thermal of youthful exuberance, and for a moment pure joy took hold. 'I'll live for both of us, Polly dear,' I promised. 'I'll make it as perfect as I can. You'll see!'

'Oh, there you are,' Sally called, coming out on deck. 'The purser's looking for you. He has a letter or something.'

I knew it would be from Arthur, who'd said he'd be in touch, so I was in no hurry.

'Come and play shuffleboard,' Sally urged, nodding significantly towards the upper deck. 'There're some really neat Princeton boys up there. Oh, come on, it'll be fun, and we need the exercise.' She took my arm, propelling me towards the stairs. 'You didn't miss much in Venice, by the way, and those canals smelled awful.'

It was afternoon before I returned to my cabin. The letter had been pushed under the door. It had a blue envelope and right off I noticed that there was no stamp. 'Diplomatic bag' was scrawled on it instead. The thrill I felt! My heart drummed, my breath shortened in excited bursts. That Hugo had written so quickly, had sensed what I must be feeling and how badly I needed reassurance, filled me with a melting love. It meant too that he had formed a plan.

I still have that letter. It is rather long, three pages in large regular handwriting.

Our being together had made him so happy, Hugo said. It had opened up such a promising future and one he had given up hope of ever finding. At last he'd been able to look ahead with pleasure. He said Polly's death, tragic and terrible, would take a long time to get over, and he knew how dreadful I must now be feeling.

As well as being lamentable, death was also

very sobering, he said. It called one's own life into sharp review, pressing a hard reality on dreams and optimistic hopes. Self-knowledge was dearly paid for; no wonder it was so highly valued, though he was unable to feel its value at the moment.

That was when I noticed the shifting tenses.

Marvellous though the prospect of a life together was — reassuring and fine to contemplate — he nonetheless and with the greatest difficulty was forced to acknowledge it could not be made to work. The fault was entirely his; he lacked the stability that was needed. It was a cruel truth to face — for both of us; and an equally cruel time to say so, when there was already so much suffering and loss. He deeply regretted that. Yet it was only fair that I should know his thoughts before I reached America. He understood there was someone with whom I'd had an understanding, and he sorely wished to avoid any irreparable or unnecessary damage.

So, Olivia had told him about Billy!

He said he was unable to shake off his past. It was part of him and he couldn't reinvent himself. 'I am an exile and I must accept it,' he declared. I distinctly remember that phrase, because it was precisely what she had said. I began to picture Olivia, leaning over his shoulder, making suggestions, even dictating bits of the letter; taking at leisure her promised pounds of flesh.

There followed the usual sorrier-than-I-can-says. He felt sure that, settled in the sort of life that I by rights and instincts ought to have (more Olivia), I would be glad I had avoided a well-intentioned mistake. He would always remember me with great tenderness. He admired me more than he could say.

I sat there with the letter in my lap, and there was nothing, absolutely nothing, I could do. I couldn't go to him and plead my case, try to change his mind, seduce him and begin a proper affair. In staying behind and breaking her promise to me, Olivia, ruinous, clinging, destructive and immature behind that smooth façade, had accomplished utterly her devilish work. And it was I who must now bear the consequences.

I didn't go up to dinner; I couldn't. I lay on my berth weeping bitter and regretful tears. My losses were piling up. Could it really be finished? All over? Half way around the world, Hugo almost certainly would stay there. Death, it seemed, was about to claim another victim: the proverbial death-in-life of a rejected woman, and for a moment I almost envied Polly her imperturbable repose. The pain was terrible. It overlaid my grief for Polly like a heavy weight, burying it deeper, under a new sorrow. But this new sorrow was also laced with anger. Olivia had never intended to give Hugo and me a chance; she'd had no intention whatever of letting him go — she would be on her own if she did. So, tit for tat, she had demanded her sacrificial victim; and she'd got it. He was, he'd said, forced to accept that it would never work. Well, it was pretty obvious who had forced him. The thing was diabolical and the pair of them, by their own admission, doomed, locked in a suffocatingly claustrophobic past and lacking either the courage or self-discipline to break away.

I felt so helpless! If I'd been able to do something, being a practical person I would have: telephoned, travelled, written, pleaded. But like Polly I was buried on that godforsaken boat and would be for the next ten days.

★ ★ ★

As I hadn't turned up at dinner, Miss Grist came down to see me afterwards.

'Oh, just seasick,' I told her.

A wise old bird, she ordered some toast, hot broth and a glass of milk; and, pulling up a chair beside the bed, sat there while I slowly tried to eat. Diagnosing grief over Polly's death, she decided to extract, insofar as possible, if not the thorn, then its painful festering, asking me to tell her, if I felt able, precisely what had happened in the desert. It was unspoken of thus far.

So I told her about the ruins, and the sandstorm suddenly coming up; how Polly had got worried about Hugo and Olivia and gone to look for them on horseback, and the horse had run off. Probably it had stumbled and she had fallen off. 'When we talked in hospital I never dreamt she was in any danger!' I said, fighting back tears. 'They had set her leg and she was sort of confused, but the reason she died — what she died of — is still a mystery!' I said it wouldn't have happened in America, though: our standards were so much higher.

What had Polly said in hospital, Miss Grist asked, obviously trying to keep me talking, give sorrow words and all that. It was supposed to be cathartic.

I repeated that Polly was confused because of the concussion. She had said Olivia and her brother weren't twins, that they weren't even brother and sister.

Miss Grist's attention was on the toast she was cutting into pieces for me. 'Did she? Why was that, do you think?'

'We thought they weren't when we first met Hugo,' I said, 'so Polly must have been reverting.'

'What on earth made you think a thing like that?' Miss Grist sounded amused.

Here I hesitated, as loyalties were involved, but quickly decided they were no longer valid. 'We felt sure Olivia went abroad to meet someone, Miss Grist; which was why she joined our group. There had to be *some* reason for it. So when Hugo turned up we thought that it was him, and that he was pretending to be her brother, as a sort of cover-up, you see.'

'No,' said Miss Grist, more firmly this time, 'I don't see.'

'It was the night I saw you in the Colosseum that I found out they were twins.'

I said they had been going around together arm in arm, publicly hugging and kissing. Then I giggled a little. 'When they went up to her room we were really shocked.'

'Was Hugo often in her room?'

'Oh sure. I mean I guess he was. But after that it didn't matter.'

Miss Grist was frowning. She even forgot to pass me the piece of buttered toast.

'Oh, they *are* twins,' I reassured her. 'We got that all wrong.'

But Miss Grist wasn't one to stumble

around in fossil fields without finding new connections. Rightly or wrongly, she picked up on things that eluded others, just didn't occur to them, especially in the 1950s.

'Did Polly say anything else in hospital?'

'She said she didn't want to see them — or else they didn't want to see her. It wasn't clear which.'

'Why was that, do you think?'

'I've no idea. As I said, she was pretty mixed up.'

'Olivia and her brother are exceptionally close, I believe?'

'Oh yes; like Siamese twins, according to Olivia. She's very dependent on her brother, very possessive about him too; it's almost an obsession. Why, she never even lets him out of her sight if she can help it. And frankly, Miss Grist,' I produced a look of grave but sympathetic concern, 'I think she may need serious psychological help.'

It gave me a lot of pleasure, that well-aimed little barb!

'I thought Hugo was your beau,' said Miss Grist calmly in reply.

I said she was mistaken there.

That Miss Grist was, even remotely, entertaining thoughts of incest never once entered my innocent young head. It was unheard of, on a par with, say, cannibalism in my hermetically sheltered world, where rape and losing one's virginity before marriage were about the biggest sexual horrors that could loom. And if I'd known what Miss Grist suspected, apart from being shocked to death, I would have very quickly set her straight. I would have mentioned Alexei, of whom she was completely unaware; and probably I would have told her, painful though that would be, about Hugo and myself, that we had been engaged. I might even have divulged what Polly had said about Olivia kissing her — in which case Miss Grist's erotic imagination might have been deployed in yet another fruitless and probably misconceived direction.

But that said, when later on I had the chance to clarify such things, I didn't, I confess, do so. Already, the ball was rolling, and whether it was from apathy or revenge, I was by then inclined to let it roll.

19

Hugging Françoise Sagan's newly published novel, *Bonjour Tristesse*, together with a copy of the *Paris Review*, I boarded the train for Lynchburg in September. I remember I was wearing a blue beret, tilted pertly to one side, and a Burberry mackintosh I'd bought on sale in London. My once-precious set of matching luggage, now being carelessly loaded by a station porter, bespoke membership of a tribe which, to my mind, I no longer belonged. I felt surprisingly grown-up, a changed person, alienated, if not exactly along Sartrean lines, then from the innocent milieu of college life. Europe had loaded me with new experience, awarding me a dramatic, even mildly tragic image of myself. And I was making the most of it.

Unlike me, Olivia did not return to Sweet Briar. Two weeks before the term began she was expelled. I never knew the exact details, but shortly after I got home Dean Allen wrote to me and, commiserating on Polly's death, said she must reluctantly ask me to confirm a fact of some importance and in strictest confidence. Which I immediately did. That

Olivia and her brother had been seen kissing and embracing and that they were often together in Olivia's room. Though I failed to properly absorb the inference, I sensed some kind of punitive campaign was under way. And yet I made no modifying comment or elaboration — partly because I saw no reason to. I simply confirmed that it was true, leaving others to act as they saw fit. Miss Grist told me later on, in confidence, that the Hartfields had been anxious to separate the twins for their own good, and that they hadn't known Hugo would be coming to Europe. (I knew that already, of course.) 'And yet they let her go to Egypt,' said Miss Grist, winding her Mickey Mouse wristwatch and looking unusually pensive.

I didn't say the Hartfields had understood that Hugo was engaged to me, and that Olivia therefore would be accompanying her brother's fiancée. Circumstances set to reassure, and, as I now saw with some alarm, conceivably designed to do just that.

Technically, however, Olivia was expelled for something else. Shortly before our boat sailed, she had telephoned Miss Grist in London to say her mother was wiring permission for her to stay in Egypt and fly home. When Miss Grist left London no telegram had arrived, but she wasn't too concerned. Talking to me on the boat, however, had raised her suspicions, and on making enquiries she discovered that no telegram had been sent.

Olivia flew to New York the very day our boat docked. It was beautifully orchestrated, but given Miss Grist's new-found arsenal of information, Olivia was easily rumbled. Unfortunately, so was poor Miss Grist. Olivia's nearly successful ruse, on top of Polly's death, suggested carelessness, and perhaps rightly so. At any rate the college felt obliged to act, and as a result Miss Grist's halcyon summers as easygoing guide and chaperone were finished. It must have been a heavy blow: half her personality was left without any congenially intemperate outlets.

It was at college that Polly's death finally took firm hold. Her wit, her deadpan scepticism, the reassuring taken-for-granted comfort of her being, like a ray of reluctant sunshine had been scotched, and I was sitting in the dark. I missed her horribly. She was my only friend and, having lost Hugo too, I felt for the first time in my life true loneliness — something very different from alienation, Sartrean or otherwise, because it is specific.

The girls were wonderfully kind. Many of them had written during the summer, having heard the news of Polly's death from others, so that when condolences were offered now, they were brief, low-key and mercifully made few demands.

Olivia's absence provoked a very different reaction. Her expulsion was never explicitly announced, so gossip and speculation abounded: she had gone to Vassar, she had polio, she was on a yacht in the Bahamas. But Pookie Payne claimed with high authority to possess the latest bulletin: Olivia, having returned home in July, had recently gone back to Europe. Olivia's family were keeping quiet about it, but everyone in Philadelphia knew — they had heard it from mutual friends in Washington. The fact was, Olivia had eloped with her unsuitable young man. 'Turns out he has a title but no money.'

I was all ears. Could this possibly be true? If so, for me it would be manna from heaven.

The other girls in the smoker were equally thrilled, if for different reasons. They thought a title sounded highly romantic; so did an elopement. And money wasn't so important; everybody made money. Besides, Olivia would have piles of it herself.

'Maybe,' Pookie solemnly intoned, pausing to get the full benefit from what was coming, 'but the point is they aren't married. Mother would have received a formal announcement if they were. They say that he's refusing to marry her until the Hartfields fork out, and Olivia may well be in on it.'

This produced its well-anticipated shock. Books were lowered, eyes widened and knitting needles ceased to click. The bridge players forgot whose deal it was. Poor Olivia was a fallen woman. How awful!

Cooking up blackmail sounded to me highly improbable, but if Alexei had indeed triumphed and Olivia had made a successful dash for freedom, I could legitimately renew my dearest hopes! Yet I had not the faintest idea where Hugo was. I'd no address in Egypt, and though I prowled through the Washington telephone directory I couldn't find Hartfield. Most people lived in the adjacent counties and the name, as it turned out, wasn't so common. I'd no choice therefore but to wait, patient, cloistered and industrious, just as Olivia had the year before, keeping my mind occupied with work. Although I didn't know where Hugo was, I told myself that he at least knew where to locate me.

The waiting game that is woman's lot began and, as a result, I confess I even missed Billy a little. I had written to him breaking things off shortly before school started, leaving it to the last minute, because of Polly, and hoping to spare him what otherwise amounted to firing both triggers of a double-barrelled shotgun off at once. Billy had written a graceful, gentlemanly reply and had never once tried to get in touch. In November I saw him with Mary-Moore, at a distance, getting into his car. I recognized the car. He didn't look particularly glum and I envied him his excellent resilience. But maybe he'd cared for me no more deeply than I had for him, which twisted, if momentarily, a knife of interest.

★ ★ ★

The months went by in rapid monotony, like watching boxcars passing with a tedious and interminable sameness at a railroad crossing. But no word came from Hugo. Work and routine enfolded me in their cosy shelter, however. I wrote my thesis on Henry James's uses of innocence. I waited tables with robotic patience, listening to tedious sopho-moronic prattle, and I spent many hours in the library reading room, curled up in an armchair, trying, as Olivia had done, not to brood; patiently awaiting rescue. It had come for her and surely it also would for me.

To a degree this homespun cocoon worked. As the weeks passed, the trauma of Polly's death receded and the wound of losing Hugo, although it didn't heal, was covered up. I plodded diligently on, concentrating fiercely on my work. But I'll skip over these irrelevant months, except to say that in the late spring what could be called my exit visa arrived: I was awarded a Fulbright scholarship. I was also chosen as class valedictorian. And so, despite my feelings of isolation, I departed Sweet Briar with a few metaphorical laurels wreathing my funereal mortarboard.

The scholarship meant graduate work abroad the following year, and, fluent in no foreign language, I chose Bedford College, a women's college and part of London University. My quiet limbo-like existence was about to change, though not in the direction that I had hoped.

★ ★ ★

The scholarship was immensely generous; so generous, in fact, that on arrival in London, having spent the summer babysitting and waiting tables to make pocket money, I found myself more comfortably off than I had ever been. Marilyn Dunn, another Fulbright scholar, and I teamed up and took a flat together in Primrose Hill. Marilyn's father owned a Chicago meat-packing company and Marilyn had a big allowance. She couldn't abide tattiness, she said, and England was *tattissimo*, English taste 'the pits', and our flat evidently no exception. Marilyn insisted on a vase of fresh flowers in every room — there were two. It was her special 'identifying' luxury, and in those days, for students, it *was* luxurious: fresh flowers cost a mint. Marilyn also bought a lot of new things for the flat: a grey Wilton carpet, an Edwardian table and chairs, and a new sofa. We painted the walls and woodwork white, and I produced a colourful Gauguin poster for over the mantelpiece. Marilyn was at University College and we saw little of each other — which didn't matter. I delighted in my new-found independence — no rules, no authorities or obligatory classes — and I adored London and tried to see everything. But above all I particularly loved the theatre.

Eventually, of course, I looked up Arthur. I was afraid of reopening old wounds, but I knew few English people and I wasn't being introduced to many. Added to which, those I did meet proved hard to get to know.

Arthur greeted me as though we'd parted only the day before, launching into some story about a rag-and-bone man he had met en route in the Underground. But despite his off-handedness and an inability to put any feeling in his voice, it was plain that he admired the flat. 'Very *chi chi*,' he declared approvingly, smelling a vase of yellow roses like Ferdinand the bull. He was himself in 'digs': a rented room somewhere in South Kensington, with a shared bathroom on the landing. 'You Americans live in clover,' he said merrily. 'May I?' And he installed a yellow rosebud in his buttonhole.

We had dinner at a local Indian restaurant. Arthur said that he thought about Polly often, and he missed her. His mother had received a note from Polly's family, thanking them for arranging things, but he had had no news of either Hugo or Olivia, or for that matter Alexei. I didn't mention the gossip I had heard at college. Were it true, I reasoned, I would have heard from Hugo by now myself. Mainly I felt relief at getting through the topic quickly and finding that I'd survived it.

There followed an exchange of happy memories of Polly: her shrewd observations, mordant humour and what at school had been so lovingly called her gollies.

'A rare spirit,' Arthur opined. 'My favourite cousin, and so droll. You know she never laughed.'

'Except that time she swallowed the coffee bean in her sambuca.'

'Did she laugh then?' Arthur looked surprised. 'I thought she was choking.'

'That's what she wanted you to think. Old Polly never liked being rumbled.' The recollection gave me a lot of pleasure. 'We got so much wrong,' I said, laughing and shaking my head. 'You can't imagine — absolutely back to front. My, what little innocents we were!'

'To Gollypolly.' We raised our glasses, and in that gesture Polly was, I believe, finally laid to rest. Mourning was over, but memories could repeatedly be raked over and, like embers, gave out their residual warmth.

Arthur still disliked his job and being a wage slave, as he called it, for Brydonne Park. 'An insatiable mistress who can never have enough attention,' he insisted over coffee in a noisy espresso bar (they were the latest fashion). 'She wants my life's blood, does that greedy vampire.'

'Do you never think of selling?' I asked. 'Eventually, I mean.' The situation was incomprehensible.

'Oh, often; daily, I expect; hourly, even. But I couldn't chuck her,' the ambivalent slave declared. Just as Hugo and Olivia had been skewered by their past, so in another way, I saw, was Arthur. It made me feel remarkably free and unencumbered; though deep down, of course, I knew it wasn't true. The truth was I was killing time.

Even so, I had to think about my future. I would qualify for a teaching job at university level the next year, and I began to cast around, applying to Mount Holyoke and Smith. I liked the idea of an academic career; it sounded so respectable. But Smith said they had no places and Mount Holyoke wanted an interview by June at the latest. However, I was determined to travel. I wanted particularly to see Venice and Florence. I owed it to myself and also to my parents, who had regarded my earlier trip as a right fiasco. 'Why isn't she engaged?' my father had wanted to know. 'Has she been jilted?' 'It just didn't work out,' I'd answered. While Mother, hoping for a revival of my liaison with Billy, deeply regretted that I couldn't go to Polly's Nashville funeral. But we couldn't afford it. 'Traipsing across America, and for what?' my father had shouted furiously. 'To see a dead person? It's throwing money away.' That hurt, but at any rate I had been saved from facing Billy.

20

In July, when the Suez crisis erupted, I was in Venice. Overnight Nasser had nationalized the Canal and appropriated British government assets. The British were having a fit. Reading about it, appropriately on the Rialto, with a flotilla of moored gondolas bobbing up and down in front of me, I naturally wondered about Hugo. Not having backed Nasser, who was now so firmly in control, he might have to leave Egypt, if he hadn't already. In fact, he could be somewhere in Europe at that very moment. The idea took hold and I began to look out for him, in the streets, in cafés and museums, even in my tiny pension on the unfashionable Giudecca. Once or twice I thought I glimpsed his curly Attic head disappearing among San Marco's bustling crowds. I even thought I saw the willowy Olivia on the arm of a very tall man. It was a can of worms, of course, but I still hoped and yearned and wondered. Without hope to feed on I would face starvation.

Back in London and anxious for more news, I telephoned Arthur. We had dinner at a French bistro in South Kensington and this

285

time Arthur paid. He had received a small promotion. Moreover he was fairly bubbling with news about Suez. War, he believed, was definitely on the cards. The British were behaving like lunatics, he said. They were absurdly gung-ho and the City was all on edge, which made it a lot more fun. At last Arthur was enjoying his work.

'Hugo may have to leave Egypt,' I said, nonchalantly sawing away at a none-too-tender grouse. 'If he hasn't already, that is.' It was the first time I had mentioned Hugo's name aloud, and it reverberated in my ears like a funeral tocsin.

'I was about to tell you,' Arthur matter-of-factly replied, 'I've had a postcard. Hugo is cooling his heels in Paris — or he was, at any rate.' Arthur said the card had arrived a fortnight earlier and Hugo wrote that he might go to the Sudan; the Egyptians had left some interesting traces there. 'He didn't give any address,' Arthur added serenely.

I had dropped my knife and fork; my face was dead white and I was near to fainting. You couldn't miss it and plainly Arthur didn't.

'I'm sorry, I thought you'd want to know,' he said, looking embarrassed.

'I thought I did.'

'It's none of my business,' he pursued, 'but

I always assumed Polly's death was what changed things between you.'

'No. Hugo changed his mind, that's all.'

'Egypt is a ghastly place,' Arthur diplomatically injected, 'and the Sudan must be worse. You're made for the civilized world, you know. That's what interests you. I'd say you had a very close shave.'

That was so kind. Arthur was an innately decent man, cheerful and upbeat, and he and I were by now so used to each other's company that we were completely at ease. In a friendly, unselfconscious way we enjoyed chatting and being together. To a degree we also shared a past. But when the following month, as we sat in a flock-wallpapered Soho restaurant eating Vindaloo curry, Arthur, who had been talking about a discovery in the Roman Forum, suddenly asked me to marry him, I was extravagantly surprised. I was also immensely flattered. I hadn't remotely seen it coming, I admit; but then who would have done?

Europeans will understand an unromantic but civilized and friendly proposal of marriage more easily than Americans, since Europeans have traditionally married for practical reasons — family, money, convenience, mutual gain of all sorts. For Americans, however, being in love is morally

287

and culturally an essential requirement.

'We get on extremely well,' said Arthur, 'and you're very good at managing things. In fact, you're astonishingly efficient.' I knew he was thinking of Brydonne Park. 'We could make a go of it, I believe.' He said I was very attractive.

I wasn't of course remotely in love with Arthur, but I was at a loose end and falling in love had nearly wrecked my life. It had wrecked completely my happiness. Was being in love then really so beneficial? When Olivia had asked that question in Egypt it had sounded rhetorical, the answer obvious, something every American took for granted. Now, however, it was worthy of serious consideration. So I slept on it, as they say.

All I know is next morning I woke up convinced it was a marvellous solution. A splendid role was being offered me and on a very considerable stage. I could imagine my mother's astonished relief: I would be Mrs Brydonne after all — eventually *Lady* Brydonne. It wasn't the American South, but, given the scale, it was even better. And I would make a go of it. I would put everything I was capable of into making the marriage a success. It would be my life's work, and I would do the very best I could to be a good wife and make Arthur Brydonne happy. Love had proved a painful and irrational business, and Marcus Aurelius, perched on his pedestal, was right: everything in moderation. Added to which, what could be more valuable than a true friend as one's life companion? So, all things having been considered, I said yes.

Arthur was delighted.

★ ★ ★

I felt sorry for Lady Brydonne, forced to leave her beautiful house and move into a cottage at the end of the park. Recently, however, heirs had begun to take possession of family houses upon marriage, since, servants having disappeared, much youthful energy was required to keep big places up. There was in this case another reason too, as I later learned; but I will come to that. Suffice to say right now that despite its outward-seeming grandeur my life was much like married women's everywhere, in that I was completely immersed in housework. I didn't mind a bit, but, ironically, life at Brydonne was in many ways less comfortable than in Wichita. For instance, the dining room was nowhere near the kitchen, and the washing-up sink wasn't in the kitchen but in another room, a scullery. Nor had we any central heating, depending instead on open fires and plug-in electric ones that were expensive to run. Those first winters at Brydonne Park, I simply froze, and 'stiff upper lip' took on new meaning. I even thought with mild envy on occasion of Lady Brydonne, sitting snugly before her cottage inglenook, leisurely turning the glossy pages of *Country Life*.

But being a practical person, I soon decided that, given our slender budget, we had no choice but to modify our habits. So we began to eat our dinner in the kitchen and to use our bedroom, where a fire was kept lit, as the sitting room. Arthur, to his enormous credit, never once protested or complained, but I often thought myself that we were like a pair of mice, burrowed into a corner of some remote and rarely visited museum. And repeatedly the importance of money was brought home to me.

Summers were different, however. The great house, having held her breath all winter, breathed out in a happy sigh, and expanding to her natural, generous girth, hinted at immense and fabulous potential, were we ever able to develop it.

Social life picked up too. Lord Brydonne, busy in the surrounding fields, bounced in and out for sherry and a chat, and Lady Brydonne took me with her to pay calls at several houses in the countryside. As Arthur spent three nights a week in his London digs, this made a welcome change, for I was often alone. I had been introduced to people locally, but I knew no-one really. A village hierarchy existed that made friendship, to my mind, artificial and predictably hive-like. More to the point, social initiative was up to me, and I was too incompetent and shy to use it.

Then, manna from heaven! Arthur's career — making lots of lolly, as we said laughingly — began to take off in the City. And with a decent income assured, Arthur decided to borrow money against the estate, securing funds both to improve the farm and, at my insistence, install central heating in half a dozen rooms. But the real treat was that we bought a little flat in London, on a top floor overlooking Ennismore Gardens. It meant that I could come up to town more often, and, given our new and expanding margin of prosperity, things might have settled down very pleasantly, had not an earlier event continued to hover, almost tragically, over our marriage — an event from which it never fully recovered, or if so not for very many years.

Shortly after our wedding, which had taken place very quietly in the village church, a serious hitch had emerged. Arthur, tactful as always, had refrained from bringing up the issue before our wedding; but as my parents hadn't come over (they weren't encouraged to) there had been no man-to-man discussion, so that eventually it was I who received point-blank the question at issue. What did my family plan to settle on me?

'But we have no money, you know that!' I had cried out, hugely surprised.

Arthur, unfortunately, did not. He'd got the idea I was very rich, with thousands of flat and fertile Kansas acres under intensive cultivation. I simply couldn't imagine why he thought this! It was true I had misled Lord Brydonne about that harvesting machine; he'd assumed my father owned it personally; and Sweet Briar was known to be a very expensive college. Maybe too, seeing my London flat so pleasantly furnished, Arthur had assumed it was paid for with my money. In addition to which, Europeans in the 1950s really did believe that Americans were made of dollar bills. Still, such slender evidence was, or should have been, inconsequential.

But there it was, and the blow crashed through the Brydonne family like a tidal wave. Arthur had made a hideous mistake, a seriously bad investment, and, poor fellow, what could he do? He was stuck with it. I'd been expected to pour thousands into Brydonne Park, bringing the old place very deservingly up to scratch. Indeed, that was the reason Lady Brydonne had so willingly decamped.

It's true, I'd known that Arthur had to marry money, but being American I suppose I'd never really believed it, or I'd vainly imagined that my meagre charms, embellished by the myopia of infatuation, overrode mundane considerations of that sort. What an absurd presumption! Our marriage got off to a most dismal start. Arthur was very polite and very correct. Lumbered with a wife of no importance, without money or background, he had to swallow it, and he did his best: he behaved impeccably. But I felt mortified and obscurely guilty, a cuckoo sitting impertinently in the redoubtable Brydonne nest; and I longed to compensate the family in some way. They had made a bad bargain: getting nickels when they'd been expecting dollars. And now, due to Arthur's blighted expectations, a loan existed that must somehow be paid off.

I thought of taking a teaching job, but Arthur wouldn't hear of it. Now we were getting on our feet, I was expected to do charitable work in Oxfordshire and to decorate the occasional London dinner table.

But I didn't feel very decorative, nor, frankly, did I enjoy working without any remuneration. Above all, I was sorely anxious to retrieve my badly damaged *amour propre*.

Eventually therefore, after a lot of brooding, I came up with an idea. I begged Arthur to back me, and he without any hesitation very generously agreed to do so. It was a highly speculative, long-term proposition, and, in addition to a considerable financial investment, would mean years of study, organization, planning and, in the end, hard physical labour. Lord Brydonne enthusiastically joined in, however, and he proved invaluable. We became fast friends. Later on, even Lady Brydonne lent a hand — a remarkably helpful hand, it unexpectedly turned out, for Lady Brydonne knew, as it transpired, her onions.

Thus, slowly, over several years and after many setbacks and mistakes, Brydonne Park's now famous Paradise Gardens were created. Arthur said the name was a tautology, that paradise was the Persian word for garden; but I maintained you needed to have both in English. I suspect what Arthur really meant was that Paradise Gardens sounded vulgar and Hollywoodish, more suited to a California cemetery or a suburban housing estate. But in the end I kept it.

Almost from the beginning the gardens were a success: people flocked, coming back again and again. They still do. In the early 1970s I added a nursery, with plants for sale, and, copying Sissinghurst, opened a small teashop. Arthur was so proud of me! Brydonne Park was making money and the garden, being a business, provided tax relief, which gave great satisfaction. Above everything, however, was the enormous pleasure of seeing an idea, worked out and refined in the imagination, rise up literally out of the ground and burst so voluptuously into bloom. It was art, but art inextricably combined with nature, and so a living thing, open to continuing change and adaptation. It was also part of a mystical partnership, for, as every keen gardener knows, it is essential that the gods lend their incomparable assistance.

' 'Paradise enow',' Arthur described it that first day, quoting from Omar Khayyam. 'A jug of wine, a loaf of bread . . . ' He had laid our simple picnic on a table beside the fishpond, together with two glasses. The wine was Haut Brion 1945, the very best in our cellar. 'To my wife in our paradise garden,' he toasted.

It was, I think, the happiest day of my life. Of course I had believed as much before — for instance, when Hugo had proposed to me that night in Rome. But that happiness was misconceived, being based on girlish dreams and high romance — at best, an intense infatuation. This was very different: this was something I had myself laboriously accomplished. And Arthur's pleasure in my success, his pride in me, covered my own achievement in a cloth of gold. It was a quieter joy, but solid and pervasive; and I was old enough to recognize its value and to treasure it.

*　*　*

And so we rubbed along, fondly and without either friction or disagreement; I mostly in the country and Arthur, during the week, in London — a typical English pattern. I took part in village affairs — church bazaars, the Women's Institute, as was expected — becoming, in effect, a model English wife. People said ours was an ideal existence, couldn't be bettered; and I began to think they must be right, because the image we presented gave me, when I thought about it, much pleasure and satisfaction. I even felt myself to be, on occasion, a person of consequence. The one drawback was our lack of children. But with plenty of other interests, we decided it didn't matter so much, although without an heir or any next of kin, the title, after Arthur, would die out. But Arthur was philosophical about that. The burden of Brydonne Park would at last be lifted, he said, shaking his shoulders like a newly unburdened Atlas — the curse removed. Besides, it was time to modernize: there would be no place for hereditary titles or entailed estates in the new century; nor should there be. 'Brydonne Park can go to the National Trust; then everyone can enjoy it,' he said, pleased but regretful too, I think. Well, that was Arthur.

21

Four days ago, when Arthur and I arrived in France, Brydonne Park had recently won the coveted Award of Garden Merit, and Arthur, chairman of his bank and firmly pro-Europe, was to give his conference's opening address. That night, we celebrated our double victory at Le Chapon Fin, Bordeaux's best restaurant, starting with foie gras and a horrendously expensive half-bottle of Château d'Yquem. It would be our only evening together. The conference was being held in a château somewhere south of Bordeaux, away from the press's notoriously prying gaze. Both Kohl and Mitterrand were coming, but as some of the smaller countries hadn't been invited, secrecy was all-important.

Full of my extraordinary encounter with Olivia that morning, I didn't let on over dinner how shaken I had been. 'Can you believe it?' I said. 'She's living here, of all places, out in the country, and married to a Frenchman. They have a vineyard somewhere around St Emilion. And there's a daughter, the spitting image of Olivia when young.' I described my mistaking mother and daughter. 'Oh, I do wish you could come tomorrow!' I said, relaying Olivia's invitation to Sunday lunch. 'Wouldn't you love to see her? It's been such a mystery all these years. God knows where Hugo is, but it's a marvellous chance to catch up. Such a stroke of fate! I can't get over it. And she looks wonderful.'

Eating his foie gras slowly, clearly enjoying it, Arthur listened, much interested, a gentle smile flickering on his prominent, bony features. Then, sipping his Yquem with obvious pleasure, he said warmly, as recalling a happy time, 'I was wildly in love with Hugo all that summer.' Adding a minute later, 'And so were you, I seem to recall.'

The English after all these years can still astonish. Their regulated, matter-of-fact delivery can be meaningless or can mask extraordinary passions, compacting them into insignificant-sounding syllables, so that whether the tip of an iceberg or the murmuring of an overheated volcano is behind an utterance is never clear. But now Arthur and I laughed spontaneously and shook our heads, marginally avoiding each other's eyes and yet united further by this newly turned-up fossil from a mutual past.

'My God, those two, what *fatales* they

were! What terrible twins!' I said. 'It doesn't bear thinking about.' And we laughed again.

'Delicious foie gras,' Arthur volunteered.

'The Yquem is pure nectar, darling.' I raised my glass, and, remembering his speech, declared that Europe's new currency should, after tomorrow, be definitely on the cards.

'Not if Thatcher gets her hands on it,' said Arthur. 'That woman is the very devil.'

★ ★ ★

I slept well that night and woke up giddy with anticipation, eager after a gap of thirty-five years to have the past smoothly filled in and to weave some awkwardly dangling threads neatly back into the general fabric. Moreover, I longed to see Olivia in situ and find out how she lived. Thrown off balance by the impact of our Bordeaux meeting, calm was now scrupulously restored. At the time, however, my youthful awe had mysteriously resurfaced, bubbled up out of nowhere, overcoming even my reserve of enmity and, feeling obscurely intimidated, I'd simply lost sight of who I was. Now, however, identity was firmly re-established: I was indisputably Lady Brydonne, and Brydonne Park, I told myself, was peer to any French château — even

300

Château Carrielle, as Olivia's hurriedly sketched-out map proclaimed.

'I await goggle-eyed the next instalment,' said Arthur impishly as he left. 'Give her my warmest regards. Oh, and see what their wine is like; perhaps we should order some.'

I was still in bed, a tray balanced on my lap. 'Whatever it's like, it won't be a patch on last night,' I answered, throwing him a kiss. That outrageously expensive dinner had helped to aid my restoration no end, and even Arthur's lightly delivered revelation had intensified rather than diminished our rapport, adding to it a conspiratorial strength, for we were nothing if not a committed team. Nor had that little confession particularly surprised. English youths famously had relationships with other boys at school, and as often as not they grew out of it. Yet given Arthur's myriad contradictions, what did I really know about his sexual preferences? As for my own, my generation in America had been so caught up in romantic love, and sex so thoroughly tangled up in it, that, in many marriages, when the romance died, as it will do, sex unfortunately got buried too. But when there was no romantic love to start with, well . . .

Buttering a croissant, I thought fleetingly of our lack of children. Arthur and I *had* wanted them, even though we pretended now we hadn't. And certainly we had tried. Not much was known about infertility then, however, and in any case it didn't bear dwelling on now, as it was far too late.

I dressed slowly, giving a lot of attention to detail. French Sunday lunches were, I knew, hallowed affairs, full of family and close friends, all of them well turned out and tucking into lots of courses and good wine. It called for some oomph on my part, as did my wish to make a splash and show Olivia my life was obviously a big success. Evidently at some level she had remained my rival.

I put on my new navy linen suit, Yves St Laurent, together with a white silk blouse and fairly low-heeled brown shoes, in case I was taken around the garden or to see grape-picking. Using a special crayon, I touched up the grey edges of my parting, applied my make-up at the window using a magnifying mirror, and renewed the nail polish — even on my toes. Well, I intended to put my best foot forward!

The car arrived promptly at eleven, a white Citroën, and as there was no traffic I quickly found myself outside the city. Rain had been predicted but the sun shone, the big clouds, like cut-outs, suggesting a white infinity beyond the punctured canopy of blue.

302

Surprisingly, the vineyards began almost at once: no piece of land, it seemed, was wasted. The rows of vines, espaliered on wires, stretched to the horizon in every direction, and although it was Sunday many grape-pickers were still at work, cutting the clusters that hung like rosy udders from the vines and stowing them in baskets strapped on their backs. The *vendange*, I knew, was famously communal, with everyone joining in: migrant workers, students, neighbouring farmers, even relations from nearby towns and cities. It culminated in a big epicurean celebration, a veritable bacchanal, which, frankly, I was very pleased to miss.

Approaching the St Emilion district, the flat terrain gave way to low hills, the ridged carpet of vines reminding me of green corduroy hills in a picture book I'd had as a child. I began to wonder whether Olivia and I would speak with any frankness about the past. Ought I to apologize for having passively misled the college authorities, whose crude insinuations must have appalled her parents? Or was I being invited so that Olivia could apologize to me? She certainly owed me one. As for news of Hugo, though curious, I preferred on balance not to know. Let sleeping dogs lie, I decided. It would be nice to catch up, to clarify generally, and to leave it at that. It was all a long time ago and something I rarely thought about any more.

Turning south onto a country road, small lanes ran to the left and right, each one marked with a discreet white-painted wooden arrow, a house or hamlet's name painted on it in black. After a couple of miles, an arrow like all the rest announced, without any fanfare, Château Carrielle, the little lane cutting through the apparently unending vineyards. As I turned into the lane, a handful of pickers paused to view the car with curiosity. This really is the country! I thought, and though famous for wine, a bit of a backwater — like Kansas, equally famous for its wheat. How odd that Olivia had ended up here. But probably the Laniers had other houses and came to this one at select periods, such as the *vendange*.

Large trees had appeared: I was approaching a small park, an oasis of mottled shade in what was becoming a monotonous landscape. The trees shielded the château from immediate view, but when it finally appeared, flanked by a magnificent yew hedge, I was taken aback. Château Carrielle wasn't remotely a château: it was a very pretty one-storey house, evidently eighteenth-century and constructed in an appealing champagne-coloured limestone. A row of arched French windows opened onto a stone balustraded terrace, and at each end a small wing jutted forward, its steeply hipped roof creating a square tower. There was a huge magnolia tree and several maples and catalpas in the park, and two lime trees set close together, forming a green canopy of leaves. A wooden table and chairs stood underneath.

I'd seen houses like this before, in books on Bordeaux gardens. Described as gentlemen's country residences, they were for some reason called *chartreuses*, and compared to a hulking, heavily frilled and turreted château, the understated elegance pleased and reassured. As for the word 'château', if you made decent claret, I would learn, you called your house a château whether architecturally it was one or not, because of the wine. Probably it was easier to sell.

Olivia must have been looking out for me. As I drove slowly up the drive, she came outside and, waving from the terrace, indicated where I should leave the car, then came towards me across the lawn. She was wearing slim gabardine trousers and a rose-coloured cotton sweater over a white silk blouse, her hair pinned back in a clip, a pair of gold earrings her only jewellery.

We smiled and kissed. 'You had no trouble with my directions, I hope?'

'None at all,' I said. 'But how charming this is. I want to see absolutely everything!'

'You'll find our garden very dull, I'm afraid. Any advice towards its improvement will be most welcome.' So she knew about Brydonne Park. Probably she'd seen articles in magazines.

I followed her from the terrace into a white entrance hall decorated with delicate plaster mouldings like cake icing, the floor a chequerboard of polished terracotta and oyster-coloured tiles. And let me say right now that from the moment I entered that house I was completely under its spell! Its spirit — for houses do have a spirit — was so benevolent and gay, so welcoming and quietly elegant, the whole atmosphere gloriously tranquil and serene. Unmistakably it was a happy house.

The drawing room, on the right, was painted robin's egg blue, with just a touch of aqua, and comfortable white-covered sofas and chairs replaced those formal sit-up-and-beg chairs and settees the French usually go in for. A large Turkish carpet in muted vegetable colours gave the room its richness, and there was a painting over the mantel-piece, a dark and leafy landscape, Barbizon school, that looked rather fine.

'How full of charm this is,' I said again, a

306

morsel of envy lodging suddenly in my throat. I'd had to take Brydonne Park as it was: a status symbol rather than a reposeful abode. As a result, my own nest had been created outdoors; though this was the first time I had seen it quite like that.

Olivia offered champagne and went to fetch it. 'Do please sit down,' she said.

'May I wander instead? I'm fascinated by your house.'

She smiled with pleasure. 'By all means.'

On a table against the wall stood that Egyptian bas-relief, and for a moment I simply floundered. Strange how something can suddenly knock you flat, and just when you imagine everything is under control and you yourself as cool as a cucumber. Then bang! and there is simply nothing you can do.

The dining room adjoined the drawing room through an open arch. It was painted yellow, and the light streaming through the open French windows made it glow like butter. The table, I noted, was laid for six and in the French manner: three places on each side, the ends bare.

Olivia must have caught my glance. 'The house is full to bursting during the *vendange*,' she said, pouring two fizzing glasses of champagne and handing me one.

For some reason we didn't toast each

other, and a short silence followed before I self-consciously took a sip. Both of us knew that any real talk must of necessity come after lunch, and that right now only small talk, never our speciality, was possible. So, unable to go forward with words, Olivia proposed a short tour of the garden.

Laid out behind the house, it combined very prettily French and English tastes. Small mop-headed acacia trees stood like balloons on sticks among the flowerbeds edged by low, carefully clipped box hedges.

'Your agapanthus are wonderful,' I said, 'and how well roses do here!' A great many were still in bloom, traditional hybrid teas and some of the new David Austin species, imported from England. White geraniums cascaded from a pair of lead urns and in the centre stood a pergola shrouded in honeysuckle. I could hear men's voices coming from large outbuildings barely visible behind a screen of trees: the *chais* where wine was made and stored.

Olivia said the others would come in shortly; there were showers and a changing-room in the *chais*. 'Caroline won't be joining us, I'm afraid. She's off with her young man. God knows where; they took a picnic. He goes back to Paris tomorrow.' The inference being it was a chance for lovemaking.

'Oh, I *am* sorry to miss her. I'd hoped to get to know her a little,' I answered, though this wasn't particularly true. 'How old is she now?'

'Twenty. She's at the Sorbonne, and loves it.'

Twenty. Our own age that fateful summer in Europe; how changed modern life was. But Olivia must have had her daughter rather late.

'And you?' she asked, bending down to pull up a weed.

'We have no children,' I said.

Quickly she changed the subject, asking with real sweetness after Arthur. She was so sorry he couldn't come. To think he'd hated banking so, and now he was sorting out Europe's money. 'He must be very adaptable,' she said.

'Arthur is unpredictable,' I laughed, adding, 'So different from Alexei, who, I remember, was so solid in everything.' I had taken a chance and it proved fruitful: the first small piece of gap-filling information was revealed.

'This will surprise you,' said Olivia, pulling up another weed and throwing it on the path, 'but Caroline's young man, Nicky, is Alexei's son.'

'Good heavens, the *principino*!' I cried, rapidly trying to calculate the years. He must be middle-aged.

'No, not the *principino*,' she laughed. 'Nicky is Alexei's younger son.' And, still smiling, she shook her head in lightly amused wonder. 'Ah, propinquity — the things it does!'

The word spun towards me like a grenade, but this time Olivia had uttered it with pleasure, as a positive accomplishment, when before it had been treated as a curse. The grenade fell unexploded at my feet.

'How marvellous!' I said. I meant it too. That something worthwhile might follow from our own foolish bungling and ineptitude would save its being a mere waste of shame and spirit, and give it utility and meaning.

'Nicky's a dear,' said Olivia lightly. 'Good-natured like his father, and he's just as tall.' She said he was in a French investment bank. 'He would have adored meeting so august a figure in the financial world as Arthur.'

We both smiled at the ready idolatry of youth, and, talk coming more easily now, sat down, glasses in hand, on a stone bench. 'Do tell me about Alexei,' I urged. 'You must still be in touch.' I wondered if they had gone off together as was rumoured all those years ago, before Monsieur Lanier came on the scene.

'We're the best of friends,' she said with real warmth. 'In fact, you've narrowly missed him. He skipped off to avoid labouring in our vineyard is what I think.' She said Alexei had retired a year or two ago and that now he was about to visit Russia — things having loosened up politically, it was finally going to happen. 'I do hope he won't be disappointed, though I don't quite know what he's expecting, or whether he wants the Russians to be better or worse off than he imagines. It cuts both ways.'

'He remarried, then,' I said, thinking of Nicky.

'Oh yes, a delightful woman; her name is Sandrine. Very attractive, also very rich — the family make motor cars — I forget which ones.' She said the Golitsyns had a château in Picardie, near the coast, not too big and with the loveliest views. 'They've kept their flat on in Paris, we stay there sometimes, but they adore the country — always have. And there are three children: Nicky and two girls.'

'And the *principino*?'

'Twice married, rackets around, not putting his shoulder to any wheel. Rather a disappointment, I'm afraid.'

'Will something come of it, do you think?' Caroline and Nicky, I meant.

'Oh, I hope so,' said Olivia, with ready understanding. 'But parents can't push these things, you know. Mine made that mistake with Alexei. They so hoped that I'd marry him, and they made their wishes all too clear.' She smiled faintly. 'I went a long way towards trying to please them, though.'

A piece of the jigsaw had dislodged, pushing out neighbouring pieces, but though confused, I hurriedly put it aside. A man was walking towards us from the *chais*. He was small and lean, wiry is the best word, his dark straight hair, evidently thinning, still wet from the shower. He wore a silk cravat and a dark sports jacket with an insignia on it. Hands in pockets, a beak of a nose, sharp eyes like a bird; he gave us the liveliest smile.

'Ah, Jean, there you are,' Olivia called out cheerfully. 'Come and meet Kate.'

I waited, looking as friendly as possible, full of curiosity.

But it was not to be. 'Jean is our neighbour,' Olivia declared as he came up. 'He's been helping with the *vendange*.' She introduced me as a friend from college and the creator of a famous English garden.

'*Enchanté*,' Jean grinned and held out his hand. Then, turning to Olivia, he said, '*Alors, il y a un petit problème avec le tracteur.*'

'Speak English, Jean,' said Olivia gaily.

'*Le tracteur* is fallen down. It cannot bring to the *chais* the grapes. *C'est le carburateur.*'

'The what?'

'It mixes air and petrol, makes the combustion,' I said knowledgeably.

Jean, raising his eyebrows, gave an admiring grin before continuing. '*Malheureusement*, Philippe must go to St Emilion to get a part from Paul Mariet. He will not be for the lunch. Paul will give him something, but he is arriving in some time for the coffee.' He turned to me. 'He sends you his big regret, Madame. He is looking so to the pleasure of meeting you.'

'And I him,' I said. 'I've really been looking forward to it.'

Olivia smiled at that. 'I'm sure he'll be back in time. Now, come and have some champagne.'

'*Avec plaisir.*'

'So there you are!' a female voice called from the drawing-room door. An attractive middle-aged woman, arms folded, was leaning against the door-jamb, smiling sceptically.

'We're just coming,' called Olivia. '*Prenez une coupe de champagne, Françoise.*'

'*C'est ma femme,*' said Jean. 'She is arrived.'

'Does Philippe always oversee the *vendange* himself?' I asked Jean, speaking slowly and I hoped clearly as we went inside. I didn't trust my French.

'*Ah, oui, toujours. Le vignoble* it is his pride and joy.'

Françoise, despite her Gallic name, proved to be Irish. She had fluffy red-gold hair, marble skin and flecked hazel eyes. She too wore trousers and a pullover, but more in the interests of service than of chic. I took to her at once. She wrote books, I learned, and she wrote them in French.

'Novels,' said Olivia.

'Mysteries,' said Françoise.

'They're excellent, anyhow,' Olivia declared. 'But Françoise refuses to translate them into English, and she won't let anyone else.'

'Who wants to write the same book twice, or to have it rewritten by someone else?' said Françoise. 'I am French now. I don't care about English or American markets any more than the Chinese ones.'

She must be very well off in that case, I decided, watching as, evidently at home, she poured herself a drink and another one for her husband, Olivia having nipped off to remove a place setting from the table. I was surprised to find she had no help, but then it *was* Sunday *and* the grape-picking season.

'I've read about your wonderful garden,' said Françoise. 'Your famous arched walk of espaliered figs. I should love to see that. And

314

the ancient Buddha — a museum piece, I read.'

'Stolen by my husband's great-grandfather, I'm afraid. One day the Sri Lankans will demand it back.'

'Oh, Buddhas are happy anywhere,' said Françoise. 'It's all the same to them.'

'*Kate a une bonne connaissance des tracteurs,*' said Jean. 'Here is a woman who knows of some things useful. *A la vôtre.*' He raised his glass to me and we raised ours.

And then the thunderclap. You've been expecting it, I know — why I'm in such a state. But I didn't. I didn't know there'd be a story to tell. I wasn't on the lookout for dramatic plots, and certainly not for opportunities to dig up the past. I wanted to infill holes, not make them, to create a smooth and solid surface — a road to move along on.

'Hugo!' Jean called out, raising his glass again.

I became, I think, a pillar of salt, my body and brain rigid with shock; and yet I must have turned round. I don't know what happened, really: it's a blank. But suddenly there stood Hugo. We were face to face and thirty-five years had passed, and they were peeling away, removing my solid crust of insulation, my long-accumulated, stolidly collected layers of ballast and perspective.

315

Hugo put out his hand. If he was embarrassed it didn't show; but then, unlike me, he had been warned. No wonder Olivia had shown such hesitation in Bordeaux.

'Why, Hugo! This *is* a surprise,' I managed.

'It's wonderful to see you, Kate.' He looked directly into my eyes. He had always done that. No scrutiny or dismay but friendliness, kindliness even, mixed with a mild curiosity. 'I'm sorry I wasn't here to greet you,' he said. His dark curly hair was turning grey, his face more angular, more filled out, was very tanned. He was less lean, more muscular and more masculine. He even seemed taller. But above all, he was still strikingly, mesmerically handsome.

After greeting Françoise, he asked Olivia if she knew Philippe had gone to St Emilion.

Yes, Jean had told her, she said. 'I've removed his place, so we can eat whenever you're ready. You two must be starving,' she addressed the men.

'I am able to eat a hearse,' said Jean.

Pouring himself a glass of champagne, Hugo took the bottle round. 'How's old Arthur?' he asked, topping up my glass and again looking straight into my eyes. 'It's a great shame he couldn't come today.'

'Oh, he wanted to!' I said. 'He'll regret it even more when he hears you were here.'

'I liked him from the very moment we met. Such a cheerful man, a very kind one too.'

'And he liked you,' I said.

'For a fellow who loathed banking he's certainly made a go of it.' Hugo sipped his champagne, but his eyes never left my face. 'And you've created a famous garden, I hear. I always knew you'd do something really wonderful.'

It cast an extraordinary glow, that compliment from Hugo.

'I had a very great deal to learn,' I said. 'About everything.'

'*A table!*' Olivia's measured contralto sounded from next door. She was holding a large faience tureen. 'Come in, come in.'

French-fashion she placed herself on one side of the table, in the middle, putting me on her right and Jean on her left, with Hugo more or less opposite me, and Françoise beside him.

'Melon soup,' said Françoise. 'You do it so well, Olivia.'

'*Olivia est un chef sans pareil,*' said Jean, looking beadily about the table.

'Speak English, Jean,' said Françoise.

'Olivia is a cook without the same.'

'*Alors*, speak French.' Françoise eyed the ceiling in resignation.

Jean had turned to me. 'My English is a

little rustic,' he said apologetically.

'You can say that again,' declared his outspoken spouse. 'No, don't.'

A general lapse into French ensued, to do with melons. They were being overproduced, the farmers threatening to strike, claiming that prices were too low. Everyone had a view. I felt pleased at getting the gist, and Hugo, smiling across the table, kept me generously inside their animated little circle. He did seem glad to see me.

Placing serving dishes on the sideboard, Olivia asked us to help ourselves, and Hugo got up to pour the wine, taking the bottle round the table.

'*Château Carrielle, oui, mais quelle année?*' asked Jean, raising his eyebrows approvingly when he'd tried it.

Hugo told him.

'I am doubly glad you are here, Madame. We are all to the benefit,' said Jean.

But Olivia was quick to say that although their wine was good and they were proud of it, I mustn't expect a *premier cru*.

'How good of you to go to so much trouble,' I told her a little later, helping myself to *blanquette de veau*. 'Everything looks so delicious.'

'Poor Philippe,' said Jean. 'He is eating *confit* at the house of Paul Mariot. It is always the duck *chez lui.*'

'Philippe adores *confit*,' Olivia declared. 'He was raised on it.' *Confit*, I learned, was duck preserved and cooked in its own grease. Françoise said that duck was to southwest France what potatoes had been to Ireland.

'*C'est pas vrai*,' admonished her husband. 'Because for potatoes there is no pearl in the oyster, so to say: no *fois gras* — no money.'

'Nor much nourishment,' added Françoise. 'To the superiority of duck.' She raised her glass.

'*Quel canard.*'

Everyone laughed. I didn't get the joke but I laughed anyhow. The atmosphere was becoming festive. There was even a touch of excitement, of anticipation, a suggestion of 'occasion', and I think everyone felt it. Of course, they were near the end of the *vendange*, but the food and wine, the benevolent spirit of the place and our ebullient if silly antics and goodwill had cast a magical net. And transported into this bewitching world, I yearned to stay there.

'*Is* it in fact mysteries that you write?' I asked Françoise across the table, when Hugo had got up again to pour more wine.

'I like to think so.'

'In that case, surely you need a corpse,' said Olivia, setting a big salad bowl on the table.

'Or a dead letter at the very least,' suggested Hugo, filling Françoise's glass. 'Or perhaps a dig-up of the past. Now there's a corpse with real potential.' Again his eyes sought mine, but this time something in his expression suggested a deeper, subterranean meaning, an undercurrent beneath the bantering surface. The past was what we had in common, of course; but was it wise to try and dig it up? I decided it was not.

'Pure Lazarus!' Françoise declared affectionately of the past. 'But I don't need a corpse, thank you, Hugo dear. And murder mysteries aren't the only mysteries, you know. There are lots of kinds. The medieval passion plays were mysteries too, remember?'

'From the Latin, *ministerium*, meaning a craft. The plays were staged by craft guilds,' said Hugo. His eyes never left my face. 'Our word 'mystery' comes from the Greek, *musterion*. To shut the eyes or mouth. In other words, a secret, as the divine mysteries always were.'

'You take my breath away,' said Françoise tolerantly. 'Well, mystery as I mean it involves the unknown. I write about the unknown,' she declared, giving Hugo a pert reproving nod.

'Then your scope is unlimited,' he teased. 'Given that definition, every life is a mystery, since its outcome is always unknown. Mind you, a corpse at the end of the story instead of the beginning makes for a pleasant change.'

Hugo and Olivia's eyes twinkled without meeting. If distanced in other ways, they still had their old telegraphic system in place, I noted.

'Every life *is* a mystery, as you say,' Françoise went on unperturbed. 'The secrets people hide, willingly or unwillingly, from themselves, from others. That sort of thing interests a novelist.'

'In your novels is the mystery always solved?' I asked, breaking the little silence that followed.

'It isn't, alas, always solvable.' She said there was the unknowable to deal with too. 'But what interests me right now is the mystery of nature's intentions. If Hugo will admit that particular use of 'mystery'?'

'Certainly, Françoise, but nature's intentions aren't remotely mysterious. Intentional or not, it's reproduction, which, as a matter of fact, is exactly what the ancient mysteries were about. Remember Demeter losing her daughter Persephone to Pluto in the underworld, and Persephone returning for six months every year to visit her mother? It's a story of fertility and regeneration. Agrarian

321

societies were dependent on it.'

'Like Isis and Osiris,' I murmured vaguely.

'Like Isis and Osiris!' Hugo gave me a rewarding smile.

'But if we know nature's intentions,' said Olivia, 'shouldn't we obey them and live in accordance with, forgive the pun, *our* natures?'

'*Mais oui*, and reproduce!' Jean was helping himself to salad. 'It is the object of every man's life. We think of nothing else.'

'Certainly not the results,' Françoise drily observed. She said they'd raised four children, and who'd looked after them?

Jean claimed they had looked after themselves; they weren't stupid. Increasingly, he reminded me of a lively terrier, running about, sniffing and wagging his tail. It was very endearing.

A superb cheese board appeared, followed by a *tarte tatin* that Olivia had made herself, when the French normally resort to pastry shops. The tart was accompanied by a honey-sweet wine. I don't remember what. I was by this time floating about cherubically on a cloud. I'd drunk a good deal, I admit, but more to the point some long-buried part of me was stirring, awakening from prolonged somnambulism, becoming alert, vibrantly alive. It wasn't of course merely the atmosphere. Hugo's presence, his sweet attentiveness and familiar boyish manner beneath the older more substantial Hugo, were powerfully catalytic; the touch of his hand, his eyes always upon me, were proving to be life-giving. I felt so happy — amazed such bliss was possible; for I had long forgotten.

★ ★ ★

'Everything is so green and prosperous,' I told Olivia as we moved into the drawing room for coffee. 'There's such happiness and wellbeing here, and it's infectious too.'

'I'm very lucky,' she answered simply. 'I've found my niche; and not everyone does, I think.'

Well, I too had found mine and yet I didn't want this enchanted interlude to end, these reborn feelings to shrivel and disappear. At the prospect, a cold fear swept over me and rolled on; for once you are prey to any emotion, they can all tumble in at will.

But Olivia's niche intrigued. At first I'd likened it to the contrived rusticity of the Petit Trianon, sure that a Versailles existed somewhere else. Yet this really was her home, it seemed, her life lived almost entirely here. Its comparative modesty was a conundrum.

Even their wine, though very good, wasn't tiptop; and in Paris they stayed at Alexei's apartment, so a Parisian address was out. Maybe Philippe was too proud to spend her money, or he was a communist or something. But whatever lay behind it, Olivia's existence suited her. She obviously revelled in country life and she was busy and happy, beautifully integrated into her surroundings — *bien dans sa peau*, good in her skin, as the French say. A sort of Demeter, I suddenly decided: a golden-haired corn goddess, the product of earth not sky. I had been gazing in the wrong direction. Yet I still thought of goddesses where she was concerned, I noted, bemused, convinced, however, it was nonetheless a trenchant observation. That sad and cosmopolitan girl, unknowable and remote, had moulted into a replete and sensual being; and it permeated every aspect of life at Château Carrielle, where existence was so closely linked to nature and the senses. Olivia's air of mystery was gone; she was at last herself, leading what Hugo had once called a truthful life. I saw he had been right.

Placing a tray on a stool beside the fireplace, Olivia sat down to pour the coffee, and Jean and Françoise settled opposite, locked in the apparently perpetual squabbles that comprised their billing and cooing.

Catching my eye, Hugo nodded imperceptibly towards a little sofa across the room, and I felt like a young girl being paid singular attention at a dance. At some deep level I remained bound to this man; I'd only ever been in love with him. Had I married later it might have been different — there would have been interim attachments, a spreading out of affections that, in diluting, balanced, even stabilized, strong feelings. What was emerging now, so concentrated and compacted, so perfectly preserved, emanated from that part of the mind, ancient and primitive, where the deepest feelings lay: sleeping dragons, vigorous and breathing fire when aroused, yet capable too of an unbounded docility.

Hugo's unceasing attentions made me wonder if he perhaps felt something similar. Could two paths possibly re-converge, renew common ground, and then go on from there? Nothing was impossible.

'Tell me about your garden,' he said, lighting a cigarette, drawing our talk into a quiet duet. Again his eyes suggested something more personal.

'Well, it's large and green; it's a bit like running a hospital,' I said. 'When one plant is cured of a disease, another comes down with something. But I love it. You must come and see it if you're ever in England.'

'I should like that,' he answered, without saying he ever did come to England. I was as much in the dark as ever. And despite my wish to hold on tightly to the present, curiosity had begun to wriggle like an irrepressible worm.

'Have you never lived in America in all these years?' I asked, convinced a more direct question would betray excessive interest.

'I never have. Do you think that's a mistake? I know Alexei does.'

'Alexei had a thing about exile,' I said. 'But then so had you.'

I was rewarded by another of his peculiarly direct looks. 'I was wrong,' he said evenly. 'And so was Alexei, I think. It's my belief he'll feel like an exile in Russia. We even have a bet on it.'

Had my future then been sacrificed to callow misconceptions — smothered under a counterpane of ignorant and fleeting childish passions? I couldn't honestly claim so. Hugo had never been in love with me; I'd known that in my bones. I hadn't believed that I *was* lovable; I'd only prayed I would become so. But Hugo had *wanted* to be in love with me, just as I had wanted to be in love with Billy, and, for that matter, Olivia with Alexei. Timing was everything, perhaps. But what was that? A random event or mad coincidence, or was it something deeply complex and unknowable but labelled 'fate' to suggest arcane control — a force capable, therefore, of manipulation, even appeasement, of hearing prayers and building up minute shards of hope?

'You and Alexei are friends now,' I said casually, keeping to surface talk, yet trying obliquely too for information, edging precipitously towards the past. 'You weren't always so.'

For the first time Hugo looked a little uncomfortable. 'My fault, puppy that I was, and Alexei rightly let me know it.' Gazing at that Egyptian relief, he suddenly frowned. 'I was wrong about a lot of things,' he said.

Hope rocketed. At the very least he must feel guilty. How could he not? He had broken my heart. And guilt was preferable to having no feeling for me at all. Guilt could be adapted, developed into something softer and, receiving the balm of true forgiveness, melt gradually, gratefully into love. Such things happened.

'Have you kept up your connection with Egypt?' I asked, aware we were within earshot of the others.

Hugo said he had revived it. Egypt was a fascinating country, but it had been no place to raise a family.

So he had a family. I didn't mind, not really; it was to be expected. Everyone had ties. What mattered was this precious interlude, a miraculous windfall of good fortune, like showers of diamonds falling from a cloudy sky. The present was everything, or it seemed to be.

Taking a coffee cup from Olivia, Hugo handed it to me, and as our fingers touched, intense physical desire surged up, overwhelming and eclipsing everything. I felt too weak even to hold the cup. It was fantastic! And something in Hugo's own manner, tense and suddenly alert, suggested he felt it too. An electrical connection, unfinished business: bridges were being thrown up, roadworks undertaken, a new thoroughfare created; you name it. But we kept to surface talk.

'You were right about the dangers of politics,' he said. 'I was persona non grata in Egypt. I went to the Sudan.'

The actual words had ceased to matter. Wisps of the past were floating in, poignant and bittersweet, a soothing and all-enveloping mist. Hugo's arm lying along the sofa back brought to mind that open carriage in Rome where it all began, for me anyhow, when, at an unconscious level, the possibility of a relationship had for the first time opened up.

After Egypt, nothing of any felt significance had happened to me, or I couldn't at that moment remember any. I had been killing time. Now, suddenly, intoxicating possibilities were budding, sap was rising, fresh green tendrils graspingly put forth. Hugo, I love you; I've always loved you, I wanted to say. Please, oh please, love me. Perhaps he was divorced.

Like a miraculously answered prayer, Hugo leaned towards me and, almost in a whisper, but with firmness, said, 'Why not stay over for a bit? I'll be in Bordeaux myself on Wednesday, so perhaps we could meet there. It would be a shame to lose you again now, after so long.' He had said something similar to me once in Rome: how it was wrong to leave our relationship undeveloped — something like that.

'Yes, it *would* be a shame,' I managed softly, my heart pounding, trying to keep my voice calm. I could easily arrange to stay over a day or two in Bordeaux. I could say there was a garden I wanted to see, one that the Laniers had spoken highly of: I'd mention a special feature — bamboo, water lilies, maybe. I was about to say that *probably* I could manage it, when to my discomfiture we were interrupted. Standing in the doorway, jeans-clad, laughing, and entwined like a pair of rampant vines, Caroline and Nicky gazed down on us as at another, not very enviable, world.

Nicky, easily as tall as his father, probably resembled in other respects his mother: his hair was dark, his eyes too, and without his father's wolfish Asiatic slant. I couldn't see his hands.

'What a nice idea,' I managed in a whisper to Hugo, wreathing it in a dreamy meaningful smile.

'Hello, children,' Olivia told them. 'You're back early. I thought you were meeting friends after lunch. There's some coffee,' she added pleasantly.

'Come in and give us a kiss,' Françoise declared.

Introductions began. Caroline, greeting me again, was distant and aloof. I could see she still regarded me with suspicion. That batty old lady, she was probably thinking.

'I knew your father,' I told Nicky. 'I hear he's off to Russia.'

Hugo's arm was touching my neck, causing exquisite shivers. His eyes stayed on me as I spoke; he never once looked away.

'Mama says he's in for a big surprise, that he's a Frenchman now,' laughed Nicky. His English was excellent, despite the strong French accent.

Plans for a Bordeaux rendezvous were flitting seductively through my head: a restaurant in a quiet courtyard or intimate little square, a pretty hotel room with a balcony overlooking the estuary. One thing was certain: Hugo was everything I had ever wanted, and I wasn't about to miss this extraordinary, never-to-be-repeated chance. It was as simple as that. And whether a mere encounter or a full-blown affair resulted, I was determined to see it through. My mind was made up. Moreover, should it go seriously forward, Arthur might have to let me go. But Arthur, I was now convinced, had interests of his own in London, and he wasn't possessive; he would understand. Arthur was a gentleman and my best friend.

'Did you have a nice picnic, children?' Françoise asked mischievously. 'There's a vine leaf in your hair, Nicky dear.'

Nicky blushed as Caroline, on tiptoes, removed a blade of grass.

Had Hugo and I been of their generation, our own lives might have gone very differently. Yet how miraculous to receive another chance! How profoundly blessed in fact we were!

'I'm writing a piece on recent excavations at Saqqara,' Hugo said, drawing the talk back between ourselves.

331

'Oh, the step pyramid . . . ' Images floated up: billowing mounted figures, heavy curtains of sand, and ruins I'd never actually seen; and lying nearby . . . I chose to focus on Caroline instead, a typical teenager, arguing with her mother. They had to meet their friends, she was saying; they didn't want any coffee. 'Your car is almost out of gas, and everything's closed,' she moaned.

'I'll be in Bordeaux Wednesday morning,' said Hugo softly. 'My plane leaves the next day.'

As I leaned forward, anxious to discover our meeting place, Caroline called out plaintively from across the room. 'Can we take your car, Daddy? We have to be somewhere, and we're already late.'

Full of curiosity, I turned towards the entrance hall, eager for a glimpse at last of Philippe Lanier and longing to complete this remarkable portrait of idyllic family life. But there was no-one there, or I couldn't see anyone and it seemed rude to crane, especially since the others took no notice whatsoever. Nicky was busy shaking hands all round and Olivia was mopping up spilled coffee on the silver tray. Only Caroline, looking very determined, headed for the entrance hall.

'Do give your father my very best,' I told

Nicky as we shook hands. Had I said that when he came in? I couldn't remember. Clouds of confusion were settling in, beginning to blanket my mind in heavy fog.

'I will indeed,' Nicky promised, letting go of my hand. 'You and the Laniers were in Egypt with Papa, weren't you, back in the 1950s?' His arm was looped again over Caroline's shoulder. 'They're always talking about it.'

'Not Philippe . . . ' I began, but Hugo interrupted, telling Caroline to take a box of grape-cutting scissors out of his car; they would be needed that afternoon. 'Best to do it right now,' he added.

'OK.' She turned to me first, however, continuing her thread. 'Egypt was a seminal trip, or so Mother's always said.' She eyed me icily.

But Philippe wasn't there, I still wanted to say, suddenly anxious to put things straight, clear up a silly misunderstanding.

But Caroline, holding up car keys taken from the hall table, and evidently intent on keeping centre stage, gave them a raucous jingle. '*Merci, Papa!*'

'Ah,' or 'oh' was what I managed instead, a sort of proto-language.

Françoise, responding to the jingling keys as to a bell, had stood up. She said they also must be going. 'Oh, and look, here comes Philippe at last,' she announced, looking towards the open window. A car had stopped outside. 'That must have been a very good lunch, *confit* or no.'

Hugo glanced hurriedly at his watch. 'I must go and give him a hand,' he said, rising and turning to me. 'It shouldn't take long; I'll be back before you go, Kate.' This time his gaze was opaque; I couldn't read anything in it. Everyone had stood up, and we were moving in a body towards the front door and out onto the terrace. In the driveway, a burly white-haired man waved from his car window, calling to Hugo in French that he had the new part.

Goodbyes were being said.

'A lady for all seizures,' Jean obliged, and Françoise said again how she hoped to see my garden one day; she was going to get my address from Olivia — she sometimes came to England. God knows what I said. My mind churned frantically and yet it was strangely empty, like a washing machine without any wash inside. If things were what they had begun to seem, if such a thing was remotely possible and what I had overheard, or thought I had, was true — well, it was unbelievable, because, if true, not only was it unheard of, but what had Hugo meant, and why on earth did Olivia invite me? There was nothing to gain and a very great deal to lose! It struck me there might be latent triumph in it on Olivia's part — that she'd malevolently set the whole thing up in order to humiliate me and rub it in — show me she still had him; he was hers; he always had been hers. And suddenly I dreaded above everything being left alone in her company. The woman was a positive devil, the situation hellish. But to leave now would look censorious, lacking in polish and sophistication, blatantly defeatist. I couldn't think what to do. The compass needle had swung too fast, cleaving like a great sword everything in its path, leaving a cerebral blank.

Yet Olivia's extraordinary calm persisted. Standing beside me on the terrace, she waved goodbye to her guests, smiling serenely, as if the most ordinary and pleasant afternoon had passed. Was it intended then that I should stumble on this extraordinary situation? Or else, having discovered a carefully guarded secret, would they hate me for it? Either way, I was angry they were so trusting. But why on earth had they done it?

'Shall we sit outside?' Olivia was saying cheerfully. Her equanimity was extraordinary. 'The clouds are gone.'

The sky, I vaguely noted, was an azure

shell; it was even quite hot. I nodded idiotically. I would have given anything for a very big whisky. It wasn't only the shock of my discovery; I was acutely embarrassed, and it was multi-faceted: on the one hand, like opening the wrong door at a tea party and seeing a horde of skeletons tumble onto the drawing-room floor — but worse, I'd been a ridiculous, absurdly assuming fool and I was so *ashamed* of myself! Hugo must have seen how wild about him I still was. How could he not? And he'd been trying once again to let me down gently. Those mysterious looks weren't remotely signs of attraction or rapport, but attempts to cover up his own deep embarrassment. What an idiot I was! What a stupid fool! And then, kept at bay till that moment, the loss of Hugo descended, the unavoidable fact of it, permanent and irretrievable, a gaping abyss cracking noisily open. Oh, oh, oh!

22

Olivia and I sat down under the canopy of limes, facing the house. The contrast was extraordinary: this serene and blissful setting masked so exquisitely its grotesque reality. Describing it now belies to a degree what I felt then, since in the past two days I've managed to scrape together some perspective. Yet even then, although I ached with such fierce disappointment and regret, my feelings were insulated by shock and, I confess, a rising and doubtless prurient curiosity. As we sat down, however, my foremost thought was what a fool I'd been. But far too proud to show it, I determined to appear every bit as calm and matter-of-fact as Olivia, who, on the face of it, was the one who ought to be upset, not me.

Olivia said she hoped the tractor part would fit; they badly needed to get the harvest in — some heavy showers were coming. Philippe was a wonderful manager though, always so calm and efficient; he was almost one of the family.

Good God, I thought, as she pulled a pack of cigarettes from her pocket; she's going to pretend that nothing's happened!

I hadn't smoked in years, but offered one I took it quick enough. Glad to get it! And when she offered me a light, I focused on the flame like a demented moth. At last there was somewhere to look.

'I hope all this isn't too great a surprise,' Olivia said quietly, pocketing the cigarette lighter and staring vaguely at some little yellow flowers in the grass. 'Probably you suspected?'

'I'd no idea! None at all.' It sounded absurdly defensive.

'I thought from the dean's letter that time that you did,' she brought out casually.

'Such a thing never entered my head. It was Miss Grist who leapt to those conclusions, and based on nothing,' I exclaimed, wondering for the first time if it *was* nothing. But why was I the one apologizing? 'That isn't what caused the trouble,' I tartly reminded her. 'It was your staying on in Egypt without permission. That's why you were expelled.'

'Yes, it *was* dishonourable of me,' she said, with just the faintest touch of irony.

'Well, yes, it was. And you know what Sweet Briar was like.' Now I was shopping the honour system. I hurriedly shifted tack. 'In fact, I thought you'd gone off with Alexei.

Pookie Payne said so — I mean her description fitted Alexei.'

'Mother had to put *something* about, I guess.' Inhaling her cigarette, Olivia almost looked at me straight. She said her parents had begun to worry about Hugo and herself the year before, fearing they were too close, too tied together. So when Hugo had returned to Paris after the Cairo riots, they'd packed her smartly off to Sweet Briar. There wasn't a thing that she could do about it.

'We knew you were there under duress,' I said. 'It got around, the way things do. But then they let you go to Europe that summer. I couldn't figure that out.'

'Oh, because of Alexei,' she answered, offhand. 'They were so hoping I would marry him. And Hugo was back in Egypt by then, and would, they wrongly assumed, stay there.'

'I knew deep down that Hugo didn't love me,' I said, adding accusingly, 'but he shouldn't have pretended that he did.'

'Oh, please don't think that, Kate! He wasn't *pretending*. He isn't calculating, not about things like that. But, oh dear, we were all so young and inexperienced.' She looked genuinely pained — really anxious to put things to right. 'Hugo and I had agreed to disentangle.' She said it was one of the reasons he had gone to work in Egypt. 'We'd made a pact to let go, to unbind and make some new, you might even say appropriate, connections. We wanted to be like other people — you do at that age — and it was working.' She said Alexei was such a fine person and that things were going ahead; they were making definite plans. 'Then suddenly there you were: so attractive and intelligent, so eager for Europe, unlike any other American we had met. Hugo was enchanted.' Olivia paused again. 'I thought I'd be so pleased at his caring for someone. I even encouraged it at first. But when it seemed to be working, I was beside myself. I hated you — you must have noticed it. I was so hideously eaten up by jealousy.' Suddenly she looked directly at me. 'That was when I knew, really knew, Hugo and I were inseparable, that I was deeply in love with him and that I couldn't let him go, no matter what. So I tried everything I could think of to make him jealous, and to discredit you. Oh, I was dreadful: underhand, malicious, untruthful. But I was desperate and I couldn't stop.'

Hearing that Olivia had been jealous of me was, I admit, pure joy. It hadn't been social inferiority after all. She'd actually *envied* me! Suddenly I felt better.

'There was a row in Luxor,' Olivia continued.

340

'Yes, I heard you,' I said drily.

'I was trying to make him give you up — convince him that it wouldn't work — and then — I couldn't help it, it seemed the only way — I was so desperate that, despite our pact, I brazenly seduced him.'

Badly jolted, I managed a smile of evident nonchalance. Poor Hugo, I thought bitterly: leaving Olivia's room after one seduction to encounter me lurking outside, attempting another. But once again Olivia had beat me to it. My little tragedy was turning darkly comic.

'I'd told myself,' Olivia went on, 'that people can come to love each other — which they do — so being in love wasn't really very important. It mainly meant that you were tied beyond your control, for better or worse; that you had a fifty-fifty chance. But unlike other people, Hugo and I wouldn't be taking a chance, because we knew exactly what we were getting. There wouldn't be any nasty surprises of personality and character to discover later on.' Olivia raised both hands in a fluttering, helpless gesture. 'The trouble, the *real* trouble, was I desperately wanted children.'

She said that if they hadn't been brought up in Egypt, if ancient Egypt hadn't captured their imaginations, none of it might have happened. But by the time they were ten years old they already planned to marry. The pharaohs had, so why shouldn't they? Of course they'd no idea what that entailed, but if they had, it would still have seemed to them perfectly natural. Her hands were folded in her lap — a familiar gesture. 'I'm sorry, Kate. The odds were against you from the start. But for what it's worth, I've partly you to thank, because you brought things to a head. If you hadn't come along I might have married Alexei, and pleasant though that would have been, the depths and heights of life would have been missed.'

It was my turn to feel envious and deprived.

Olivia said her parents had tried everything to stop them and, not surprisingly, they'd been disinherited. You couldn't blame them, though. 'Mother could hardly say, 'The twins are getting married,'' said Olivia, smiling faintly. Luckily, they had small trust funds by then, and that had helped. 'We were married in Bordeaux as Monsieur and Madame Hugo Lanier, twenty-one years ago last month.'

'And no-one here knows?' I asked, surprised.

Olivia said Françoise, with her nose for mysteries, probably suspected something; that Sandrine and Alexei knew, and, answering my look, no, Caroline didn't. Nicky was in the dark as well.

'Surely that could be dangerous,' I suggested.

But Olivia brushed it off. 'If they should marry? Well, if Alexei's past is anything to go by, there'll be a surfeit of dominant Russian genes.' She said the danger had been in having Caroline, not the children Caroline herself might have. Olivia said what was proving awkward was that the Hartfields had left a trust for Caroline and the income began when she was twenty-one. They hadn't yet decided what to tell her, but she'd be very comfortably off. 'Too comfortable in my view,' said Olivia. And suddenly she smiled, one of her rare brilliant smiles of dazzling radiance. 'I was so happy to have her! So relieved when everything was OK, because no matter what Hugo claimed about those Egyptian dynasties, I was terrified. I couldn't bring myself to risk it a second time. I became superstitious: once blessed was enough. And I am blessed,' she said warmly, looking with pleasure across the lawn towards that charming, sun-bathed house.

'So, here we are, peas in a pod I imagine Mendel would have given a *te deum* to see. And we couldn't be happier.'

That was evident, I said.

'I've often thought of you,' she went on. 'I felt so dreadful about what happened, because you got trapped in our vacillations, and when you told me about that boy back home, I feared we'd upset a sizeable apple cart.'

Billy had married Mary-Moore Montague, I told her, and things couldn't have worked out better — for everyone. Especially myself, I added, in a deserved tribute to Arthur. 'More propinquity,' I smiled urbanely. So there!

'I'm so glad — so truly glad,' she said with feeling. 'I would have felt so guilty if it hadn't.'

I couldn't see why, I said.

Olivia paused, she even unfolded her hands. 'I knew Arthur had to marry money, or he thought he did,' she said. 'But I knew too that you would be wonderful for him. You could sort out Brydonne Park, resolve his contradictions, as you call them, and make him happy — and yourself into the bargain. Besides, you deserved a larger stage. So . . . ' she cast me a sideways glance. 'I told him you were very rich, that your family owned thousands of acres in Kansas. I've no idea how big Kansas is, but I gave you a very big chunk.' Olivia actually blushed. 'That, of course, was all the push he needed.'

The anguish and humiliation resulting from that untruth rolled painfully over me — the shame and inferiority I'd felt; my guilt at having, even inadvertently, misled the Brydonnes, who doubtless believed I'd tricked poor Arthur into marrying me.

'Then you made my marriage,' I said simply.

'You could say that we made each other's.'

It was a strange acknowledgement: the knife-edge of irony sheathed in what could only be reciprocal gratitude.

And Olivia was quick to set a happy seal. 'So everything has come out for the best.'

I wasn't going to let her off the hook so easily though. Why should I? 'Except for Polly,' I said solemnly.

'Oh, yes, that was dreadful, dreadful!' she cried, genuinely pained.

'She was very fond of you, you know.'

'Yes,' Olivia said again, but this time more slowly. 'If only I had realized earlier. I would have been better prepared — more careful.'

'Well, it's a long time ago now; over thirty years.'

I was regretting having brought it up; I had sorrows enough on my plate. But, surprisingly, Olivia didn't let go. Surely Polly must have said something in hospital about the accident. She had often wondered. 'I never saw her again, you know — after it happened.'

Polly hadn't said much; she was very confused, I told her. But then, unable to forgo a knife-sharp opportunity, I added perversely, 'She said you'd kissed her.'

Olivia looked surprised.

'Oh, I knew you hadn't,' I hastily tacked on. 'There was a big sandstorm going on. Polly was concussed.'

'But she didn't mean *then*; she meant at Luxor, when we were together in that hut, and I was so upset. She was so sweet, so concerned for me, and so sad, too — such a sad little person — and enormously sympathetic. I was deeply touched. I gave her a hug and kissed her on the cheek; I was so grateful to her.' Olivia paused. 'And then, she kissed me back — on the mouth. Only a peck, though, very shy. Still, after that I should have been more careful.'

For the first time that day Olivia looked uncomfortable. 'I may as well tell you the truth,' she said, pulling her cigarettes out again; but when I refused, she changed her mind and put them back.

A singular thought occurred to me. For so reserved a person, once Olivia began to talk, which was rare enough, she was unusually forthcoming. In our Cairo conversation after

346

Polly's death, and her confession to Polly at Luxor, she had revealed quite a lot. In fact, when one thought about it, Olivia possessed a remarkable gift for intimacy.

But now she hesitated, her gaze fixed on some private inner vision where, evidently, a careful screening was under way. Then very quietly, without any expression but gazing straight at me, she said, 'The truth is, Polly saw us in those ruins.'

'Saw you? Whatever do you mean?'

'She came looking for us. In that sandstorm, remember?'

'You mean . . . ?' I didn't know how to go on, but in any case, Olivia's gist was pretty clear.

'We were sheltered in this alcove — the collapsed stones made a sort of niche — and we could hear her calling.' Olivia pulled the pack of cigarettes out again, and this time, with careful concentration, lit one and inhaled it deeply before proceeding any further. 'Being in that storm alone was dangerous. Polly must have known that, and yet she still came looking for us. It was tremendously brave.' Another deep narcotic draw. Olivia's voice fell almost to a whisper. 'Yet we paid no attention whatsoever.'

A long silence followed that I was not inclined to break. I simply waited.

347

'Suddenly I heard this high-pitched little cry,' Olivia said. 'It sounded exactly like a bird whose nest has been destroyed. I looked up and Polly was standing there — only a silhouette, because of all the sand — but standing there, holding her horse by the reins, and — well, just *standing* there. But near. Oh, very near!' Olivia's interlocking fingers were squeezed tight. 'We should have answered her calls. And we should have been more careful!'

Polly's words in hospital were zooming in a glaring neon rubric through my head. '*Go away. Go away now ... Go away from Hugo ... Hugo doesn't love you.*' Polly wasn't in the least confused; rather it had been a conscious warning, full of concern and wishing to protect me from the truth, unable to tell it me outright. '*We're lousy detectives, Kate.*'

'That's not all,' Olivia said tersely, a moment later. 'You may as well know everything. In fact, I want you to.' She jettisoned the unfinished cigarette, crushing it on the lawn with a surprising intensity. 'You see, Hugo went after her.' Olivia sounded almost apologetic. 'He had to. He was desperate to put things right, to calm her and give her some sort of explanation. Well, you can imagine; because if it came out, the scandal would have been appalling — everyone's life devastated.'

She was right about that. Even then the thought gripped me with icy fingers.

Olivia said that sand was bucketing down, blowing horizontally, the wind was so fierce; and yet Hugo managed somehow to find Polly. She had just remounted. Hugo called out at the top of his voice, but the wind was against him, and Polly couldn't hear. She turned her horse around and, anxious to stop her, Hugo rushed forward and tried to grab the reins. But lunging so quickly like that had frightened Polly's horse: it reared up or shied, and then it bolted.

A sad and elegiac gravity entered Olivia's voice. 'Polly seems to have hung on for nearly half a mile.'

'*Sandman!*' Polly had cried, as at a monstrous apparition. Which is exactly what Hugo must have seemed. Very likely she was trying to get away from him. She would have been so shocked by what she'd stumbled on — especially feeling about Olivia as she did. And Hugo rushing at her like that, given what she knew, could have made her believe she was in serious danger. She could have panicked and lost control of her horse. I shuddered openly, thinking of the terror and bewilderment she must have felt; but I had no desire to bring any of this up. What, after all this time, would be the point? Vindictiveness? Rubbing in salt?

'Still, in the end it was an accident,' I murmured gently.

'Yes, it *was* an accident,' Olivia quickly agreed. 'But we contributed to it; we helped it along. Hugo has always felt responsible.' Again Olivia's eyes met mine. 'I won't tell him I've told you, if you don't mind.'

'Olivia, why on earth did you invite me here?' I suddenly cried out. 'Was it because of that . . . ?'

At first, Olivia looked surprised. She said that if I'd run into her in London, I would have invited her; it was only natural. 'Well, I admit it's more complex than that,' she added a moment later. 'But Hugo and I live like other people do. We're not ashamed of our situation — not at all. No-one has been harmed by it — Caroline is fine — in fact, a lot of happiness has been created.' But in her eager defence of their position, a desperate note had sounded, and Olivia's lips had tightened in the suppression of feeling.

'Something I never anticipated,' she continued after a moment and in a surprisingly collected voice, 'something I never imagined possible, is what a heavy burden secrets are:

how they prey on you, weigh you down and cut you off from others. But worst of all, they cause such guilt — undeserved guilt, too. Because even when you know rationally, beyond any doubt, that you are innocent and not to blame, that no-one has been hurt, only made happier, still the guilt seeps in.' Olivia's hands fluttered up like disturbed birds. 'The truth is, and it's been a hard thing to accept — a very hard thing, bordering on tragedy — but the fact is, no-one can escape the times they live in. It isn't possible. Society is such a powerful thing — the collective will! You've only to go against it, and my God you're made to feel its wrath! Hugo and I have paid a big price — in compensation or in appeasement, if you will: the loss of our identity, of our past, the loss of our inheritance. And yet it hasn't been enough. Nothing is ever enough. Guilt stalks society's boundaries like a despotic policeman: keeping you firmly within the fold or else reminding you that you're a pariah, feeding on the edges by grace and favour, and you had better watch out!'

Olivia said gay men must have felt something of this before the law was changed; and perhaps a few still did. 'I'm not complaining,' she added calmly, seeing the dismay on my face. 'It's been worth it — oh, well worth it! And that must be so for others too.

'I asked you here for all those reasons, I suppose,' she said gently, returning to my question. 'Also, you're part of our past — and that means something, or it can. Hugo was against it at first, but I told him how friendly you'd been when we met. And then there's this *connection*, this link, because you know who we really are.'

Olivia shook her head in mild amazement. 'I can't tell you how wonderful it is to be sitting here with someone who knows everything, someone with whom it's possible to feel completely at ease. The difference that makes!' She said Alexei and Sandrine had been superb; that their friendship was invaluable.

'I thought the truth might come out today, or it might not,' she went on. 'I told myself it didn't much matter which, but I'm very glad it has come out, and perhaps, after so long, we can be friends again, and you and Arthur will come for a visit sometime? We would both like that so much.'

'Thank you, Olivia,' I said, sadly aware she'd left my feelings for Hugo out of her equation. That was the fly in the ointment. 'Thank you for telling me all this.'

'I hope you'll stay to tea.'

'What?'

'I said, I hope you'll stay to tea,' Olivia repeated. 'Philippe's longing to meet you. He's heard so much about you.'

The socially self-possessed Olivia had slotted back smoothly into place with unnerving alacrity. Then I noticed she was looking past me, and, turning, I saw Hugo and Philippe coming towards us across the lawn.

I had been utterly swept up in Olivia's story: touched, dismayed, yet feeling admiration and compassion. But now I woke up fast. The prospect of facing Hugo filled me with undiluted horror, and my embarrassment and humiliation were mercilessly elbowing forward. I had always blamed Olivia for what happened, yet clearly this had been unjust: Hugo was at least as much to blame. As things looked now, maybe he was to blame for everything. It was childish of me, and no doubt self-defensive, but suddenly I almost hated him.

Hugo glanced quickly towards Olivia, then at me — an examining awareness — before cheerfully introducing Philippe, who, speaking no English, heartily shook my hand midst an enthusiastic litany of *bonsoirs* and *enchantés*. But my departure noises were well under way. I pleaded the hour, Sunday drivers, and Arthur's return that evening (which wasn't true). I expect it sounded wooden and unnatural, and, on Olivia's account, I regretted that. I would have liked to meet her halfway. But already I was retreating inside myself, beginning to rock my shocked and wounded heart, my trampled pride and, yes, my badly deflated ego that, earlier on, had ballooned so foolishly. But above all, I yearned for some solitude in which to think things carefully through, and find my way out of this labyrinth of confusing turns and blind misleading alleys.

'You have our address,' Olivia was saying. 'Do let's stay in touch.'

I would send mine when I wrote to her, I promised.

Hugo insisted on walking me to the car, and there was nothing I could do about it.

'I expect you've forgotten about what happened all those years ago, Kate,' he said, as we marched side by side across the lawn. 'Your life has moved on at a great pace. But I want to apologize. I was a callow and confused young man, and I behaved very badly.'

To my mind, it was the worst thing that he could have said.

'We were very young,' I answered. 'It was a teapot tempest, nothing more.'

'Thank you for that,' he said. 'I didn't

behave very well, though. I didn't *know* myself very well — only that it was important to do so. And then, you see, I thought I'd lost her, and I nearly did.' He'd thrust his hands in his pockets, his head bent. 'If you and Arthur *are* able to join me for dinner on Wednesday, it would be a very great pleasure.'

Unfortunately, we had to go home, I said. Arthur had his report to write and my garden needed constant attention. I was its abject slave. Of course, Hugo's invitation had always included Arthur, but my own ridiculous and self-indulgent fantasy had removed him.

Standing beside the car, Hugo and I shook hands, as kissing, even Hugo sensed, thank God, would in the circumstances have been a travesty.

'It's been a lovely afternoon, thank you so much,' I said.

'Give my best to Arthur,' Hugo answered, 'and do let's keep in touch. You're looking wonderful, by the way.'

As I drove down the driveway, I could see the pair of them in the rear-view mirror, standing before that delightful house, his arm around her. They were smiling and waving, the afternoon sunlight casting a dappled light over everything. What an extraordinary photograph they made: the ideal *House and Garden* couple.

23

How I wish that you, privy to this frantically delivered tale, could speak, because, frankly, an impartial view would help no end, especially now everything's been assembled, you could even say like so much dirty linen, washed, sorted, and hanging in good order on a line, ready for critical examination. Two days ago my mind still spun in a whirligig of conflicting thoughts and feelings. I felt ill, seasick; I'd had a pretty choppy voyage, so much to think about and react to, buffeted by such unaccustomed feelings. And then, that encysted disease breaking out, causing a brain-inflaming fever. But I've sat here long enough, my feelings veering riotously, trying to divide the unreal from the real. Now, at last, I'm prepared to take a good hard look and resolve once and for all this extraordinary and unfortunate business.

One thing is certain. Whatever my personal feelings for Hugo or Olivia — and they are complex — I'm no longer shocked by their being married — the *fact* of it, I mean. Most certainly they have flouted a big taboo, one protecting the fabric and good health of society, and rightly against the law. Yet I don't find their particular attachment dreadful or even dangerous. As Olivia said, it's hurting no-one. Caroline seems to be all right and apparently there's no danger to Caroline's children. Hugo and Olivia have paid a big price to have their way, but they are also rarely blessed. Right from the beginning they had everything — love, affection, friendship, mutual devotion — things the rest of us look for so hard all our lives. Mightn't it have been a mistake to throw that out and start all over again; dangerously cavalier?

Judging isn't up to me, however. As far as I'm concerned, that's not the point. The point is the effect all this has had on me. If there's to be a judgement, it's actions towards me and the damage done to me that are at issue. Where all this leaves me.

I see now that Hugo luring me to Egypt was largely a means of getting Olivia there, but he also hoped that we could make a go of it. He was divided, reason against emotion, head against heart, and he was wavering. That's understandable. Look at Billy and me and Olivia and Alexei; we were all of us wavering, wavering and hoping, trying hard to love each other enough, when all the time the heart refused point blank to compromise. But Hugo lied outright about the Hartfields' disapproval of Alexei. The truth was just the opposite, and lying, he'd always claimed, was dishonourable, if a person was entitled to the truth. I think I was, and yet he lied specifically to mislead me. I even wonder if Olivia isn't the stronger of the two. Not that it matters, but probably Hugo isn't quite the conscientious character I'd imagined, and Olivia is much sturdier. And yet Olivia lied to Arthur purely to get her conscience off the hook, and that lie set the life I live in motion. Was that fair to me, was it fair to Arthur, and weren't we their innocent victims?

Surely the point is to get on with life, which is precisely what I have been doing all these years. Now, however, I've a chance to settle down as a victim, put my feet up, and take early retirement in a comfortable cocoon; it's fashionable and it's convenient. But I know better, having spun one years ago. It successfully blocked pain, but as no air got in the wound never properly healed. At Château Carrielle, air got in at last — pain too — and the cocoon finally burst. For that I am truly grateful; it is a genuine release.

Could Henry James have got it right, then, about the importance of suffering? Moreover, is it, emotionally speaking, the essential growth hormone — the catalyst or mordant without which we can't feel *anything*

358

properly? It's true that even love affairs require it. And maybe what Christianity picked up on wasn't love so much as suffering. Its *aide-mémoire* is a crucifix, after all. What an irony, though, if suffering is what's required to keep alive and happy, to keep the heart open and our feelings properly functioning. I don't like the idea myself. Yet if it should prove true, I still maintain you need to get the dosage right. But it's an odd situation when you think about it.

★ ★ ★

When Arthur came in last night, after his farewell dinner, we telephoned room service and for old times' sake ordered up two sambucas. Then, nestled in armchairs opposite the ersatz Louis XV fireplace, I regaled him with an edited account of my visit. Château Carrielle wasn't remotely a château, I said — but that was only the beginning of the fiction. I described the house, the lunch, my great surprise at seeing Hugo, who sent his best, and what I'd learned about Alexei; finally leading up to the extraordinary revelation of their marriage. 'It all falls together, doesn't it?' I ended. 'How they behaved and the havoc that they caused.'

Arthur smiled, casting his mind back. For a

financier who must of necessity be conservative in judgement, he's a surprising optimist. The silver he looks for most is inside clouds. 'We were all of us unhappily in love,' he said. 'But it was worth it. We would never have got together but for that trip.'

I thanked him for that. It's true he'd never have thought me rich but for that trip. But he hadn't meant that, so why bring it up, any more than sexual preferences or my own recent devastation and distress? We have always honoured each other's privacy.

How curiously things have come out, though. Olivia and I have in a way swapped destinies: she is the farmer's wife and I the titled lady living in a stately home. Life certainly bestows some unexpected compensations. But Hugo and Olivia undoubtedly have theirs. They have answered their natures fully, turning their backs on wealth and social position, successful careers and cutting a figure in the world — things most people give their eye teeth for — in order to be together. From the beginning, those two were each other's vocations. And they are happy — well, as happy as people ever are. They have their own little Eden in the Bordeaux boondocks, and sex has put them there. But possibly Polly haunts it: beady eyed, mischievous and about as dangerous as a garter snake, but reminding them of their connection with, even responsibility for, her death. For there *is* a connection.

Recently, it's been discovered that after a serious fracture a bit of fatty tissue can break away and, entering the bloodstream, operate as a blood clot, causing an embolism. That's probably what caused Polly's death — if you leave out personal responsibility, which I can't. And yet where does responsibility end? For it was I who persuaded Polly to go abroad. Is that another instance of propinquity? Olivia was certainly right about that, because propinquity is like a chain, and in chain reactions, the closer the link the more intense the reverberations. Everyone is affected though, being linked; Hugo and Olivia no less than others, as they have at considerable cost discovered.

I used to imagine those two walking on the earth like gods, to be imitated and looked up to, and I assumed that there were many others like them — the Titans and celebrities of this world. Youth is so easily deceived by surfaces, so keen for definite models, for certitude, and for the everlasting. They are the building blocks of life, hiding the fact that our perceptions and connectedness, forged chains so tightly soldered and vital to our reality, are unsound, and from another view, illusory — mere random twists braided by chance into a rope of sand. So much of living is designed to hide that truth, but what else can we do?

I told Arthur before we went to sleep how glad I was to be going home, how much I was looking forward to it. 'I want to see my arbour in full fig,' I quipped, 'and all the autumn colours. It's my favourite time. I think autumn is the best of all,' I insisted brightly.

'That's the ticket!' Arthur said, still perusing his notes. Then he added softly, patting my hand with a surprising tenderness, 'So chin up, my darling.'

THE END

We do hope that you have enjoyed reading this large print book.

Did you know that all of our titles are available for purchase?

We publish a wide range of high quality large print books including:
Romances, Mysteries, Classics
General Fiction
Non Fiction and Westerns

Special interest titles available in large print are:
The Little Oxford Dictionary
Music Book
Song Book
Hymn Book
Service Book

Also available from us courtesy of Oxford University Press:
Young Readers' Dictionary
(large print edition)
Young Readers' Thesaurus
(large print edition)

For further information or a free brochure, please contact us at:
Ulverscroft Large Print Books Ltd.,
The Green, Bradgate Road, Anstey,
Leicester, LE7 7FU, England.
Tel: (00 44) 0116 236 4325
Fax: (00 44) 0116 234 0205

THE RECKONING

Patricia Tyrrell

In a phonebooth beside a dusty Arizona highway, fifteen-year-old Cate listens in on yet another conversation between Les and her mother. But this is no ordinary parental discussion, for the woman hasn't seen her daughter since she was three years old, and the man is the homeless drifter who abducted her from beside her sleeping parents over a decade ago. Now Les has finally decided that Cate should go home. But how will Cate cope with learning to love a mother she can't remember? How will her English mother square the memories of her three-year-old daughter with the hard-bitten, poorly educated and cynical teenager? And what will happen when Cate's awful secret is revealed?

KITH & KIN

Stevie Davies

Mara and Frankie are cousins and best friends, growing up in the stifling atmosphere of Swansea in the Fifties, within an extended family that thrives on gossip, petty feuds and innuendo. Mara is a difficult but loved child whilst Frankie is rebellious, fired by an intense emotional hunger. The two develop a strange mutual dependence in which love, jealousy, hate and rivalry intermingle. They come of age in the Sixties — a decade in which notions of family and kinship are being overturned in favour of 'free love', sexual experimentation and social revolution. But that dream turns sour and a bitter battle of wills results . . .

LINDBERGH'S LEGACY

Katy Hayes

1926, on the south west coast of Ireland, in the aftermath of the bloody civil war: Marie-Rose O'Brien is about to give birth to her first child, as her handsome police sergeant husband, Cormac, patrols an uneasy peace. Shortly after the birth of baby Michael, the young family witness Charles Augustus Lindbergh's first flight across the Atlantic, as his plane passes over Ireland. Inspired by this, and fascinated by Lindbergh and all that he stands for, Marie-Rose tries to instil a sense of adventure in her son. It is this ambition, along with the pride he inherits from his father, which is set to run through the generations to come . . .